Always
Remembered

Always Remembered

JANELLE MOWERY

summerside
PRESS™

New York

Always Remembered

ISBN-10: 1-60936-747-2
ISBN-13: 978-1-60936-747-3

Published by Summerside Press, an imprint of Guideposts
16 East 34th Street
New York, New York 10016
SummersidePress.com
Guideposts.org

Summerside Press™ is an inspirational publisher offering fresh,
irresistible books to uplift the heart and engage the mind.

Distributed by Ideals Publications, a Guideposts company
2630 Elm Hill Pike, Suite 100
Nashville, TN 37214

Though this story is based on actual events, it is a work of fiction.

All Scripture quotations are taken from The Holy Bible,
King James Version.

Cover design by Garborg Design, GarborgDesign.com
Interior design by Müllerhaus Publishing Group, Mullerhaus.net

Printed and bound in the United States of America
10 9 8 7 6 5 4 3 2 1

Dedication

To the men who bravely fought and died in the
Battle of the Alamo, and also to all those who have
fought and continue to fight for our freedom.

Acknowledgments

I would like to thank the many people who helped with this latest endeavor:

Bruce Winders, for being generous with his time and knowledge while answering my many research questions.

Nancy Toback, for helping to smooth the rough edges of this book.

Elizabeth Ludwig and Mercedes Nanson, my Spanish language advisors.

MerriDee Shumski, Julie Fowler, Gary Moon, Rachel Moon, Elizabeth Moon, Missy Moon, and McKenzie Moon, for their unending prayers and encouragement.

And last but far from least, my husband, Rodney, who is not only a gift from God but remains patient and supportive during the crazy life of a writer, which enables me to achieve more than I ever could on my own.

Chapter One

"Let's go, Mama."

Rosa Carter paced in front of the table where her mother sat darning a sock. "Let's get away from this place. There's so much of the world yet to be seen. Places much safer than this."

"Don't be silly, Rosa." Mama glanced up briefly from her sewing. "You know I just got married." She worked the needle and thread more quickly. "I can't leave now."

Rosa stopped directly across the table from her mother, hands on hips. "Didn't that battle here a couple months ago scare you? It did me. We need to leave before something worse happens."

"Battles scare everyone, child. You can't run from conflict." She jabbed the needle into the material with force and winced. "Besides, I'm married. . . ."

Rosa planted her hands on the table and leaned across the worn, wooden planks. "Yes, I know you're married, but I don't know why. How could you marry a man who was probably a member of the group who killed my father?"

Her mother's slap snaked out faster than a rattler, but Rosa refused the impulse to massage her stinging cheek.

"You watch your mouth, Rosa. You may be my daughter, but I'll not let you speak of my husband like that. Carlos swore to me he wasn't a part of that massacre. He's done nothing but work hard to take care of us. You should be thankful rather than sully the name of a good man."

Rosa pushed away from the table to keep from being struck with humiliation again. "If he's such a great man, why is he making us sneak around to get information about the Alamo, the very thing that got you banned from entering the fort ever again? I'm only eighteen, Mama, and yet he's forcing me to place myself in danger by going there alone, wanting me to flirt with the men so they'll tell the secrets of their situation. If the information he seeks is for a sincere and legitimate reason, he shouldn't need us to go behind the backs of the men inside the Alamo."

Mama rose and threw the sock on the table. "He doesn't mean anything evil by it. He's always had a heart for this land and often got into trouble as a boy because of it."

"How would you know that? I thought you two met shortly before you married last month."

Mama looked away. "Ah, he told me so." She again met Rosa's eyes and shook her finger. "He and our people want the Texians to abide the law and free their slaves, and also make sure the land is not taken from our people. Texas must remain a part of Mexico, but the Americans want to steal it from us. Just look at how many Americans have already come and taken our Mexican land, many of them illegally."

"Now you're sullying the name of Papa. . .who was killed by the Tejanos. How could you have forgotten so soon? It hasn't even been a year. Did you forget that you and your parents lived in America too? You and Papa met at the shipyards of Louisiana. If you could make a living in America, why can't Americans make a living in Mexico?"

Angry tears welled. Rosa wiped them away with the back of her hand. "Papa came with the best of intentions, because he knew you wanted to move back to this area. When that empresario Mr. Austin invited him to come here, offering a large piece of land by the Mexican government, Papa grabbed the opportunity to make you happy. He wasn't one of the men who crossed the border illegally. Have you forgotten all that? Did Carlos put these ideas in your head?"

Her stepfather's form filled the doorway, darkening the room. He paused for a moment to stare at Rosa then entered and stood next to his wife. Broad across the shoulders, the man's strength scared her, as did the scowl on his face.

"Come, Carmela. We'll walk and give Rosa time to think. My motives shouldn't need to be explained. And obviously her father never taught her respect or obedience."

The words cut deep, adding fire to her anger as Carlos led her mother outside. How could Mama have fallen for such a man? She'd changed since the two met. Mama would never have hit her in the past. Since Carlos entered their lives, gone were the days of she and Mama as the best of friends, chatting about anything from cooking to men. Many times they giggled like schoolgirls as Mama told her about Papa's hesitant attempts at courtship, and Rosa described the kind of man she hoped to meet. The thought made her heart ache. Not only had she lost her father; now it seemed she might have lost her mother.

She took Mama's place at the table and worked to finish the sock before starting on another. She still had too many to do before heading to the fort with the clothes she'd been asked to clean and mend.

If only her father hadn't brought them here from Louisiana seeking a new life with cheap land. If only she and her mother had left San Antonio de Béxar when they'd first talked about finding an easier way of life after her father was killed. If only he hadn't fought with the Texian army. If only they hadn't lost. If only. . .

The list could go on, but dwelling on regrets would only make her angrier. The land was beautiful, just as her father said. She wished she could stay on the land Papa bought no more than ten miles from Béxar, but with all the unrest, the beauty wasn't worth the danger. They would probably end up in the ground next to her father. Now the land was left for anyone who wanted to steal it from them. Because they'd hesitated to leave, Mama had met Carlos, and now they must make their way through life washing and mending the clothes of the cavalry and volunteers living in the Alamo fort. At least she did.

Too many questions by Mama made her look suspicious. Colonels James Neill and William Travis heard one of those questions and banned Mama from the fort. Rosa couldn't believe she was allowed to stay. But since they now had different last names, the colonels must not have made the connection.

Rosa finished the last of the socks and began folding the men's clothes, binding them into separate stacks. This would be her last day for such a task. At least that was her plan. When she returned from the fort, she would work harder on changing her mother's mind. She'd remind her of their former friendship and beg to resume that relationship. With any success, the two of them would leave in the morning for a town, any town, east of the Mississippi. If she failed to convince her mother to leave, Rosa would go by herself. Or hopefully find a family with the same plans so she wouldn't have to travel alone. Maybe she could get her friend Ana Maria to leave with her. She'd ask the next time they were together.

Before she finished with the clothing, Carlos returned alone. This time, he shut the door behind him then strode to the table to tower over her. She made a pointed look at the door then up at him.

"Where's Mama?"

One corner of his mouth turned up, but the scowl remained. "You will see her again. Maybe."

A chill sped down her spine. "What does that mean? What did you do to her?"

The smirk turned into a sneer. "If you want to see her again, you'll get answers to my questions." He pulled a slip of paper from his vest pocket. "Here's what I want to know next. Memorize the questions. Get the answers. I'll be waiting for your return."

"And if I don't?" She hated the tremor in her voice.

"You'll find another home."

"What about Mama?"

"You'll not see her again."

She swung at him, but he caught her wrist. "What have you done to my mother?"

"Your mother is safe. For now."

She glanced at her sore wrist. He turned her loose but still towered over her.

"I only wish to help those who rightfully belong here. But all of those"—he waved his hand toward the door—"immigrants, those who have come here and illegally claimed our land, they must go! They are no good. They refuse to adapt to our ways and obey our laws, as was agreed." He smacked his fist into the palm of his other hand. *"Se han convertido en rebeldes sin valor."*

Those were fighting words. "They're not worthless rebels. They're trying to make a life here the best way they know how."

"You've been blinded by greed, just like those rebels. We have many men who want to own and work the land, but it's been filled with foreign settlers. They're thieves. Your mother sees this. Why can you not understand?"

"I understand that the Texians came here and worked hard to make something useful out of this wilderness, and now you want to steal it back from them. All this sneaking around asking questions makes you look like the thief, not any of those hardworking men out there."

The slap from Carlos hurt much worse than the one from her mother and sent her reeling back, almost knocking her to the floor.

Trying not to cry, she stared at Carlos. What had God said about turning the other cheek? She knew what His Word said about forgiveness, but with Carlos, that might be asking too much. And as of today, she was out of cheeks.

"I want to see my mother."

"Not until you get what I want."

If she wanted to protect her mother from harm, she'd have to do exactly as Carlos asked. She scooped the paper up from the table and read his list of questions, which raised some of her own, but she wouldn't ask and risk another slap.

"What if I can't get the answers to all of these today?"

"Get what you can. Get the rest soon."

She looked him in the eyes. What did her mother see in him? He was nothing like her gentle father. "I'll do it."

He nodded and turned to go. She did have one question.

"Wait. I can't. . .*won't* stay here alone with you."

His lips twitched, making her anger flare again.

"I'll be staying with your mother. You'll be here alone. I'll stop by to check on you, see what you have for me."

He strode into their bedroom and returned minutes later with an armful of Mama's clothes. He walked out without a word, leaving her fuming as she watched out the open windows of the adobe home to see which direction he headed. West. As if that knowledge would help. In the six months they'd lived in Béxar, she'd seen enough to know there were too many buildings to search, many of them walled-in properties, and even if she did happen to find her mother, Carlos would stop her. She knew very few people in town, and the only person who might help would be Ana Maria—and another female wouldn't be much assistance.

With no recourse, she gathered the clothing into large baskets and toted them out to their small cart. She returned and tied a shawl around her shoulders to ward off the chill in the air. Then she wrapped the loaves of bread she and her mother had baked. Food was a good way to loosen a man's lips. It was the only thing she was willing to give for information.

She chided herself at that thought. How could she have allowed her honor to fall so far? She thought she used to have such high principles. But at the slightest pressure from Carlos, she gave in, yielded her values. And because of that, she'd become a traitor. . .to herself and her country. What would her father think? She'd wanted so much to be like her father. He was a man of integrity. She'd allowed herself to become nothing like that. She was a woman of duplicity. He'd be disappointed. Shame made her determined to end her disgraceful actions. . .after today. Right now, she needed to save her mother.

After a long look at the fort, Rosa grabbed the handles of the cart and tugged, rocking it a bit to get it in motion. She headed in the direction of the bridge crossing the San Antonio River. Once she dropped off the clothes, she'd look for the young man who'd shown so much interest in gaining her friendship—and likely a deeper relationship. She wouldn't leave without the answer to at least one of Carlos's questions.

* * * * *

Miles Fitch leaned against the wooden palisade on the south side of the Alamo and looked out at the land he'd come to love, a love passed on to him by his father, who would have also enjoyed the view. The Alamo sat on a hill, which allowed him to see quite far, though the huts and houses of La Villita blocked some of his view to the west. Instead, he ignored the small village and focused south, where the cottonwood and oak trees growing tall in the distance teased as they waved in the wind that added a slight chill to the air.

His mother would have loved a morning such as this. Too many months she'd had to stand over the cook fire when the day was already scorching. He couldn't count the number of times he'd seen her stand to stretch and rub her back then tuck away her wayward hair the wind had tugged loose. He missed the waves she'd give him when she realized he was watching. Never again would he hear her sweet voice drift to him on the breeze as she sang her favorite songs or called him in to eat.

His throat tightened. He would like nothing more than to avenge the deaths of his parents, but there was no chance he would ever learn the identity of the men who killed them. But the death of Santa Anna, leader of the Mexican forces, would suit him just fine as their substitute. To stand over his body would bring him a tremendous amount of satisfaction. Then he could get on with his life.

"You're at the wrong wall if you're looking for that young beauty you seek on a daily basis."

Miles tucked away his wrath and grinned at the man he'd come to admire in the two days since the colonel arrived with his men. He held out his hand to Colonel David Crockett. "I wasn't looking for her. . .yet."

Crockett clapped him on the back. "Not sure why you bother. I have yet to see you say a word to the young lady. Looking won't get you far with her. Or with most any woman, for that matter."

"She's never given me a second glance. Doubt I interest her much at all. I think she has eyes for one of Travis's men."

The colonel leaned on the palisade next to Miles. "Gotta give her a reason to look, son. Watching from the shadows ain't much of a reason." He moved his rifle to the other arm and adjusted his powder horn. "No more lecture." He tipped his head the direction Miles had been staring. "Pretty land, ain't it? I'd like a piece of it for myself."

"We had a piece of it, my folks and me."

"What happened?"

He shook his head as he pushed away the ache of loneliness for his family. "They were killed during one of the skirmishes between the Mexican army and the Texians while I was staying with some Indian friends of the Tonkawa tribe. I was told not to go back or I'd be buried next to them."

"I'm sorry."

"Yeah. Me too. But I aim to get our land back. That's why I'm here. I learned about this fort from our trips to pick up supplies. Up until about a week ago, I've been staying with my Tonkawa friends, since I really had nowhere else to go. I heard about the battle back in December where the Mexican army was beaten and sent home. I figured I could help with the next one. If I can help defeat Santa Anna, I'll get my land back, and I'll do whatever it takes to live on my land again."

"And I'll do what I can to help." Crockett closed one eye as he aimed a look at Miles. "Indian friends, you say?"

Miles picked at the bark on the wooden palisade as he pictured their faces in his head. He hadn't seen them in a long time. "My father and I ran into a brave and his son hunting deer. Shared a meal and, over time, shared a friendship. The brave sent his son to stay with us to learn our language and ways. Then I went to stay with them to learn theirs. Good people."

"That's not the kind of story you often hear."

"No, I don't imagine. Most shoot first. Fear is the motivator that kills great possibilities."

Crockett squinted an eye at him again. "How old did you say you were?"

Miles hitched one shoulder. "Twenty-one. But my father was a wise man and great teacher. What I learned from him in a short time probably makes me sound older than I am. He was a good man." A man he would never be able to learn from again. He scanned the horizon. "You think Santa Anna's coming?"

"From what I've heard about the man, he'll be here."

"They're saying we should expect him around spring or later. You agree?"

The corner of Crockett's mouth twitched as he tilted his head. "You don't get to be president of Mexico by sitting back and letting things happen. Wouldn't surprise me if his army was already stirring up dust."

Boots scuffed the dirt behind them. They both turned.

"Colonel Crockett, Colonel Neill and Lieutenant Colonel Travis are looking for you."

Miles's heart sank when he recognized the messenger. John Prine was the man who held his girl's interest. Miles caught Crockett's wink before he left to find Neill and Travis. John wasted no time striding toward the gate on the south side of the fort that faced La Villita, the small village across the river from the southeast side of San Antonio de Béxar.

Miles grabbed his rifle from where he'd propped it against the palisade and trailed behind to take up his usual vantage point near the long barracks. There he'd watch the two together and wish it were him making her laugh. He'd been spying on them since he'd first laid eyes on the dark-haired beauty. One day, hopefully soon, he'd learn her name. And one day he'd take Crockett's advice and get her to notice him. Until that day came, he'd continue to pray the good Lord would grant him the perfect opportunity to make her acquaintance.

A woman screamed, evaporating his girl from his thoughts. Miles veered toward the gate and raced past John to see if he could offer his help.

Chapter Two

The man held Rosa much too close. She slapped his face with one hand and scratched his cheek with the other. He finally turned her loose, only to grab at her again. She twisted away, but he caught hold of her shawl and jerked her back. She squealed as he pulled her to him.

"Hold up." The attacker struggled to restrain her as she wriggled to get free. "Stop fighting."

A handful of men had gathered around, but none made an attempt to help. Instead they laughed and cheered on her attacker.

"Hold her, Starks."

"She's gonna get away, Starks."

She swung her arms. Her elbow caught something hard, jarring her with the impact. He yelled and stepped back, holding his hand over his eye. She tried to run, but he grasped her skirt and yanked her backward. Off balance, she tumbled to the ground.

Something flashed past her face, and she was suddenly released. Seconds later, a young man crouched next to her, dipping his head to look into her eyes.

"You all right, miss?"

"Of course she's all right. Now get out of the way."

Rosa watched her rescuer plant his hands on the ground and sweep one leg at her attacker. His legs knocked out from under him, the assailant landed hard an arms' length away.

While the rescuer made sure Starks stayed down, her informer, Soldier John Prine, helped her to her feet. "Did he hurt you, Miss Carter?"

"No. I'm fine." She turned to the young man who'd rescued her. "Thank you so much."

"What's all the commotion out here?" A big man she recognized as one of her laundry patrons rushed up to them. "Speak up. What happened?" He examined faces before spotting her. He strode to her side. "Name's Jim Bowie."

"Rosa Carter."

"You hurt, Miss Carter?"

"No, sir. Just a little unnerved and dirty." She brushed dust from her sleeves as she glanced at the cart. Thankfully it hadn't been overturned.

Bowie stared at her face. "I know you." His scowl softened. "Were you able to mend my trousers?"

She managed a smile. "Yes, sir."

"Good." He looked around, his face turning stern again. "Can you tell me what happened?"

She peered down at the man on the ground. "He attacked me."

Mr. Bowie pointed at her rescuer. "You, come here."

"No, not him. The other one." She met the gaze of the young man. "That one saved me."

The young man stood and began to speak, but the attacker interrupted.

"I thought she was someone else."

Mr. Bowie grabbed the man by the shirtfront. "You mean to tell me you treat other women like that too?"

"No, sir. I just wanted her to stop fighting me."

"So you could do what?"

"Ah—talk to her?"

"What's your name?"

"Tom Starks, sir."

Mr. Bowie shoved him away and looked at Rosa. "What would you like me to do with this ruffian?"

She shrugged a shoulder. "I don't know. I just don't want him to do it again. Not to me or any other woman."

Mr. Bowie put his hand on the handle of a large knife in a sheath attached to his belt. "You hear the lady, Starks? You ever lay a hand on a woman again, you and me will do more than stand here and talk. They'll be carrying you out."

Starks's throat worked. "Yes, sir."

"Now, git."

The man left at a run. Mr. Bowie stood in front of her. "Let me apologize for the stupidity of that man. I'm guessing his brain quit working at the sight of a lovely young lady."

He held out his hand to her rescuer. "Thank you for helping her. What's your name?"

"Miles Fitch."

"Good man, Mr. Fitch. You busy this afternoon?"

Rosa's soldier friend, who'd been standing with all the other onlookers, stepped to her side. "Miss Carter and I already had plans to meet up today."

Jim Bowie frowned at the soldier. "Aren't you one of Travis's men?"

"Yes, sir. The name's John Prine."

"That's fine. I want you to stay with Miss Carter, help her while she's here. Then see her safely home." He turned back to her. "You should have a proper escort, young lady. Women should never wander around alone. Especially pretty ones like you." He dug in his pocket. "What do I owe you for my trousers?"

Her face heated while she quoted the amount then dug through the stacks for his clothing. He placed the coins in her hand and took his trousers.

"Thank you, Miss Carter. Let me know if you have any more problems with the men."

John stepped into her view of Jim Bowie's back. "You ready to deliver the clothes? It appears we're spending the day together."

The prospect of an entire afternoon with Soldier John wasn't at all appealing. If it weren't for the need to pry information from him to free her mother, she'd turn around and run home.

She forced a smile. "Let me get my things."

The man who helped her stood holding her shawl. She turned and let him place it around her shoulders. What was his name?

"Thank you, Mr.—"

"Miles Fitch. And you're welcome. If you ever need anything—"

"I'll take care of her, Fitch. Go back to your post."

Something flared in Miles's eyes. Rosa had a feeling if she weren't here, John may have ended up on the ground much like her attacker. Instead, Miles nodded, picked up his rifle, and started walking away without a word.

"Wait. Please come back, Mr. Fitch." She couldn't let him leave like a chastened little boy. She reached inside her cart, pulled out a loaf of bread, and handed it to him. "To show my appreciation."

"Call me Miles." He sniffed then smiled. "I think I've been overpaid. Thank you, Miss Carter."

"You can call me Rosa."

His blue-gray eyes held her captive, as if he could see right through her and found her to his liking. If that were true, the feeling was mutual. His buckskin clothes and days-old beard made him ruggedly appealing.

John stepped between them and extended his elbow then grabbed the handle of her cart. "Time to go."

Gritting her teeth, she placed her hand on John's arm but

took one last look at Miles before she took a step. John led her across the compound toward the long barracks and chapel.

"You shouldn't encourage that man. He may end up being your next attacker."

She almost laughed at the jealousy she heard in John's voice. "Oh, I don't know. He seemed the perfect gentleman."

"Those are rare, especially in a place like this. Not everyone here is a trained fighting man. I believe some are outlaws looking for a place to lay their head, get some food in their bellies, and a reason to shoot someone."

Rosa tamed the first thought that came to mind but still felt the need to scold. "Pretty harsh description of those here to help."

"Maybe so, but accurate for many of them."

The way he belittled his comrades grated on her, but she decided to forgive him since he was smitten and wanted her to himself. Besides, the conversation gave her the perfect opening for one of her questions.

"I've never gotten over how large this place is. Its size makes it look like there aren't many men here."

He chuckled. "I think you'll be surprised to know there are around one hundred and fifty men here already, and we're expecting more."

Rosa couldn't believe how easily John answered her unasked questions. He didn't suspect a thing. "That many? How in the world do you manage to feed all those men? Do you have stores of food stacked somewhere? I can't imagine cooking for so many at one time."

"You and everyone else. That's why the men eat in shifts. That leaves men free to stand post at all times."

"And there's always enough food for a hundred and fifty men?"

He blew out a long breath. "To be honest, I doubt it. As a man, I know our appetites, and it takes a lot to fill the hole. I've walked away wishing I could've taken more, but I wanted to make sure there was enough for others."

"Very thoughtful of you." She needed more details. "So, do they get to eat much meat?"

"We eat meat." He motioned to the left with his head. "We have a cattle pen and horse corral over there behind the long barracks. Some men like to hunt. The men probably don't get as much meat as they'd like, but meat is available."

She'd love to see that pen but didn't want to appear too inquisitive. "So, will my loaves of bread be appreciated?"

He smiled down at her. "Without a doubt. They'll probably ask for more."

One more question. . .for now. "I can help with food. I just wish I could also help with weaponry. I hope you have enough to withstand a large army."

Shame washed through her for what she was being forced to do for her mother's welfare. Carlos deserved a beating of his own.

"We'll be fine. Most of the men have been trained or raised to shoot well."

That answer was the most reserved he'd ever given. Was he getting suspicious? It was time to pull back from her inquisition and become more entertaining. She'd try to find the answers to the rest of Carlos's questions later.

"After hearing all that you men go through, I've decided to be content to have only a stray dog as an extra mouth to feed and a broom as my weapon to chase it along to its next victim."

John burst into laughter. "I wonder if it's the same dog that used to come around here. Quite entertaining. It would beg on its back legs while turning circles."

Rosa listened to John's incessant chatter just enough to laugh and respond in all the right places, all the while hoping the men would hurry to the long barracks to retrieve their belongings so she could get home. She slowly turned, taking in all the buildings making up the walls of the Alamo. Most of them were flat on top, which served as walkways where men stood to keep watch.

While waiting, she wandered to her right and stopped at the opening leading to the chapel. The ruins of the old church drew her almost every time she entered the Alamo. This was the closest she'd ever gotten to the church and hoped the day would come when she could get close enough to touch it. In her mind, she pictured what it could have been. She knew *Alamo* was the Spanish word for "cottonwood," but that was all she'd known about the fort until Ana Maria told her the place began as a Catholic mission to minister to the Indians in the 1740s before it became a barracks for a Spanish army in the early 1800s. Learning details about the mission's history made her love the fort all the more.

"You really like that old building, don't you?"

Irritated at John's interruption, she couldn't understand how anyone could look at the chapel and not see its beauty. "Look at it, John. The ornamentation on the front is incredible. The arched doorway, the four pillars and niches. . .you can see the love that went into its creation. I don't think I've ever seen a more lovely building."

"Yes, it's nice."

Rosa frowned at his lack of appreciation and wished he'd leave her alone long enough to enjoy everything about the fort. Instead, she led John back to the long barracks to continue her wait for the men to retrieve their clothes and ply John with more subtle questions. She prayed the information she gained today would appease her stepfather so he'd allow her to see her mother. . .if she was still alive.

* * * * *

Miles had been enjoying his loaf of bread until he heard Rosa's sweet laugh. What had been honey in his mouth turned to dust.

Colonel Crockett strode up to him. "Colonel Neill would like to speak with you."

"What about?"

"He has an important job for you." He broke off a chunk from the loaf Miles offered. "I knew you'd find a way to get that young lady to notice you, Fitch." He took a bite. "Good for you." He disappeared through the opening that would take him to the palisade.

Miles pushed to his feet. What kind of job would Colonel Neill need to see him about? How did the colonel even know he existed? He handed what was left of the bread to two young men who looked like they could use the sustenance then wiped his suddenly moist palms on his trousers. His mouth felt full of the dust he'd thought about moments earlier. He took a deep breath then took the first step to face the man who held his future in his hands.

Chapter Three

Miles stood near the half-open door, hesitant to interrupt Colonel Neill's thoughts. The colonel sat at the table in his quarters hunched over the document in his hand, intently focused.

But he couldn't keep their leader waiting. Miles cleared his throat as he rapped his knuckles on the door.

Neill turned and squinted. "Yes?"

"I was told you wanted to see me, sir?"

"I do." Neill laid the paper on the table. "If you're Miles Fitch."

"Yes, sir." Miles left his rifle propped at the doorway and stepped forward. "I am."

The colonel waved him in and pointed to a chair. Miles stood before the colonel, lifted his hand to salute, decided against the formality, and then dropped his arm to his side. He wasn't part of the army.

He sat on the edge of the chair, unable to feel comfortable in the commander's quarters, his back stiff, waiting in silence for Neill to speak first. The man's hair stood on end in front, as though he'd been running his fingers through it many times.

"I have a job for you, young man."

"Yes, sir," he consented before he even received his orders.

Neill relaxed against the back of his chair and eyed him for several agonizing moments. Miles met the colonel's stare with confidence, though his gut bucked and twisted like an unbroken horse.

Neill finally nodded and tapped the table with one finger. "You may or may not know that I'd given orders not to discuss anything about the goings-on in this fort to anyone outside our walls. However, word has come to me that there's been talk of our plans and situation in the town of Béxar."

Miles sat forward, his interest piqued. What kind of fool would turn on his comrades. . . ? "Unfortunate, sir."

"Yes, very." The colonel's scowl deepened. "I've already had to ban one woman from entering the fort for that very reason. I overheard her asking too many questions. It appears vital information is still leaking out."

His mind rushed to Rosa, but he pushed the distasteful thought away. The young woman was merely a laundress. "No sir, I hadn't been aware of any of this before today. I've only been here five days."

The colonel leaned forward and rested both arms on the table, his dark eyes intense, almost angry. "I want you to find out who's doing the talking."

Resolve gripped him with a fervor he'd never known.

Neill continued, "Is it one of the soldiers or one of the volunteers? Are they being paid for the information? I need you to find out so I can get it stopped before they ruin any chance we have at winning this battle. Find him today if possible. Tomorrow at the latest. Any questions?"

Dozens of thoughts and questions darted through Miles's mind. He landed on one. "I'm honored, sir, but why me?"

The colonel sat back and pursed his lips. "You came highly recommended by Crockett. Says you're bright and reliable. I asked him to do this, but he said you'd be the better man for the job."

Miles's brows shot up. "Me? Better than Colonel Crockett?"

"Under the circumstances, and after hearing his argument, I agree. You see, the men fall silent and aren't forthcoming when any of the leaders are around. Why, even you look nervous and stiff in my presence."

He nodded at Miles's attempt to relax by sitting back in the chair. "You've been here a little longer than Crockett and know some of the men better. Enter into conversations with them. Get a feel for their loyalty or treachery. Follow them into Béxar if you have to." He leaned forward again and pierced Miles with his eyes. "Do whatever you must, but get me that man."

Or woman? Miles nodded, fully committed to the mission, heart and soul. "Can I ask how you learned of the information leak, sir?"

The colonel speared him with another soul-searching look. "The men working the kitchen. They went to town looking for food and overheard a conversation."

He waited for more, but the colonel stared off, his eyes fierce and resolute. No other questions came to mind. He needed time to think— to snare the two-faced snake in his own trap.

"Can I depend on you, Fitch?"

"Yes, sir!" He sat straighter at the honor of being asked to do such an important task and at the respect afforded him by Neill and Crockett. He'd do everything possible not to let them down. Chances were, Neill would have the traitor hanged.

* * * * *

Rosa trudged alongside John, his presence an annoying distraction from her important meeting with Carlos. *Go away!*

Who knew what she'd find at home? She sure didn't need John getting an earful of venom from her stepfather. Or, worse, a fist to the face that would raise his suspicions about her and her family.

She tried for a smile. "I'm fine now, John. I can get home by myself."

"That won't happen. I was given a direct order to see you safely home, and I'm going to do just that. Besides, now I'll know where you live."

29

Yet one more thing to fear. She didn't need him stopping by whenever the whim hit. As they drew nearer to the house, Rosa grew much more alert, eyes darting down each street and beside every house, looking for a glimpse of Carlos or her mother. Though she wanted to see Mama, she didn't need John connecting the two of them. He was sure to have heard about Mama's ban from the fort.

She stopped in front of the house. "Here we are. Thank you for walking me home. I'll see you in a couple days when I return to the fort."

John wheeled the cart next to the house then stood by the door. "I hoped you'd ask me in. I'd like to meet your parents as well as spend more time with you."

She tamped the impatience mushrooming inside her. He'd gotten much too insistent as far as she was concerned. "I'm sorry, John, but they aren't home, and you know I can't allow you inside when it's just the two of us. As I said, I'll see you soon."

His expression resembled that of a scolded child. Then his eyes narrowed. "Actually, this might be the perfect time to go inside." Hinting at impropriety, he stepped closer and took hold of her upper arms. "Some time alone without prying eyes is just what I've had in mind since we met, dear Rosa."

He pulled her close and slid one arm behind her back to keep her there.

She struggled to wrest out of his strong grip, but he placed his other hand behind her head and managed one quick kiss before she shoved her fist into his abdomen.

He took a step back, gasped, and coughed. Then he grinned. "You're stronger than you look."

It was all she could do not to look for a club and land it upside his head. "And I'll give you much worse if you ever try that again."

His smile remained. She didn't scare him one bit. "All right. I guess that will have to be good enough. For now."

He leaned forward as though to peck her on the cheek, but she placed one hand against his chest and took a step back, her teeth clenched. "Good-bye, John. Leave!"

The relief of his departure was short-lived. Now she had to face Carlos. Part of her hoped he wasn't inside. But more than anything, she wanted to see her mother. She lifted the latch and pushed open the door.

At first it appeared no one was home. Then Carlos pulled back the curtain covering his bedroom. "Is he gone?"

She stared into his harsh eyes. "Yes."

"Is he the man you use to ask all the questions?"

What had this beast done with her mother? "Yes."

"So?" Irritation washed across his face. "Did you learn anything new?"

She would tell him nothing unless he gave her what *she* wanted. "Where's Mama?"

Carlos smirked. "Information first."

She loathed Carlos and trusted him even less. "I don't want to do this anymore. That soldier is getting much too friendly."

His jaw muscles worked. "If you want to see your mother again, you'll get me that information." He took a step closer. "Tell me what you learned today, or I'll—"

"But that man is trying to. . .do things to me." Oh, why was she pleading for mercy from this cruel man? "Isn't there another way?"

"I don't care what you have to do with that soldier. Just get my answers."

Anger exploded until she saw tiny flashes of white in her eyes. "I won't do it. Not until I have proof that Mama is alive. I see my mother or you don't get the answers to your questions."

At first she thought he would hit her again. Then a slight smile curled the corners of his mouth. "Sit down."

"I want to see my mother."

"I know. I had a feeling you'd act like this." He pointed at a chair. "Sit. I have something for you."

She narrowed her eyes, but she had to comply if she wanted to see Mama. She slid out a chair and sat. Carlos reached behind his vest, pulled out a folded sheet of paper, and tossed it onto the table. She eyed him a moment then reached for the paper. In the dim lighting, she couldn't be certain, but there looked to be a smudge of blood near one corner. She prayed she was wrong as she unfolded the sheet and recognized Mama's handwriting.

> My Dearest Rosa,
>
> I want to tell you first and foremost that I am well.
> But I miss you. Please, please do as Carlos asks. I hate
> that this has happened. Get his information as soon as
> possible so we can be together again. I love you, dear Rosa,
> and hope to be with you soon.
> Mama

Hot tears stung her eyes then rolled down Rosa's cheeks. She didn't know if she wanted to crumple the message in her fists to show Carlos what she thought of his actions or hold it tightly against her chest as if to hug her mother.

Fury at the situation propelled her from her chair. She lunged at Carlos, swinging her fists.

"Where's Mama? What have you done with her?"

Carlos grabbed her wrists, squeezed, and held them high until she was rendered helpless. He forced her back to her seat then leaned over her, his nasty breath washing across her face.

"As I said before, you'll see her when I have my information. Now, what did you learn today?"

As Rosa stared into his eyes, hoping he recognized every ounce of hatred she felt toward him, she wavered as to what or if she would tell him. Deep down, she knew in their battle of wills, Carlos would win.

* * * * *

Half an hour later, Rosa led her friend Ana Maria out into the woods. Ana Maria must have sensed Rosa's unrest and held her questions as long as she could. But Ana wasn't known for her patience, or a lack of words for that matter. Rosa smiled when the silence came to an end.

"So, why are we out here again? A club? Why do you need a club? You have rats in your house?"

"Only the two-legged kind."

"Two legs? What's wrong with your rats?" Several seconds passed. "Oh, wait. I understand now." She laughed and swatted Rosa's arm. "You're awful."

No one could accuse Ana Maria of brilliance, but she was a devoted friend. And when it came to listening and offering sound advice, Ana was the first person Rosa sought.

"I'll just feel better knowing I have some way of protecting myself, even if it's a stick of wood." If only she had Papa's rifle, but she was certain the Tejanos had taken it when they killed him.

"You've never wanted protection before. What happened?" She grabbed Rosa's arm, turned her around, and took a long look at her face. "You have a mark on your face. Who did this to you? Who has you scared?"

"Carlos."

"No! Your stepfather? Why?"

Rosa refused to explain everything. Though she loved and

trusted Ana, she couldn't take the chance of the news getting out, which would stop her from gaining needed information and possibly cause harm to her mother.

"I said something he didn't like."

"That's still no reason to hit you. What did your mother say?"

Rosa continued her search for just the right stick for a club. "She wasn't there."

"And you didn't tell her?"

"I haven't seen her yet."

Ana stopped her again. "But you're going to tell her, aren't you? She'll protect you. You won't need a club."

"She won't go against her new husband, Ana. So I'm going to try to take care of myself."

"Oh, Rosa." Ana pulled her into a hug. "All right, I'll help you. And if he ever touches you again, you let me know. I'll find my own club and lay it upside his head."

Rosa returned the hug, wishing it were her mother on the receiving end. Hopefully soon.

Chapter Four

Miles stood at the opening that led from the palisade into the court-yard and eyed the group of about thirty men shoveling food into their mouths. He found it interesting that although every man at the Alamo was here to fight the same battle, they still split up and grouped themselves according to the leader they followed. The men in Travis's army sat to one side, while Bowie's volunteers had clustered a short distance away. It was as though they wanted to be part of the same group yet still distinguish where a certain line was drawn. He hoped before the battle began, they'd mesh into one cohesive unit.

He examined every face. Were any of them the men he sought? Would any of them be traitorous enough to give out important information to the enemy? Would he be shrewd enough to ask the right questions and be able to discern who could be the turncoat? The last question stiffened his gut. Time to find out.

He meandered toward the kitchen and sniffed appreciatively at the scent wafting toward him, though he wasn't all that hungry at the moment. Finally he sat on the ground with the group of men.

"What did they manage to cook up tonight? Appears edible."

One man swallowed hard. "Beans and johnnycakes again. But the beans are decent today. They put in chunks of cooked meat. Don't know where they got it, but it's tender and tasty. Better hurry and get some 'fore it's gone."

Miles knew him as Peacock, so nicknamed because of the feathers protruding from his hat, as well as the fact that his hair stuck up in the back whenever he removed his hat. Peacock proceeded to scoop another spoonful into his mouth, sopping up the bean juice with the remainder of his johnnycake. No one else bothered to slow down enough to speak.

Miles went for a plate and returned with his grub. The look of it nearly turned his stomach, but he figured by the way the food disappeared from the other plates, it must be as good as Peacock described.

He sat and took his first bite. His brows went up as the food went down. He hadn't tasted grub this good since his mother last cooked for him. They must have found a new man to work in the kitchen.

"Told ya so." Peacock grinned. "They letting anyone in for more?"

"Don't know, but it never hurts to try," Miles said around a mouthful.

As Peacock went off to beg more food, Miles took another bite and caught sight of Rosa's attacker leaning against the adobe wall near the doorway of Jim Bowie's quarters. The man repaid him with the same stare then gave a slight nod.

Peacock returned with empty hands and dropped next to Miles, his boots scuffing dirt into the air. "Said no more till everyone's had a turn at the pot."

Miles handed him his johnnycake. "I had some bread earlier."

"I heard." Peacock took the cake and shoved almost half in his mouth. He motioned toward the attacker. "Heard you and Starks had a go-round. That's how you got the bread."

Crumbs spewed from Peacock's mouth as he spoke. Miles brushed some from his leg, ignoring the bread part of the conversation and turning his focus to the man. He also noticed they had the attention of every man in the group.

"Was that his name? I'd forgotten."

Peacock nodded. "Tom Starks. You didn't know the name of your opponent?"

"No time for introductions." Miles eyed Starks a moment longer before scooping up a forkful of beans. "He tried to have his way with a woman. I stopped him."

"Heard you used some fancy move to take Starks down." A man by the name of William Morrell, who held a higher rank than private, leaned forward to make eye contact. "The men said you had Starks in the dirt faster than they could blink."

Miles swallowed his mouthful. "You men sure hear a lot."

"You gonna show us that move?" William set his plate on the ground beside him and made ready to stand. "Might be useful one day."

"Sure." Miles caught Starks's glare and almost smiled at the thought that it was supposed to fill him with fear. "But how about later? Tomorrow maybe."

Something didn't feel right about the way Starks remained near Bowie's quarters. Did he intend to retaliate for his earlier humiliation? If so, *he* should be Starks's target, not Bowie.

"I've got plans tonight." And Starks would be part of those plans.

Peacock bumped him with his elbow. "You gonna finish that grub or play with it?"

Miles handed him the plate. "It's yours. The girl's bread filled my belly."

Peacock wasted no time slurping down the food. Now that Miles had the group's attention and slight appreciation, he decided it was time to put his orders into effect.

"What's the word on Santa Anna's arrival?"

He received a few shrugs along with a murmured, "Spring."

"Is everyone ready?"

One man belched and rubbed his belly. "The sooner the better."

William picked up his plate and stood. "Spring is good. A little more time to get ready wouldn't hurt." He wandered toward the kitchen without more explanation.

Miles looked around at the faces. "What did that mean?"

Most of them shrugged again, their expressions showing they really didn't know.

"It means you should mind your own affairs instead of everyone else's," Starks warned. He stared for a few seconds then pushed away from Bowie's door and headed toward the gate.

Some of the men chuckled. "Appears you made a new friend, Fitch."

Miles never took his eyes from Starks. "Seems so."

As Starks disappeared through the gate, Miles got to his feet, brushed off his trousers, and grabbed his rifle. There was something off about the man. Could be he was the traitor.

As he headed off after Starks, one of the men called out, "Better watch him, Fitch. He has a gun this time. Your leg can't stop lead."

He waved over his shoulder and kept walking, unwilling to lose sight of Starks. It would be dark soon, making it easy for a man to duck into shadows and disappear. He hurried through the gate and had just started past the north edge of La Villita as Starks crossed the bridge over the San Antonio River, passing Rosa's soldier friend at the halfway point. John and Starks shared a brief greeting.

John wasn't nearly as pleasant as he approached Miles. He thumped Miles on the chest while still walking. "Stay away from Rosa."

Miles's steps slowed then stopped. "Or what?"

John stopped and turned slightly but didn't return to face him. "Trust me, you don't want to find out." Then he continued into the Alamo.

Miles rushed after Starks, shaking his head at the empty threat. Or was it so empty? He'd never seen John do more than follow orders and give undue attention to Rosa. The man might be a better fighter than he thought.

Starks strode through Béxar, turning down a couple different streets. Miles trailed behind, just close enough not to lose sight of him.

He'd never been in this part of town. He and his parents usually came just to pick up supplies on the outskirts and stay a night or two in their hut outside of town to rest up for the trip back to their land.

He was surprised at how many properties were walled. The farther into town they walked, the more the properties were spread out instead of close together. Scattered here and there were adobe homes or mud huts with grass-thatched roofs. The bell tower of a church in the distance demanded to be noticed. Many wonderful scents, especially roasting meat, wafted through town and would have normally made him hungry, but Rosa's bread and the cook's beans had sufficiently fill the hole in his stomach.

As they passed one street, Miles glanced to his right and thought he saw Rosa. He paused, tempted to make sure it was her and maybe spend time getting to know her. Then Starks turned onto another street, and Miles remembered his task. He made a mental note of where he saw her then rushed ahead and peeked around the corner in time to see Starks enter a cantina.

Still three buildings away, his hand running along the rough bricks as he rushed to catch up, Miles heard the greeting Starks received, as though he were the local hero. Without a doubt, he was a frequent patron. And apparently well-liked. Miles lingered outside. When he thought enough time had passed, he peered over the swinging doors. Starks sat at a table against the left far wall, involved in a card game.

Miles pushed through the doors. Smoke hung in the air so thick it seemed one of the clouds from outside had moved indoors. Brown stains decorated the wooden floor. As he moved farther inside, trying to keep to the shadows with his back or profile to Starks, waves of rancid body odor replaced the pleasant scent of food from earlier. He chose a table at the opposite side of the building and dropped onto a chair.

"What'll ya have?" The barkeeper scowled at him through bushy brows.

"Ah, coffee?"

"Coffee? We're no restaurant. You want coffee, go down the street."

Miles hadn't given a thought to the fact that he didn't drink before entering the cantina. But in order to stay, he'd need to keep up appearances. "Whiskey."

A minute later, the barkeeper slammed a glass in front of him and poured. "Two bits."

Miles pulled out the coin and tossed it on the table. Once the barkeeper left, Miles strained to catch bits of the conversation, but all he could hear was the elderly man sitting at the next table strumming at an old, out-of-tune guitar. Boredom set in as the drinking, shuffling, and bidding continued.

Miles jumped when the big clock behind him announced the top of the hour, making him realize he'd almost fallen asleep. He tried not to stare when a scantily dressed woman approached and leaned on Starks then slid her hand inside his vest. Miles was about to look away when he saw her pull out a folded piece of paper. He straightened for a better look.

The woman bent down, her arm around Starks's shoulders. They shared a private conversation ending with a quick kiss. The woman nearly swayed as she left out the back.

Miles shoved to his feet, hurried out the front door, and then raced between the two buildings to get to the back. He spotted the woman stumbling down the street. She paused to lean against a building. Miles took that opportunity to rush toward her. "Miss? Can I talk to you a minute?"

"Huh?" She executed an off-balance half turn.

He easily snatched the paper from her hand and turned to make his getaway. Something hard hit his head, making his knees buckle from the pain as the night grew even darker.

Chapter Five

Heart heavy, Rosa wrung the water out of the last of the few socks and clothes she'd picked up from the men earlier. She hung them over the rope strung across the corner of the small house then dumped the water outside the door. She shoved the door latch in place, more than ready for some rest, especially from the battle going on in her mind.

What had once been a wonderful life had turned into a nightmare, and she couldn't understand why. What had she done to make God mad enough to kill her father and turn her mother's love toward another man? Every minute of her life was now spent trying to decide whether she should be shaking her fist at the Lord or falling at His feet pleading for the turmoil to end. And during all her indecision, Carlos had taken her mother away. If she did pray for forgiveness, would it bring her mother back unhurt, or would the chaos continue? Exhaustion didn't help with her uncertainty, so she just said a quick prayer for help.

The curtain dividing her bedroom from the rest of the house felt heavy to her weary body. She slid it closed and loosened the first button of her dress with arms that felt one hundred pounds each.

Loud banging shattered the silence. Rosa jumped. She ran to the other side of her bed in search of her makeshift club. She held it with both hands, ready to protect herself to the last breath.

"Open up, Rosa. It's me, Carlos."

That news only made her want to keep the door latched.

"I need your help, Rosa. Hurry."

With only a moment's hesitation, the thought that her mother might be hurt made her drop the club and run from her room. She shoved away the latch and opened the door.

Carlos rushed inside with a man draped over his shoulder and a rifle in one hand. He didn't stop to explain but headed for her room and dropped the man on her bed. He then pressed two fingers against the man's throat.

"Still alive. Get some warm water and see what you can do for him."

Rosa moved next to him to get a better look at what the man might need. "Miles?"

The name came out in a whisper, but Carlos heard.

"You know this man?"

She headed for the stove. "I met him today."

"Where?"

"At the fort."

The water in the pot she'd heated earlier was still warm. She poured some in a large bowl, grabbed a clean cloth, and returned to her bedroom. Carlos trailed her every step. After setting the bowl on the small table beside the bed, she pulled her chair close and wrung out the cloth before gently wiping away the blood and dirt covering Miles's face.

"What happened to him?"

Carlos moved a few steps to set the rifle on the table and then returned. "Don't know. I found him on the ground covered in blood. I guessed he was from the Alamo since I didn't recognize him. Clean him up and help him. Use his gratitude to get information from him."

His demand for more information didn't surprise her, which explained why he even cared what happened to Miles, but Mama was so much better at nursing. She needed her here. That thought gave her pause, and a chill ran down her spine. "Why didn't you take him to Mama?"

"He's heavy and you're much closer to where I found him."

That answer slowed her pounding heart. She leaned closer to Miles, trying to get a better look at his wound. Carlos moved to the other side of the bed. Something clattered at his feet. He bent and picked up her club. She cringed.

"What's this?"

She focused on Miles, unwilling to meet her stepfather's scowl. "Protection."

"From what?"

"Men."

He grunted. "You mean me?"

"All men."

"Where'd you get it?"

She sighed. If only he'd leave so she could relax and get on with her task. "I went out to the trees awhile ago and found it where someone had been chopping firewood. I think they forgot that piece."

He was silent for almost a full minute. She could feel the heat of his stare. Then he placed one end of the club under her chin and forced her to look at him.

"Don't ever try to use this on me." He propped it in the corner and strode to the door. "I'm leaving. I'll stop by tomorrow to check on him."

When the door closed behind him, she blew out a long breath and went to latch the door again. The man was a puzzle. She grasped the fact that Carlos wanted answers about the Alamo and Miles might be able to provide them, but why would Carlos trust her not to confess to Miles her real reasons for visiting the fort? Carlos didn't seem all that worried about her turning on him. He even left behind Miles's gun and her club. But then he had Mama. . .which ultimately meant he had all the control.

She returned to work on the gash above Miles's ear and across his temple. The blood had stopped oozing, and she could see the cut wasn't deep. Relief washed through her that only a bandage would be needed. She'd watched her mother stitch a gash closed in the past, but she'd never done it herself.

Once she had all the blood and dirt cleaned away, she cut some cloth and folded it in half. She used several strips to hold the bandage in place. With the obvious injury patched, she glanced over the rest of Miles's body. No rips in the buckskin and no other bloodspots. She felt his forehead and cheeks for a fever and found none.

She returned to the chair and stared at the handsome face. When they'd met that afternoon, he looked much older and so rugged. Now, lying helpless on the bed, his youth became much more apparent. He couldn't be more than a couple years older than her. She held his hand in hers and examined the palm, which was calloused in several places. The man had known hard work.

The longer she held his hand and stared at his face, the stronger her feelings grew for him. That thought made her release his hand, though she still couldn't look away. His eyes fluttered open, and she gasped. He tried to sit up, moaned, and dropped back to the bed.

"Be still," she warned.

His hand went to his head, and he stared at her. "Rosa?"

She couldn't help but smile. "Yes."

"What happened?" His voice sounded raspy.

"I'm not sure. My stepfather found you like this and brought you here."

"Where am I?"

"My house."

He tried to sit up again. "I should leave."

She pressed her hand to his chest. "I don't think that's a good idea. Rest for the night and see how you feel in the morning."

He didn't fight but relaxed against the pillow. In seconds his eyes closed and he was asleep. She watched his chest rise and fall for a minute then studied his face again. How could she care for a man she didn't know? But without a doubt, her heart ached for how much he might be hurting. She examined her handiwork. At least she'd done her best to take away some of his pain.

The fact that Miles had been beaten and was in her house, in her bedroom, filled her with surprise. With much effort, she tried to withstand the urge to touch his face but couldn't resist running her finger across his brow, as if she needed the contact to prove he was really there.

She brushed his hair back from his forehead, drawing closer to him so she could examine his face. His strong, whiskered jaw reminded her of her father's, except Miles had a small dimple on his chin. His wide mouth and soft lips held her attention for several seconds before she leaned to his ear and whispered a short prayer for his quick healing. He stirred, making her pull away to make sure he was still asleep. She cupped his cheek, relishing the rough texture on her palm.

"You helped me with that man in the Alamo. Maybe you could help me with so much more. In fact, maybe you're the answer to my prayer."

She stared at his face a moment longer then rested her hand on his arm, telling herself she did it only to know the moment he awoke.

* * * * *

Miles shifted and winced. His head throbbed with each heartbeat and felt as though spikes were being driven into his temple. He opened his eyes. A thin shaft of light streaked across the ceiling. . .a ceiling he didn't recognize. Very slowly he turned his head to peer around. Nothing looked familiar.

He tried to lift his hand to touch his aching skull, but something held it down. He tugged harder.

"Oh!"

A woman's head came into view. *Rosa?* So he wasn't dreaming last night. She stood and peered into his eyes, a beautiful, warm smile on her face.

"How's the head feel?"

"Like my horse is standing on it."

Her smile grew. "Can I get you anything? Water, maybe?"

"That would be nice."

Once she disappeared from view, he wished he hadn't said anything to send her away. But a minute later, she was back and helping him lift his head. Stars sparkled in his eyes from the movement. He took a quick sip and lay down, closing his eyes against the pain. Her cool hand on his forehead made him open his eyes again. She was incredibly beautiful with her black hair hanging loose about her shoulders. Her dark brown eyes held the warmth of a thousand candles. His heartbeat increased, making his head throb worse.

"No fever. That's good."

"Thank you for all you've done."

"You're welcome, but I haven't done much."

"You've done plenty. In fact, I really should be going."

She gently shoved him back down with a hand on each of his shoulders. It didn't take much effort. He felt as weak as a new kitten.

"Let me fix you something to eat. If you feel better after that, I'll help you back to the Alamo. Otherwise, you can stay right there until you're up to the walk."

Once again she disappeared, leaving him feeling deprived. He'd fought the longing to pull her into his arms. That thought alone made him know he needed to leave. He took his time sitting up, the effort making drums beat in his ears. Shoving the blanket aside, he swung his feet to the floor and stayed in that position until the room stopped turning.

As he sat, he did a quick inspection and found he was fully clothed with his knife still in its sheath. What about his rifle? He looked around and saw it lying on a table, right next to his hat.

He tried to remember what had happened the night before. The events came back slowly at first, and then it all rushed back. If whoever hit him didn't take his gun and knife, then they were only after the note or trying to keep him from having it.

Noise from the kitchen forced him to his feet. The room wobbled a few moments then righted itself. What he could see of this room and the rest of the house was sparsely furnished but very clean. Either Rosa had just moved in or she didn't have the money for embellishments, which would explain why she did laundry for the men at the fort. What bothered him most were the masculine touches, especially the worn boots near the door. Maybe he would find out who they belonged to while he ate.

With careful steps, he made his way out to the table. The more he stayed upright, the better his head felt. Now if he could just get rid of the weakness pulling at his limbs. He dropped onto a chair.

Rosa turned and gasped. "You weren't supposed to get up. I would have brought your food to you."

He smiled. This was exactly how he pictured his life. . .sitting at the table waiting for the woman he loved to join him. The thought brought him up short. He'd fallen in love with a woman he knew only from a distance.

"Go back to bed."

Rosa's demand shook him back to the present. When had she found time to pull her hair back into a bun? He preferred it loose, but she was still a beauty.

"I can't do that. I need to return to the Alamo."

She eyed him for several moments, as if trying to read his mind. "Are you expecting to start another battle soon?"

"No." He hated seeing her fear. "At least we don't think so. We don't expect any fighting for several months." He hesitated to ask any questions but wanted to know. "Were you here for the battle last year? Did your father fight?"

She turned back to the stove and stirred something that smelled like it came directly from heaven. "He didn't fight in the one here. He was killed in another battle early last year."

So who do the boots belong to? "I'm sorry."

"Thank you." She lifted the skillet and emptied the contents on a plate. After setting a slice of bread on top, she brought the feast to him. "Hope you like it. I didn't have much to put together for you."

"If it tastes anything like it smells, it'll be a true blessing. Thank you."

He dipped his head and said a quick prayer. When he looked up, he found her staring again, a puzzled expression on her face.

"I realize you made this, but I also like to thank God for His provision."

"Oh, I understand. I just haven't seen anyone do that for a while. It's nice to see."

His heart warmed even more toward her. "You don't attend a church in town?"

She made a face. "No. I haven't gone since Papa was killed. Mama hasn't wanted to go, and—" She shrugged. "I haven't made much of an effort to see what churches are here."

He could identify with her hesitation. His own anger about his parents' deaths made him drag his feet for months. He appreciated her shameful expression. He shoved a forkful of the eggs and meat mix into his mouth to stem the desire to lean over and kiss her. But once he tasted her food, he wanted to kiss her more.

"This is wonderful. I almost hate to say it, but I think this might be better than anything my mother ever made."

Her face flushed around a wide smile. "When's the last time you saw your mother?"

His eyes went back to his plate. "She and my father were killed in a skirmish almost a year ago."

"Oh, goodness. I'm so sorry."

"All this fighting hasn't been good for anything, it seems."

He dug into the eggs with gusto to keep his mouth too busy to have to talk about their deaths. The slice of bread had been warmed and spread with honey. He finished it in three bites then pushed the plate away and sat back.

"You're an amazing cook, Rosa. Thank you."

"You're welcome. Did you—"

Something slammed into the door, making both of them jump.

"Unlatch this door, Rosa. Let me in!"

As she stood to do the man's bidding, Miles reached for his rifle. He had it pointed at the door as Rosa let in a large, barrel-chested man. He eyed Miles, his nostrils flaring.

"I know that isn't loaded so you might as well put it down."

A quick check proved the man right, but Miles kept it in his hands in case he might need to use it as a club. Rosa stood between them, her eyes to the floor. Miles couldn't tell if her expression held anger or fear. Possibly a mixture of both. She motioned to the man.

"This is my stepfather, Carlos Mendes. He found you and brought you here last night."

Miles gave him a nod. "Thank you, sir."

Carlos's face never changed from the scowl. "Now that you're better, you need to leave. I can't have you here alone with Rosa. It doesn't look good." He glanced at Rosa. "You see to it he makes it back. He still looks wobbly."

"Yes, sir."

He sent another scowl toward Miles then stomped from the

house. Miles waited for Rosa to look at him, but she picked up the dishes from the table and put them in the sink. Then she headed to the door, took the shawl from a hook, and draped it around her shoulders.

"Do you feel ready for this long walk or should I try to borrow a burro?"

"I can make it." He did feel better, although his head still hurt. He was more worried about Rosa. Her entire demeanor had changed since her stepfather's visit. "Did I cause trouble for you, Rosa?"

When she finally looked at him, he could see she fought tears. He wanted to wrap her in his arms.

"You haven't caused any trouble."

He could tell she wanted to say more. He waited, but she remained silent. "Should we go?"

She nodded and opened the door. A glimpse of his reflection in a small mirror made him stop.

She returned. "Is something wrong?"

He made a face. "This bandage. I'm not sure the men need to see this."

With much care, he unwrapped the strips then pulled away the folded cloth, revealing the ugly wound.

"You should keep something over that for a while longer."

"My hat should work."

"And if it starts to bleed again?"

He replaced the folded cloth then tugged his hat over it to hold it in place. "How about this?"

She shrugged and gave a slight shake of her head. "Man's foolish pride. It will have to do."

He stepped out into the bright sunlight, which stabbed his eyes and head like a multitude of knives. The pain matched what was occurring in his heart. He hoped she'd talk to him about whatever was happening to steal her joy. He had a feeling her stepfather stood right in the middle of her difficulties.

Chapter Six

As much as Rosa wanted to hurry, she kept her steps slow and measured for Miles's sake. Like Carlos had mentioned, Miles was still a bit unsteady. She wondered if he'd make it up the hill to the Alamo or if he'd let her go for help. They returned to the fort in near silence. Except for her commenting on the cool weather and Miles telling her again she was a great cook, conversation was limited, though Miles had tried to find out more about her stepfather. She'd responded with a simple "I don't know" when he'd asked where Carlos had been during the night, shutting down his attempt to ask another question.

The fear she'd slip up and say something that would give her away as a spy sealed her lips. The knowledge that she'd been forced into this position because of Carlos did little to calm her self-loathing. And now that she had feelings of affection for Miles, dread that she'd be caught as a two-faced traitor increased tenfold while her revulsion of herself and of Carlos grew one hundred-fold.

Miles must have grown frustrated with the quiet because, within mere yards from the Alamo's gate, he stopped her by grasping her arm.

"Is something wrong, Rosa?"

"What makes you ask that?"

His hands moved from her arms to her cheeks. "Because you won't look at me or talk to me. We were doing fine until your stepfather interrupted. Since then you've been distant. I might be able to help if you talked to me."

Oh, to be able to talk to someone. Especially someone like Miles. But she couldn't. If she told him or anyone of her situation, he'd talk to his leaders and she'd be banned from the Alamo just like her mother. If that were to happen, who knew what Carlos would do. . . or if she'd ever see her mother again.

She stepped back, away from his touch, and tried to smile. "Everything will be fine once I get you back inside the fort." She motioned toward the gate. "Shall we?"

He hesitated, trying to look into her eyes. She turned away and heard him sigh. To keep him from asking any more questions, she continued toward the Alamo, leaving him standing in place.

Walking through the gate felt odd without a cart or armful of laundered clothes for the men. For some reason, she now felt even more scheming and deceitful. She stopped and looked around. The desire to turn and run washed through her. She might have done just that, but John seemed to come out of nowhere. He hooked his arm around her waist and drew her aside.

"My dear Rosa! I knew you wanted to see me as much as I wanted to see you." He turned her to face him and pulled her close. "But I thought you'd wait for me to come escort you here so you wouldn't have to walk alone. I want no man accosting you."

She tried to push him away, but he'd hooked his arms under hers, making her efforts useless. Every time she tried to move her arms, he tightened his hold, lifting her arms higher until they were almost around his neck. From the corner of her eye, she saw Miles watching them, his mouth open. Horrified at what he must think, she struggled harder.

"Let me go!"

John grinned and leaned down, bending her backward and off-balance. "Just a quick kiss and you can be free."

"Turn her loose!"

John looked up, and his grin disappeared. "This is none of your business, Fitch."

Rosa sent Miles a desperate look. He glanced at her then glared at John. "Rosa, would you like me to leave?"

"No."

Miles took a step closer. "Then this is now my business. Let her go."

Breathing heavily, John hesitated then allowed Rosa to stand upright, though he kept his arm around her waist. "She's my girl, Fitch. We shared a moment yesterday. She agreed to allow me to escort her."

Miles stabbed her eyes with his. "Is this true?"

"No."

John pulled her against him again. "It is. Tell him, Rosa."

"I agreed to nothing. In fact, I warned you to keep your hands off me."

She pushed against him, but he refused to let go. Miles took another step forward and shoved his fist into John's chest. His breath left in a gust, making him release her. Rosa raced for the gate. As she ran, she hiked the front of her dress to keep from tripping.

Tears ran down her cheeks. What had she done? Now John would no longer offer information, and she doubted Miles would tell her anything. Without news of the Alamo, Carlos would never let her see her mother again. It was time to search for her mother or leave town. And she had a feeling Carlos would make sure she didn't find her mother.

* * * * *

Miles struck John in the stomach right after the blow to the chest, just to make sure Rosa could escape. John swung at him. He ducked, making his head throb. John rushed him and wrapped both arms around him. In an effort to end the fight quickly, Miles bent forward then back again, throwing John off balance and tossing him to the ground.

With a quick hit to John's abdomen to keep him down, Miles stood and looked around for Rosa. Not seeing her, he ran out the gate. She was already across the bridge, racing toward town.

"Rosa!"

She never slowed.

"Rosa, wait!"

She picked up her pace.

Miles stood in uncertainty. Should he go after her? He wasn't sure his waning strength and throbbing head would get him all the way back to town. With that thought, he decided to either go later in the day or the next morning. But without a doubt, he'd go check on her.

When she'd disappeared from his view, he turned and walked through the gate. As much as he wanted to rest, he needed to find Colonel Neill. He didn't get another step when he was slammed from behind and thrown to the ground. Fists pummeled his back, arms, and neck.

"I told you when I saw you at the bridge to stay away from Rosa!"

As John continued his pounding, Miles muscled to his hands and knees then shoved to one side, tossing John from his back. He pushed to his feet and faced John, already standing with his fists ready and a grin on his face.

"You wanted to know what would happen if you didn't stay away."

"I'm still waiting to find out."

John's grin changed to a glower. "She's mine. Walk away."

"I've seen no ring on her finger or heard of a promise of marriage. That makes her free to be courted by others."

John's nostrils flared. "I've made my intentions known. That should be enough."

"Only for you, it would seem."

"You're not man enough for her."

"When's the last time you peeked into a looking glass?" He relaxed his stance though his head throbbed from the beating. "It's funny, but in all the hours I've spent with her, she never once mentioned your name."

With a growl, John rushed at him. Miles used his right leg to kick at John's while giving him a shove as he blasted past. John almost lost his balance but caught himself with a hand to the ground before hitting the dirt. He spun and threw a handful of the dirt into Miles's face then followed it with three quick punches.

Miles reeled back, rubbing the dust from his eyes. John landed two more hits. The crunch of boots made Miles twist away, avoiding the sound until he could see. John stood a few feet away, his fists at the ready. He looked like someone used to fighting. Miles widened his stance, ready for the challenge.

John came at him, his fists jabbing. Miles bent left to avoid the blows and drove his fist into John's abdomen. He followed it with a downward punch to John's jaw. John didn't fall but spun around and pounded his elbow in the middle of Miles's back before chopping his forearm down on Miles's neck.

Miles dropped to his knees then whirled, his leg catching both of John's. Before John could recover, Miles jumped on him and continued throwing lefts and rights until he had very little strength remaining. He pulled his right arm back, ready to end the fight with one last, powerful blow.

Someone hooked his elbow, stopping the hit. His other arm was grabbed, and the men hauled him off John. Miles tried to wrest out of their grip. He wanted that last blow.

"Hold on, son."

Miles glanced to his right. Crockett held tight, a grin on his face. He motioned to John with his head.

"I think he's done."

Blood oozed from John's face as he rolled to his side. He paused several moments before making his first attempt to push from the ground. A couple of men moved to his side to help.

Crockett led Miles away. He turned his head and pointed at one of his men. "Get his gun and hat and bring them along." Several steps later, he leaned closer. "There aren't many men who'd dare to compete with John. He's a trained fighter."

"It wasn't his fists that made him lose."

"Huh?"

"It was his mouth that got him into trouble."

Crockett laughed and thumped him on the back, hard enough to make Miles grimace. "I like you, son. But it might be a good idea to mend your relationship with that young man."

"Why's that?"

"We've got enough turmoil going on inside this fort. The men in here facing an upcoming violent physical battle don't need to be divided mentally or emotionally by two men they respect. They need to see and feel unity, if not by their leaders, then by their fellow fighters."

Miles could see the wisdom in the request. "Yes, sir. I'll see what I can do."

Crockett squeezed his neck, making Miles wince again. "You're a good man, Fitch." He led him to the barracks. "Let's get you cleaned up. Neill's been waiting to see you."

Half an hour later, Crockett accompanied Miles to Neill's quarters. The colonel motioned them inside.

"Been waiting on you, Fitch." He eyed Miles from head to toe. "You look terrible, son. You better sit down before you fall down."

"Thank you, sir." He dropped onto the nearest chair.

Water still ran down his ears and neck from the near drowning by Crockett, who all but shoved his head into a water barrel. Crockett shut the door behind them then stood against the wall in a position where he could see out the window. The man was shrewd, among many other qualities. Miles could learn much from him.

"You have some information for me, Fitch? By the looks of you, I'd say you came by something the hard way."

"Yes, sir. You could say that."

"Got a name for me?"

"Possibly. Man by the name of Tom Starks. I ate with some of the men last night and didn't like the way he was leaning so close to the doorway of Bowie's quarters. I couldn't tell if he was trying to listen or waiting to get revenge for a little skirmish they had earlier in the day."

Crockett shifted enough to face Miles. "Ain't that the same man you knocked down yesterday?"

Miles cringed, wishing he hadn't said anything. "Yes, sir. He'd attacked a girl so I stopped him."

Neill leaned on his table. "That all you got on him?"

"No, sir. I followed him to a cantina in town and saw him give a woman a piece of paper. She looked like she'd had too much to drink, so I thought it would be easy to find out what was written on the paper. But as soon as I had it, someone struck me on the head and knocked me out. When I woke up, I still had my knife and gun but the paper was gone."

"And you think Starks took it back?"

"Near as I can figure. He might have seen me follow the woman."

Neill sat back, crossed his arms, and appeared to mull the information then nodded. "I'll have someone check on him. You have any others you suspect?"

Rosa came to mind, but, except for her odd whispers in his ear while she thought he was sleeping, she hadn't yet done or said anything to cause him to distrust her. He needed proof.

"No, sir. Not yet, but I'll keep studying and questioning the other men."

"Good. Stop by again tomorrow."

"Yes, sir."

He stood and grimaced at how his body had already stiffened from the fight. He opened the door and limped out, Crockett right behind him.

"Hit your bunk for a rest, Fitch. Don't know that you'll accomplish much for a while anyway."

"I'll do that."

He hobbled to a quiet spot at the far end of the long barracks and hunkered down. He doubted anything could keep him awake, except Crockett's request to mend the relationship with John was doing a pretty good job of it. He had no idea how becoming friends would be possible.

Thoughts of John led to Rosa and the possibility of them having a romance, which was odd, considering the fact that she wanted nothing to do with John. So, what was she doing with him? She claimed not to want his attention, yet she walked and talked with him often. Suspicions floated around in his head, making rest impossible.

Chapter Seven

Rosa had been wandering the streets of Béxar for almost an hour with no success in finding her mother. And the trouble was, she could have already passed where Mama was being held and she would never know it. With the cool weather, most windows and doors were closed. Very few people could be found outdoors.

The rocks in the dirt streets bruised the bottoms of her feet. When she could afford them, she'd need new shoes. The ones she now wore, as well as the bottom half of her skirt, were covered in dust.

She'd lived here since her father died and hadn't seen this much of Béxar, especially the south and west side of town, though there wasn't much to see beyond the cathedral except the creek she didn't know existed until today. She loved all the trees dotting the landscape. Many of the oaks offered shade and cover for homes—and, for the moment, a place to lean while she rested and rubbed her aching feet.

As tired as she was from lack of sleep the night before, she refused to give up her search until she'd at least walked every foot of the town. If she still hadn't found Mama by then, she'd go back to the house and pack. The best she could do after that was leave a note saying she'd be in contact when she found a new place to live. Surely Carlos wouldn't kill Mama if Rosa were no longer around. But even as the thought crossed her mind, doubts assailed.

Soft singing drifted from a window, halting Rosa's steps. The voice sounded so much like Mama's. She rushed to the small mud hut, stooped under the low-hanging thatch, and peeked inside. In her haste, she bumped a small clay pot from the sill. It fell with a thud. A crack showed as it rolled a short distance. The woman of the house swung around, a scowl on her face.

"Ladrón! Desaparece! Dejar!" The woman picked up an onion from the counter and flung it at her.

Rosa ducked. "I'm sorry." She backed away. "I'm so sorry. I'm leaving. But I'm not a thief. I promise."

Tears fell as she left as ordered. She raced down the street, all hopes dashed at finding her mother. She ran all the way home, bursting through the door with thoughts only of tossing her few belongings into a satchel. Surely someone would be leaving town and would let her travel with them. Would Ana go with her?

She slid to a stop at the sight of her stepfather sitting at the table. The scowl he wore deepened at the sight of her.

"Usted es un mentirosa!"

"I'm a liar?" A cold chill skittered down her spine as her face heated. "What have I lied about?"

Carlos leaned forward, his forearms planted on the table. "There aren't over three hundred men inside the Alamo. There might not even be one hundred." His nostrils flared. "What else have you lied about?"

Fear surged until she thought she might be sick. How did he find out? And had he already hurt her mother because of her deception?

"But that's what they told me! Maybe they suspect I'm a spy."

He slammed down his fist, rattling the lantern on the table. "I don't believe you! What else? Do they have large amounts of food stored up or not?"

She swallowed hard and shook her head. "I don't know! They said they had food."

He stood, and she backed against the door, afraid he might slap her harder than he had the day before. He slowly made his way around the table until he stood right in front of her.

"You will get me the rest of the information I want, and you will get me the truth. If you don't, your mother will be dead to you." He closed his fingers around her throat. "Do you understand?"

"I told you the truth, Carlos. . . I can only bring you what information they give me." Already against the door, she couldn't back away any farther. She swallowed past the pressure from his hand and nodded. "Yes, I understand."

"Get it done soon. I will be here this time tomorrow." He reached around her and opened the door. "And remember, I have ways of finding out if you're lying to me."

He slammed the door behind him, and she leaned against it, nearly panting as her heart pounded. After several deep breaths, anger flooded through her. If he had ways of finding the truth, why didn't he use the other person for his information? Why did she continually have to risk her life and dignity for his corrupt purposes?

Carlos stuck his head through the open window. "If you get me what I want, Rosa, I will make sure you spend some time with your mother. But that is the only way you'll get to see her."

When he'd disappeared, she collapsed onto the closest chair and put her face in her hands. She couldn't leave now or she'd run the risk of being the reason her mother was hurt or maybe even killed.

Why, Lord? Why are You doing this?

Those were questions she'd asked many times since her father's death. Nothing made sense anymore. Nothing was easy any longer. But life still went on, and she'd have to learn to deal with the blows as they came, just as her father always had.

Her father. Such a godly man, never failing to trust the Lord during the tough times. He always said things would work out, that God was still on His throne and in control. Difficult as it might be, she'd try to follow his example. She'd have to, or she'd despise herself for the rest of her life.

She stood and moved to the window. The sun hung low in the sky, which meant she'd have to wait until the morning to do her stepfather's bidding. The nights were too dangerous for a woman to be out alone. To fill the hours, she'd make more loaves of bread. Maybe they'd loosen the lips of some of the men, hopefully one in particular.

As she shoved the door latch in place, she prayed John would still look forward to her company and offer up information. But because of how she'd treated him earlier, doubts filled her. Her thoughts moved to Miles, but she believed him too smart to be tricked. Because of her foolishness, she may never see her mother again. Just how far would Carlos go to make that possibility a certainty?

A knock at the door made her jump. *Please don't be Carlos again.*

"Who is it?"

"It's Ana. Let me in."

Rosa shoved aside the latch and opened the door. "Is something wrong?"

"That's what I planned to ask you. I saw Carlos stomping down the street. Did he hurt you again?"

Not physically. "No, I'm fine."

"Are you sure? You look upset. In fact, I've never seen you so tense before. Have you told me everything?"

Rosa moved to the kitchen and pulled out all the items she'd need for making bread. Ana stood beside her and took the bowl.

"How many loaves this time?"

Rosa smiled and gave Ana a hug. "Four?"

"Done. Maybe you can get rid of your tension by hitting the dough."

That made Rosa laugh. She could always count on Ana to make her feel better. Maybe now was the time to ask what she'd been wondering.

"If I were planning to leave Béxar, would you come with me?"

"Why would you leave? Your mother is here."

"But if I were?"

Ana turned and gave Rosa her complete attention. "I don't know, Rosa. My family is here. It would have to be an awfully important reason for me to leave." She took Rosa's hands. "Please tell me what's happening. I promise I won't say a word to anyone."

As they worked on the bread, Rosa tearfully told Ana everything—the threats from Carlos, her mother's disappearance, John's unwanted attentions, and Miles spending the night in her bed.

Ana gave her another hug. "No wonder you want to leave. But how can you do so with your mother still missing?"

"I can't. I won't. Not until I know she's safe. And I'll do what Carlos demands to make sure she's not hurt. But after that, I think I'll leave. I can't stay here." Her voice hitched. "Though Mama has already said she won't go with me."

"Oh, Rosa. I'm so sorry this has happened to you. Is there any way I can help, besides leaving? I'm not sure I can do that. It's something I'll have to think about."

"I understand. And just being here is help enough. I don't know what else you can do."

Ana kneaded the dough for several moments then stopped. "I know. I can try to follow Carlos. Maybe I can find your mother before you have to let Carlos try to sell your soul."

"Oh, would you? That would be wonderful."

"I'll do it. At least I'll try."

Ana left when four loaves were formed and in pans, allowing Rosa to bask in the sweet friendship and the hope lifting her spirits.

* * * * *

Miles sat up, rubbed his eyes, and looked around. The sun had become a red ball near the horizon. He'd slept too long and hadn't accomplished a thing. . .except to feel better. His head didn't hurt nearly as much as earlier. He pushed to his feet. Time to get something done, like find more information for Colonel Neill. Visiting Rosa would have to wait until morning, which was a shame. He'd dreamed of another chance to taste her cooking. But more than that, he needed time to speak with her.

Rifle in hand and stomach rumbling, Miles walked through the long barracks, taking his time as he passed the rooms in case some of the men were talking, but he heard only silence. He ducked out the door and headed toward the kitchen in search of something to eat. Hopefully the cook had managed to put together a meal as tasty as the one the night before. And with any luck, the men would be in a good and talkative mood.

Halfway to the kitchen, he spotted John sitting on the wall of the southwest corner, his foot propped on the cannon wheel, watching his every step. Miles eyed him for several seconds while Crockett's request to befriend the man rolled through his mind.

With no idea what he would say, he strode across the court and up the incline of the cannon ramp. He stopped a few feet from John, who had tensed as if ready for another fight, and leaned against the wall, his rifle resting across his arms. Miles glanced down and noticed several of the men were watching. Some looked ready to race up the incline to stop them if he started anything, yet more proof of the wisdom of Crockett's request.

John's puffy and bruised face made Miles wonder if he looked as bad. "I'm not here to continue the fight, Prine. In fact, I want to apologize. It won't happen again."

"Does that mean you plan to stay away from Rosa?"

How could he say no without starting another fight? "Look out there, John." He took the time to glance around at the land he loved. All the trees growing in town amazed him. The oaks, the only trees still holding on to their leaves, added plenty of green to the view. "As far as I'm concerned, that's what we need to be fighting for. If we're fighting each other, we're not only splitting our alliance, but also that of the men down there ready to do battle for that land."

He ignored the shocked look on John's face and recognized the moment he'd softened and maybe even agreed. Then a thought came to him, something his father once told him.

"Everyone in this fort is here for the same reason, as though we're one body. If you and I continue to quarrel and clash, we'll hurt this body of men as surely as if we remove an arm or leg. If we work together, we'll be much stronger, both individually and as a group." He turned to face John. "The day is coming when we'll possibly be in the biggest battle of our lives. What do you say we face it together?"

John sat silent a few moments then nodded. "Makes good sense. I agree. But you didn't answer my question. Does this mean you're going to stay away from Rosa?"

He stared down at the town of Béxar and pictured Rosa cooking and doing laundry inside one of the houses. How could he never see her again?

"I'm not going to lie, Prine. I plan to see her one more time. If she tells me there's no chance of any kind of relationship with me, I'll walk away and never talk to her again, but only if you'll promise never to force yourself on her again." He turned and held out his hand. "I hope you can accept that."

John looked intently into his eyes until Miles thought he'd ruined everything by what he'd just said. Then John reached and shook his hand.

"I think I can live with that."

"Thank you." Miles was about to walk away when John stopped him.

"You're a better man than I first thought, Fitch."

Miles clapped him on the shoulder. "And the men down there have a good man to follow."

He headed back to the kitchen with a feeling of contentment, and the men seemed much more at peace, as well. The tension on their faces had dissolved into smiles. But the nod he received from Crockett was the most satisfying of all. Now, to take care of Neill's request.

On the way to eat a meal with the men, and hopefully pry some information from them, he received several thumps on the back as well as tips of the hat or nods from men too far to reach him. Halfway across the court, one man clapping his hands stopped Miles from taking another step. He turned to face a smirking Tom Starks.

"Very nice, Fitch." Starks put his hand over his heart. "Got me right here."

A sarcastic reply came to mind, but Miles didn't want to be put into the position of having to apologize to or befriend this man, too.

"Thank you, Starks."

He tried to move on, but Starks stood in his path once more.

"You heading to town again tonight, Fitch? Cuz if'n you are, maybe we can walk together this time instead of you trailing so far behind. Give the appearance of being friends. Kinda like you and John up there."

So Starks did know of his presence in town. But was he the one who nearly cracked his skull? He took the few steps needed to keep anyone else from hearing what he had to say.

"I wouldn't be seen walking anywhere with you, Starks, for fear of being mistaken as your friend."

He moved away before Starks could respond or take a swing at him. William Morrell, who'd wanted a lesson in fighting, stepped out of the room next to Bowie's. He looked down and brushed at his sleeves and shirtfront before continuing on.

"Care to join me at tonight's meal, sir?"

"I would, Fitch, but I've got my heart set on some better cooking and"—he looked around—"some better-looking company. Hopefully one that smells better too."

Miles grinned. "I understand completely. Maybe tomorrow. Enjoy your evening, sir."

"I intend to do just that."

William hadn't quite made it out the gate before Starks went after him. Miles wavered between getting his food and following Starks. His stomach voiced a strong disapproval, but he decided to trail Starks. This time he'd be ready for any kind of an attack.

Starks must have expected him to follow. By the time Miles made it across the bridge, Starks was nowhere to be seen. The man must have run to get away that fast. Miles headed straight for the same cantina, hesitated a moment, and then peeked inside. No Starks. He looked up and down the street then started wandering the town in hopes of running across the man. He peered into the two other cantinas he came across and still didn't find Starks.

If he were a wise man, he'd march straight back to the Alamo and see if there was anything left to eat, but as far as he could recall, no one had ever called him wise. As though he had no control, his feet led him to Rosa's house. The windows were dark. If his nose wasn't mistaken, the faint scent of freshly baked bread hung in the air. His mouth flooded at the thought of Rosa's bread. He'd be on the watch for her in the morning.

He stood in front of the house trying to decide what to do next. Just as he was about to return to the Alamo, he spotted William leading a woman along by the hand. They knocked on a door. In seconds, the door opened and they disappeared inside. Miles smiled. William's wishes had come true.

The scent of cooking meat wafted on the air. Miles followed the scent and found himself in front of a small cantina he hadn't noticed before. He pushed inside, not caring if Starks was there or not. The man behind the bar eyed him. Miles made motions of eating. What was the word for *food*? He'd heard it so many times at the fort. He scolded himself. He had much more Spanish to learn.

"*Comida? Usted quiere un poco a comer?*"

Miles smiled at the man. "Food. Yes, please." He pulled out some coins and placed them on the counter. "How much?"

The man slid a couple coins onto his palm and pointed at a table. Miles nodded and sat, hoping it wouldn't take long. In minutes, a steaming plate of beans, rice, and spicy chicken was placed before him.

"Thank you."

He said a quick blessing and shoveled up the food as though he hadn't eaten in a week. As he swallowed the last few bites, he thought the leaders at the Alamo would be wise to hire the cook in this place. The food, though simple, was some of the tastiest he'd had in a long time.

He pushed the plate away, stood, and rubbed his belly as he turned to the owner. "Very good. Thank you."

The words had hardly left his mouth when a gunshot went off, followed by a shout and a scream. It sounded close. Miles raced out of the cantina and down the street. More yelling led him toward Rosa's house. Heart pounding, he rounded the corner to see lamplight streaming from Rosa's doorway.

Chapter Eight

Rosa screamed when her door burst open. She screamed again when the intruder fell, firing and dropping his pistol. She tossed her club aside and grabbed the attacker's pistol. Hands shaking, she pointed the gun toward the man as he stood and raced back outside. Unwilling to take any chances, she kept the gun aimed at the door. She tried to control her breathing as her heartbeat pounded in her ears.

Calm. Stay calm. He might be back.

Pounding footfalls came closer. Then someone was in the door. She pulled the trigger. Nothing happened. She tried to pull the hammer back.

"Rosa?"

She tossed the gun aside and reached for the club she'd dropped.

"Rosa, stop."

Someone grabbed her. She screamed once more.

"It's me, Rosa. It's Miles."

The club was pulled from her hands, and she heard it drop to the floor. Miles? Was Miles really here? Strong arms held her close.

"I'm here. Are you all right?"

When he held her away from him, she looked into his eyes. He'd never looked so good.

She nodded and tried to speak then cleared her throat. "I'm fine."

"What happened?"

She relived the attack and started shaking all over again. "It was him. That man at the Alamo. He kept shouting your name then broke into my house."

"Starks?"

Who was Starks? And who were all the people filling the house? Many of them were neighbors, several were strangers, all pushing inside and asking what had happened. She wanted to tell them to leave. She only wanted Miles. But they came closer, pushing against her. Miles used his body as a shield, holding her in his arms as he tried to keep everyone at bay. Tears filled her eyes. Everything was out of control.

"What's going on?" Her stepfather's voice bellowed, and everyone grew quiet. He shoved his way through the throng, his dark brows drawing into a deep scowl when he saw her. He pulled his pistol and aimed it at Miles.

"You scoundrel! Get away from her!"

Horrified, Rosa tried to stand between the two men, but Miles refused to release her. She held up a hand.

"Wait! It wasn't him. He wasn't the one who broke into the house. He's only trying to protect me."

"Protect you? He looks to be doing much more than that. Back away from her!" Carlos's voice hadn't calmed at all. The order came out as a roar.

Miles held up his hands. "I meant no harm. I heard the gunshot and came at a run."

This time, Rosa was able to move between Miles and the gun. "It's true. He arrived after the other man broke down the door."

"What other man?" Carlos looked around. "Is he here?" He bent and picked up the discarded pistol. "Where'd this come from?"

"It belongs to the other man. He fell and it went off. I grabbed it." Her voice shook, partly from fear of Carlos.

Carlos shoved the pistol into his waistband. "I want everyone to leave, especially you." He pointed at Miles with his pistol.

Another man Rosa recognized from the Alamo approached and

put his arm around Miles's shoulders. "Come, son. I think it's time to take our leave."

He nodded at Carlos and led Miles out the door. Miles craned his neck to see her, but the man pushed him outside. All the other people followed them, soon leaving her alone with Carlos. Her stomach constricted as she waited for his next move or comment.

He sat on the nearest chair, set his pistol on the table, and ran a hand through his thick hair, looking extremely weary. He pointed to another chair. "Sit. Tell me what happened."

She did as told and prepared to relay the entire incident. What seemed to have taken a lifetime had all happened in mere minutes.

"A man who sounded much like you demanded that I open the door." She left out the part where she ran for her club. "He slammed against the door a couple of times and it finally gave. It was a man from the Alamo. He fell inside, and the gun went off. I grabbed it, but I think he was so surprised, he ran off. Then Miles came inside."

"Miles? You two are so familiar with each other, you call him Miles?"

"No, sir. It's what he asked me to call him."

"You don't know why that man broke inside?"

"Only that he'd attacked me once before. I suppose he wanted another chance."

"You never told me you'd been attacked."

Rosa made a face. "I didn't think it would matter. You've already told me to do whatever was necessary to get your information."

Carlos nodded. "You're right." He pushed to his feet. "All right. If you'll fix me some coffee, I'll fix the door. Maybe I can make it strong enough to keep the young men out."

Stunned at this softer side of Carlos, Rosa stood and heated some water. As she went about the task of brewing his coffee, she realized it hadn't taken him long to get to the house. Did that mean her mother was also nearby?

* * * * *

Miles walked silently next to William Morrell, his mind focused on what might be happening to Rosa. Carlos raged like an angry bull. Surely he wouldn't take it out on his stepdaughter, would he?

"What were you doing in that house, Fitch? You could've gotten yourself killed tonight."

"Yes, sir. I realize that. But it's like the girl said, I ran inside after I heard the gunshot."

"What were you doing in town? When I left the fort, you were about to eat with the men."

How could he answer that without divulging the task Neill entrusted him with? "I ended up eating at a cantina instead." That was true enough, and it didn't give anything away.

They were both quiet for several moments. He'd never been so glad to see the glowing torchlights from the Alamo. Miles was ready to be inside and find a quiet place to run the events of the night through his thoughts.

"For such a quiet fella, you sure get into lots of scrapes."

Miles smiled. "Yes, sir. Sure seems that way."

William clapped him on the back as they passed through the Alamo gates. "Why don't you save all that energy for the fight ahead of us?"

"Good idea."

He hadn't gotten far when someone called his name. Crockett stepped out of the shadows and motioned him over. Much as he liked the man, Miles wanted some quiet time.

After the two shook hands, Crockett led him away from everyone. "Find out anything tonight?"

"Only that Starks broke into the house of the young lady he attacked the other day. He ran off before anyone could catch him."

Crockett stopped and gazed at the stars a few moments. "Interesting. Why would he do such a fool thing?"

"I don't know, but if I ever find him. . ."

"Hold on, Fitch. I'll talk to Bowie. I'm sure he'll put the word out to bring Starks to him. He'll take care of the problem. But you didn't see him talking to anyone in town?"

"No, sir. He disappeared as though he knew I was following him."

Crockett blew out a breath. "This is taking longer than I thought it would. Maybe if we keep Starks out of the Alamo, the leak of information will end. Time will tell."

He slapped Miles on the back. "Since you had such a long rest this afternoon, why don't you go up and help Hector keep watch?" He pointed at the southwest corner. "Two pairs of eyes are better than one. See ya in the morning, Fitch."

Pushing away disappointment, Miles made his way up the ramp toward Hector and the eighteen-pounder cannon. The two shared a nod.

"I'm Miles Fitch."

"Hector Rojas."

Miles tried to make himself comfortable. The Tejano had the best position. . .sitting on the wall and propping his feet on the cannon. Miles ended up leaning his forearms on the top of the wall.

The town of Béxar didn't look nearly as large from this vantage point. While wandering the crooked streets, the town seemed much larger, though the houses were spread out quite far, especially to the north. He tried to picture which house belonged to Rosa. There weren't many lanterns still burning, making it impossible to find the right place.

He regarded Hector from the corner of his eyes. The man looked tired. "I can take this watch for you."

"I'm fine."

Miles peered out into the darkness on both sides of the town. No lights could be seen except the flashes coming from fireflies. He stifled a yawn. This night would be awfully long with so much tension. Good or bad, he decided to break the silence by seeking an answer to a question that held his curiosity since he'd arrived.

"Why are you here, Hector?"

"I was assigned to this post."

"No, I mean—"

"I know what you meant."

Yep, this was going to be a long night.

"I apologize, *señor*. I think maybe I've been asked that question one too many times."

For the first time, Miles considered the feelings of the Tejanos, the native Mexican Texans, in the upcoming battle. He'd always looked at them with a bit of suspicion. Now he had a sense there was a deeper reason for their presence.

"I'm sorry too. I really didn't mean to imply anything with that question."

"I think maybe you did. I think maybe you thought of us, of me, as traitors? You look at us as possible spies, yet you forget to consider your own kind."

Odd how he'd used *spy* and *traitor* in his comment, the very descriptions of the person he sought. "My own kind? You mean an American? You have someone in mind?"

The torch next to Hector revealed he held up two fingers. "You ever seen a two-headed snake?"

"No, sir."

"A two-headed snake has two heads, two brains, but shares one body. Most times, the heads move as though disoriented, as though they can't agree. And many times, they attack the other head and try to swallow each other."

Miles knew a moment of impatience. "I know you're trying to make a point."

"I am. Someone you know has an American father and a Mexican mother. Who's to say she isn't any different than any number of men here, being pulled both ways?"

"She? You mean Rosa?" Miles tensed, ready to fight for his girl once again. "And you dare to call her a snake?"

"No, señor. My mistake. I only used the snake as my example of the possibility of her indecision as to which side she wants to fight for."

"So you're saying she might be a traitor?"

"To which side, señor? Every man in this fort is fighting for what they believe, as are the men we will fight. It's possible she doesn't yet know which side she's on. Haven't you thought the same about all the Tejanos in here? But I won't hold it against you. I have a feeling you have a reason for doubting us."

Hector's voice held a tinge of sympathy. He probably had a fair idea about Miles's reason for being here. He resumed his position leaning on the wall.

"My parents were killed in a skirmish with some Mexican nationals. At least that's what I was told. I was also told not to go home or I'd end up next to them." He looked at Hector. "Even though that land belongs to me now."

"Just as I'd feared. But let me assure you, señor, that I was not one of those nationals."

Miles adjusted his stance so he could see both the town and Hector. "Help me understand, Hector. What would cause a man to fight against his own people, his own president?"

Hector slid off the wall and shifted to stand beside him, leaning on the wall in much the same way. The move gave Miles a sense of camaraderie, as though Hector had decided to trust him.

"You can ask that same question to six different Tejano men and get the same number of answers. It's wrong to lump all of us into the same mold, to assume we all think and act the same way. You could ask the same question to any of the American men down there and get several more answers. You have one of your own."

Hector's wise words managed to stuff Miles's doubts down his throat. Shame washed through him. "You're right. I'm sorry again."

"No need. Open eyes lead to understanding."

Miles immediately liked Hector. He was a teacher, much like his own father had been. "May I ask your reason for being here?"

"You may." Hector shifted his feet. "I used to be a follower of Santa Anna back when he and I shared the same political ideas. He used to be a federalist who wanted each state to be self-governed. When he became president, he changed to a centralist and wanted complete control over all of Mexico. Shortly after that, he became more of a dictator, with sole and absolute, and sometimes abusive, power." He rubbed his hands together as if to warm them. "Money and power. Two things that can turn a good man into another kind of two-headed snake."

Hector took a long breath. "What really put me over the edge was when Santa Anna ordered his troops to rape and rampage the village where members of my family lived because they were planning a revolt against his tyranny. He used that massacre as a message to anyone who might be planning their own rebellion. My brother and his family, much like yours, were killed."

Miles prayed his mother and father didn't suffer such atrocities. "I'm sorry, Hector."

"Me too." He pushed upright and rubbed his lower back before gesturing to some of the men resting on the ground below. "The reasons for them being here? Some will echo mine. Others have grown up in this region and have gotten used to the easy access of American goods and ideas. They've developed a working relationship with many businesses in Louisiana. They fear those freedoms will be removed if Santa Anna wins." He returned to his position on the wall. "Others are landowners and want to secure their claims. As I said, many reasons from many men. None are necessarily wrong, just different."

Miles examined the reasons of the men he'd met. Some were like him, wanting to keep the land where they'd been raised or once owned. Others wanted to preserve their own version of freedoms. Those who'd just arrived, the volunteers who came to fight, were here to expand the land of America, while others wanted to be in a battle to feel a sense of purpose and belonging. Like Hector said, many men and just as many reasons.

"Do you mind one more question?"

"Not at all. You're a good listener."

"Why would Santa Anna come here to the Alamo first instead of someplace else, like Goliad? This seems a little out of the way, whereas Goliad brings him right into the heart of Texas."

"*Sí*. This is true. But did you hear about the battle fought here back in December?"

"Yes. The Texians beat the Mexican forces in a decisive victory. That's part of the reason why I came here."

"Did you know that the leader here at the time, General Cos, was Santa Anna's brother-in-law? I doubt Santa Anna took that loss too well. It was a slight on the family name. One he didn't take lightly. He'll want to come back with an absolute triumph to win back the good family name. And trust me, he will want it to be complete and bloody."

"And will he? Have a chance at winning, I mean?"

"I think he will bring everyone he can, whether they come willingly or not. He will want a show of force."

Miles frowned. "Knowing that, you still want to fight here?"

"I want to fight for what I believe is right. Don't you?"

"I do. Absolutely." He held out a hand. "Thank you for explaining all of this, Hector. I'm honored you took the time."

Hector accepted the handshake. "You're a good man, señor. I will enjoy the new friendship."

Miles settled in for the night, his eyes continually drifting toward town. He planned to stay put until he spotted Rosa on her way to the Alamo. It was time they had a long talk.

Chapter Nine

Rosa placed the four loaves of bread at the bottom of her basket, covered them with cloth, and then put the men's laundered clothing on top. After a disappointing morning searching for her mother and coming up empty-handed, she lifted her chin with determination. She'd get the answers to her stepfather's questions so she could see her mother again. Failing that, she might have to resort to threatening Carlos's life. How, she didn't know, but she'd find a way.

Only steps out the door, she heard her name. She turned to see Ana Maria running toward her as fast as her skirt allowed. Ana grabbed her in a hug without slowing, nearly knocking them both to the ground.

"I just heard what happened last night. Are you all right?"

"I'm fine. Carlos fixed the door even better than it was. I feel safer."

Ana held her at arms' length, examining her face. "Why did that man break in? Did he want to hurt you?"

"I don't think so. He was hollering Miles's name. I assume he thought Miles was inside with me."

"What did Miles say?"

"We didn't have much time to talk. Maybe we can today."

"Oh, Rosa." She pulled her into another hug. "I'm scared for you. Why don't you stay at our house where you'll be safe?"

Rosa stepped back. "Thank you, Ana, but really, I'm safe right here."

"Well, maybe I should go with you to the Alamo. That should keep anyone from attacking you."

"I appreciate the offer, Ana, but I'm afraid having you along might not only draw more attention and questions, but it could also add suspicion. I don't need any of those today." She squeezed Ana's hand for added assurance. "I'll be fine. I'd better go so I won't be out too late."

Nearly out of breath from hurrying through town and up the hill to the Alamo, Rosa nodded to the men at the gate as she entered. She scanned the grounds, searching for John as she made her way to the barracks to hand out the clean clothing and gather any items they might want washed. She hoped for plenty of dirty laundry. It would give her more money and allow her to stay inside the fort longer and talk to many men who might offer information, even if it came from an overheard conversation.

Rosa scanned the Alamo compound until a movement by the kitchen drew her attention. John stood for a few moments looking at her. She smiled, hoping the gesture was enough of an invitation for him to join her. He headed her way, making her confidence soar, only to crash when he tipped his hat and turned away, disappearing through the opening that led to the chapel and palisade.

Tears threatened. Just as she'd feared, her actions yesterday, along with her denials of a courtship, had caused John to reject her. Hope of finding answers and saving her mother all but disappeared. The only chance of information would have to come from the other men in the fort, most of whom she didn't know.

"Excuse me, miss. You have my shirt?"

She swiped at the tears and forced a smile. "Yes, I sure do."

He, along with a few others, received their laundry and handed her a few coins. They didn't offer any other dirty clothes, nor did they stay any longer than necessary. She waited, hoping someone would have work for her. But it was as if they intentionally avoided her. She received many stares and a few nods, but no other men came near. Either John or Miles must have said something to them, maybe warning them away from her for one reason or another. But if the warning came because they suspected her of spying, she had no chance of helping her mother.

With very little optimism, she trudged to the kitchen. "Hello?"

The two men inside turned then took a step back, proving to her the men had been warned to stay away.

"I have bread for the men, if you'd like to serve it to them."

The two exchanged a look then nodded. Only one made the effort to claim the loaves. Basket empty and eyes full of tears, Rosa raced from the Alamo, probably for the last time. If the men wouldn't come near her, let alone talk to her, there was nothing more for her at the fort. Fear increased the flow of tears. What would Carlos say or do when she gave him the news? With each step toward Béxar, she felt farther and farther away from her mother.

* * * * *

Miles spent his early morning hours walking the perimeter of the fort with Colonel Crockett, gaining a new appreciation for its size. But that appreciation gave way to worry as he realized the difficulty of defending the Alamo with so few men. One feature that would help was the fact that most of the limestone walls of the complex were at least two feet thick and anywhere from nine to twelve feet tall. The chapel itself had been made with four-feet-thick limestone blocks. He'd counted about seventeen cannons the Mexican army left behind when they were defeated and prayed they all worked. They could mount a good defense with that kind of artillery.

The north wall gave them some concern. A large section had crumbled, probably from artillery fire during the battle back in December. Work crews had done their best to shore up the weakened wall by piling dirt and timber against the breach. But with the eight-pound cannons placed near the breach and the additional cannon at the northwest corner, he hoped Santa Anna might find attacking the wall unappealing.

The other weak part of the Alamo was the palisade on the south side, but even the log barricade seemed quite sturdy. From what he and Crockett could figure, the fort was safe and well fortified except for the lack of able-bodied men.

Miles stopped and examined the north wall of the fort, tipping back his head to estimate the height to the top, guessing it over eight feet. "I think the palisade is the only area we need to worry about."

Crockett nodded. "I agree. My men and I will defend that part of the wall."

"I'll help."

Crockett clapped him on the back. "I'll be glad to have you."

They were about to turn the corner when Colonel Neill rode by them, tipping his hat as he passed. Miles noted the bedroll and saddlebags. Stunned, he took several moments to react. He turned to Crockett for an explanation.

"He's going on furlough."

"Furlough?" He glanced back and caught one final look at Neill before he disappeared over a small hill. "Now? We're about to go to battle and he's leaving?"

The lines around Crockett's eyes deepened. "His family's been stricken with an illness. He's going home to care for them. He left Travis in charge while he's away. He claims he'll be back in two or three weeks, long before he figures Santa Anna will arrive."

Miles examined Crockett's face. "Will he be back before then?"

Crockett shrugged. "Time will tell."

"And what about my task of finding the traitor?"

"Neill told Travis and Bowie all about it. You still have the task, but now you'll report to me and I'll pass along any news."

They continued along the wall toward the gate when Miles caught sight of Rosa running toward Béxar. He'd been watching for her to arrive when Crockett invited Miles to join him for the examination of the walls. He looked at Crockett, who smiled and motioned with his head.

"Go on. But I want a report when you get back."

Miles ignored the wink and raced after Rosa. He slowed as he reached the edge of town so as not to garner too much attention. Some of the families sat visiting outside their homes. As the mothers chatted while grinding corn, the children played in the open area of the street chasing each other around.

One young boy tussled with a puppy. He stood and tried to walk away, but the puppy latched on to his britches and started tugging backward. The child strained against the jerks, finally falling forward, his hands planted in the dirt as he pulled the opposite direction. The puppy won when the boy's trousers dropped to his knees, making the child shout for his mama. All the ladies laughed as one woman rose to help. Miles smiled and tipped the brim of his hat to them. The scene warmed his heart.

He caught up to Rosa just as she reached her house. He touched her arm, only to have her pull it back.

"What happened, Rosa? It seems you're always running from the Alamo. Did someone hurt you? Did John bother you again?"

"No. He never even said a word to me. He just walked away." She set the empty basket on a bench and crossed her arms. "Did you threaten him or something?"

"Not threaten, exactly. I just asked him not to attack you again."

"There must have been more to it than that. He wouldn't come near me or even talk to me."

The comment filled him with confusion. Was this the same woman who, only yesterday, begged him with her eyes to make John leave her alone? The same woman who said she had no relationship with the man?

"I was under the impression you wanted nothing to do with him. What changed?"

The contents of Rosa's laundry basket suddenly held her complete interest.

"Rosa?"

She refused to look at him. Frustration and impatience took root and quickly grew. This time he wanted answers, and he planned to stay until he got them. He rested his rifle against the house and sat on the bench next to the basket.

"I'm not leaving until you talk to me."

She spun around and, with hands on her slim hips, glared at him. He leaned against the adobe, propped his head with his hands, and gave her a warm smile. He saw the moment she softened, even appeared to fight her own smile. He set the basket on the ground and patted the empty place next to him. She groaned and dropped beside him.

"What do you want to know?"

He leaned over and bumped her with his shoulder. "I like this much better."

"What? That you forced me to talk?"

"No. I like that you're no longer so far away."

She shook her head and swatted his arm, still fighting the smile he wanted to see. Then he caught himself. As much as he wanted to relax and enjoy Rosa's company, he had some very serious questions that needed honest answers.

He sat a little straighter and cleared his throat. "Rosa, I have to ask again, why are you so upset about John not speaking to you when, just yesterday, you wanted him to leave you alone?"

She stiffened. "Look at my bad manners. I haven't even offered you something to drink. Can I get you some water?"

"Rosa—"

She stood. "I'll be right back."

She disappeared inside the house. What should have taken only minutes seemed to take forever, until he thought he'd have to go in search of her, yet more proof she was hiding something.

* * * * *

Rosa wasted as much time as she dared, knowing where Miles's question would lead. Her stomach churned as she struggled with the decision of whether or not to tell him everything. If she did confess, could she bear the look of revulsion bound to be on his face, aimed directly at her, and with good reason? But what were her choices?

On one hand sat her mother's freedom and safety, which might already be in jeopardy since she had rebuffed John. She could think of no other way to gain the information Carlos sought. On the other hand sat her friendship and possible relationship with Miles, which already had no definite promises. But to confess she'd played the traitor with his friends at the Alamo guaranteed the severance of that friendship. She had no doubt the conversation would end with him stomping away with disgust.

Lord, help me! What do I do?

After taking several deep breaths, she finally returned outside with two glasses of water. Her hand shook as she handed one to him. Instead of sitting next to him again, she hovered nearby and stared into the distance, wishing she were anywhere but here.

"Rosa, please come back here and talk to me." His voice was tender and sensitive, making her heart break for what was about to happen. "You can trust me."

When she turned to face him again, it was with tears nearly overflowing her eyes. He set aside his glass and stood, and though his hands reached for her, he stopped short of actually touching her. He was already unsure of her, and she hadn't yet said a word.

"Tell me, Rosa. What has you so upset?"

"I can't tell you. You're a soldier at the Alamo."

His mouth opened and closed a couple times as his throat worked. "What does that mean? This obviously has something to do with the Alamo." He grasped her arms. "What have you been doing, Rosa?" His nostrils flared as he took a breath. "Laundry isn't the only thing you've been collecting from the men, is it?"

She hesitated, glancing around to see if anyone was watching, then shook her head, unable to speak the words. Her stomach threatened to empty itself.

Miles dropped his arms to his sides. "So, it's just as I feared."

She almost didn't hear him. His statement was uttered more to himself. She fought for something to say, but nothing came. Finally, he motioned to the bench.

"Let's sit, Rosa. I need you to explain."

She dropped to the bench, feeling very much like her legs would no longer hold her, and set down her glass of water. Miles looked at the ground then removed his hat and scratched his head before sitting beside her. The way he clamped his hat back on his head made his irritation clear.

"All right." Miles's voice was quiet but deep. "Tell me."

"I—" The word came out as a croak. She cleared her throat and started again. "I don't know where to start."

"The beginning would be good."

Disappointment oozed from his voice. She fought her tears and failed. They dripped from her cheeks. She'd already lost her mother. In the last few minutes, she'd become resigned to that fact. And even though she never really had Miles, now she would lose him as well.

"My stepfather is a loyal follower of Santa Anna. He wants to make sure Santa Anna's army wins this battle." She paused to wipe the tears from her cheeks. "He forced Mama and I to start doing laundry for the men at the Alamo so we could look things over and try to get information about the situation there. Mama was banned from entering the fort again because of all her questions. She wasn't very subtle."

"I heard a woman was banned. I didn't realize she was your mother."

Rosa nodded and picked at her fingernails. "I didn't plan to go back either. I don't agree with my stepfather. My father was invited here and given some land by the empresario. Then the Mexican government wanted it back. When my father wouldn't leave, even joined another group of American men to fight them, he was killed. I can understand them wanting to keep the land as part of the Mexican territory. But I can't agree with their methods. What they did to my father was murder and thievery."

"I agree. It's almost the same thing that happened to my parents."

She looked at him with a tiny sprout of hope. At least he understood that much. Maybe he would be able to appreciate her dilemma.

"When I told my stepfather I wouldn't go back to the Alamo for more information, he took my mother away. He told me I wouldn't see her again until I found out the answers to all his questions. I haven't seen her for days. She could be hurt. . .or even dead for all I know."

This was the first time she'd ever said the words out loud, and they stabbed at her heart. Her teardrops gave way to sobbing. Miles pulled her into his arms and held her close. He waited for her crying to slow before speaking.

"I had no idea, Rosa. You should have told me before now. I could have been helping you."

She leaned back to look into his eyes. "You'd give me information for my stepfather?"

"Never. I still can't believe you'd give out information that could harm the men in the Alamo."

Rosa's hope evaporated, especially when his arms fell away and left her feeling cold and alone. "Not that it mattered. I told Carlos the opposite of everything I learned from John."

Miles's lips twitched. "That was taking quite a chance, considering your mother's circumstances."

"I know. I guess I thought I could have it both ways."

"I understand. And I'm glad you took the risk. But I think I can help in another way."

She didn't have much faith in his words. Without information, she would continue to be without a mother.

Miles twisted on the bench and faced her. "What time does Carlos come every day to talk to you?"

She shrugged. "Around late afternoon. Why?"

If Miles thought he could beat her mother's whereabouts out of Carlos, he was mistaken. Her stepfather was a big man. Miles might be strong, but there was no way he could best her stepfather in a fight.

"Good. I'll come back this afternoon and hide. When Carlos leaves after talking to you, I'll follow him. Sooner or later he has to go see your mother. I'll find out where she's staying and try to free her."

Optimism returned. "That sounds like a wonderful plan. But what do I tell Carlos when he comes looking for answers?"

"What is it he wants to know?"

"He's wondering where you stand with ammunition and supplies."

Miles nodded and appeared deep in thought. Then he looked at her. "Has he ever mentioned when Santa Anna will arrive?"

"No. He would never say anything to help your chances of success against Santa Anna."

"Understandable. That's why we've been trying to stop the leak of information about the Alamo. We don't want to hurt our chances."

"I'm sorry."

He gave her a tight smile and patted her hand. "All right, when he comes today, tell him you've been told you'll get a tour of the Alamo in the morning, that you'll learn as much as you can and pass everything along to him sometime tomorrow."

"That's a great plan." She couldn't resist wrapping her arms around him for a quick hug. When he only patted her arms, she pulled away, trying hard not to show her disappointment. "I think it will actually work. Thank you, Miles."

"Don't thank me yet. I haven't found your mother." He rose to his feet. "I've got to go back to the fort for a while. When I return, I'll tap on the window and wave to let you know I'm here and ready."

She stood and gave his hand a squeeze. "You'll come back after finding her and let me know, won't you?"

"Of course." He pulled his hand away and reached for his rifle. "I'll be back soon."

She watched him walk away until she could no longer see him. Too many emotions to count bounced around inside until she felt completely battered. But she latched on to the hope that he was coming back to help.

Chapter Ten

Miles trudged to the fort with heavy steps, the short walk feeling more like several miles. He didn't really need to go back. He could have waited in town for Carlos to return for his information, but he needed some time alone to think, though that was difficult with a handful of men and women hawking their wares, hollering at him from both sides to come over and look at their goods.

Many of the men sat beneath the trees, their sombreros pulled low as they rested while the women and children called out to those passing by. He waved them away, hoping they'd grow quiet. But he couldn't ignore the young child who ran up to him and tugged at his trousers. The beautiful little girl with a cherubic face held out a colorful beaded necklace. Unable to resist, he dropped a few coins into her hand and pocketed the necklace. Her sweet smile was the only bright spot in his day.

Anger warred with compassion. How could Rosa betray the men ready to defend the fort as well as freedom for everyone? But would he do the same thing to protect his mother? He gripped his rifle tighter. There was always an alternative. . .wasn't there?

He blew out a breath as if it would also blow away his troubles. But he had to ask himself. . .did he really want anything to do with a girl who would turn her back on what she knew to be right? That was a question that would need to be explored more deeply. . .a question that required an answer as soon as her mother was safe.

The fact that she kept her treachery from him hit the hardest. She was using John, and possibly him. Her secrecy and deceit were no different than a lie. But then, she also said she'd given Carlos false information from everything she'd learned. He detested lying, but in this case, he appreciated her courage. . .if, indeed, she had fed Carlos misleading information.

That thought slowed his steps. If Rosa gave her stepfather false information, then that meant they still had a real informant out there. And it very likely could be Starks, though Miles didn't think Starks had been back to the fort since he'd tried to break into Rosa's house.

His head spun at the apparent connection between Rosa and Starks. But if they had been working together, why would Starks have tried to break into the house? Unless Starks discovered she'd been lying about the information. He shook his head. He couldn't wait to get to the fort and find Crockett. Maybe the two of them could make sense of what he'd learned. And maybe if he could just get some rest, he'd understand all of the news. But it appeared sleep would be many hours away.

Halfway through the courtyard, Miles turned and spotted Crockett coming out of Bowie's quarters. Crockett waved him over then led him into the room. Bowie gave him a nod and motioned to a chair.

Crockett closed the door and sat in the only other unoccupied chair. "Your girl doing all right? She looked upset."

"With good reason, apparently." Miles quickly filled in both men on what he'd learned. He ended with, "And now I've got to go back soon and see if I can find her mother." He shook his head. "What a mess."

Bowie nodded. "It is. And you know we can't allow her back inside the fort now, right?"

Miles squirmed in his chair. "Normally I'd agree with you, but she really does need the money she's making. I have no idea how she's getting what little bit of food she has."

Crockett leaned his forearms on his thighs. "I guess we could allow her in, but only if she's escorted by you the entire time. We can't take the chance she'll continue trying to get information from any of the other men."

"That won't help the relations between John and myself."

"It has to be that way. We can't tell him about the information leak just so he can escort her. How do we know he hasn't been the one purposely feeding her everything she wants to know?"

"All right, I'll come up with some kind of explanation."

Bowie started to talk then fought a bout of coughing. Miles exchanged a quick look with Crockett while waiting for him to be able to speak. Bowie cleared his throat one last time.

"What about that other fella Neill told me about? Any more word on him?"

"Starks? As far as I know, he hasn't been back to the fort since he broke into Miss Carter's house."

"He did what?" Bowie looked at Crockett. "You knew about this?"

"I did. I've told the boys at the gate to take him into custody if he shows. That's the same man who attacked the young lady at the gate. You warned him not to do it again."

Bowie scowled. "You don't say." He had another round of coughing then wiped his mouth. "Well, by gum, I'll teach the boy a better lesson this time."

"That's not all." Miles had their complete attention. "If Miss Carter really did give her stepfather false information, then, according to what was overheard, we still have a traitor. Chances are, it's Starks."

"That boy needs to be stopped." He pointed his beefy finger at Miles. "You see him again, you bring him to me. . .any way it takes."

"Yes, sir. In the meantime, I need to get back to town. I promised Miss Carter I'd help her find her mother. I need to get there before her stepfather shows."

"Let me know how it turns out."

Miles gave Bowie a nod, stood, and walked out with Crockett right behind him. After a quick look around to make sure they wouldn't be overheard, he stopped Crockett from leaving.

"What do ya think? Am I reading this girl right?"

Crockett smiled. "Worried your heart's in the way?"

Miles took a deep breath then nodded. "Exactly."

Crockett moved closer and patted his back. "She's in a tough spot, Fitch. I don't know that I'd be doing anything different. And now that you're aware of what she's done, you'll be much more alert to her attempts at deceit. . .if there are any more. But I do think it's important that you help her find and free her mother. No woman should be put in such a position."

Miles tried to smile. "Yeah, that's how I felt too. I'd better go. Thanks."

"You bet. Come find me when you get back."

"All right."

With a much lighter step, Miles hurried back to Rosa's house. More than ever, now that he'd had time to think things through, he wanted to help her and her mother. Once that problem was resolved, he'd get a better idea of her true character. Her actions thus far had him puzzled.

He skirted the street with all the people selling their goods, so he wouldn't be coerced into buying something from that little girl again, though he did like a colorful band he saw on one man's sombrero. When things calmed down, he might have to return to get one for his hat.

As he approached Rosa's house, he slowed and looked all around for any sign of Carlos approaching. A few people milled farther down the street, while others meandered past. He waited until the street grew quiet then moved toward the window. He held his breath and quickly peeked inside, but he didn't see anyone at the table.

He tapped three times and waited a moment. Rosa came from the left, smiled, and waved. Then another lady appeared beside her, staring with mouth open. Miles frowned and tipped his head. After another quick look around, he motioned for Rosa to meet him at the door.

She swung the door open. "You made it."

"Who is that? Isn't Carlos coming?"

The girl appeared at Rosa's side and looked him up and down. Rosa put her arm around her.

"This is my friend Ana. She was just about to leave. Give us another minute. Where are you going to hide?"

"I don't know yet. I'll find a good place. Just. . ." He eyed Ana. She looked somewhat familiar, but he couldn't place where he'd seen her. "Get ready."

With a quick nod, he strode a few houses down the street and prepared to wait behind a large oak tree. In moments, Ana appeared, looked around, then hurried away to the west. Miles finally relaxed. Everything had to go right or Rosa's mother's life could be at stake, and Rosa's as well.

The warmth of the sun overhead felt good but also made him sleepy. He shifted several times in an attempt to stay awake. Almost an hour passed before he spotted Carlos advancing up the street. Miles took a step back to ensure concealment then leaned forward again after Carlos turned toward Rosa's. Everything in him screamed to follow to keep Rosa safe, but he stood his ground to make sure the plan wouldn't fail.

Impatience grew as he waited. Their conversation was taking too long. It should have only taken a few minutes for Rosa to tell Carlos she'd have information for him tomorrow. As he took a step to get closer, Carlos appeared, slamming the door behind him. He stood in front of the house several seconds, looking at the ground, before he lowered his hat and headed up the street.

As Miles trailed Carlos, staying two streets over instead of right behind the man, he noted that about every twenty steps, Carlos would turn and look behind him. He'd wait a few seconds then continue down the street, a sign he didn't want Rosa following. His actions continued for several streets before Carlos, apparently no longer suspicious, strode on until they were on the far north side of town. He entered a house without knocking.

Wanting to make certain this was where Rosa's mother was being held, Miles hunkered down in the shadow of what appeared to be a vacant house down the street from where Carlos disappeared and waited. He frowned at the fact that the house hadn't been locked. Did Carlos keep his wife tied up when he wasn't around? His confusion grew when Carlos returned outside only minutes later then turned and kissed a woman before walking away.

With a moment of indecision, Miles headed back to retrieve Rosa. He needed to know if the woman really was Rosa's mother. He rounded the corner of a building and slammed into someone.

Chapter Eleven

The collision caught Rosa by surprise and knocked the breath from her. She gasped for air and would have fallen had not a pair of hands grasped her arm. Fear of Carlos forced her to look up at her captor. Relief that it was Miles weakened her knees.

"Rosa? What are you doing here?" Miles's quiet voice was also stern. "You were supposed to stay at the house until I came for you."

"I know, but I couldn't wait. I watched the way you were following and thought I could do the same. Better to follow you than Carlos." She held his muscular forearms to steady herself, her heart pounding. "Did you find my mother?"

"I think so. Carlos left a few minutes ago. You need to knock on the door to make sure it's her."

"Oh Miles, thank you." She threw her arms around his neck, and though she wanted to kiss him, she resisted. "Show me which house. I need to see Mama."

Miles finally smiled and shook his head. "What am I going to do with you?"

She grinned up at him, her joy bubbling over. "I'm sure you'll think of something." She nudged his arm. "Let's go."

"All right, but slowly. I want to make sure Carlos isn't coming back, and I don't want anyone to see us enter that house."

She turned him around and pushed on his back. "I promise to behave. Now let's go."

At the corner of each house and building, Miles stopped and looked around. Impatience made her want to impel him to go faster. Caution made her resist. She caught herself wringing her hands and finally clasped them together and held them to her lips. Miles motioned her to follow. Eagerness had her almost running in place. Finally, he pointed at a house but held up his hand to make her wait. As he looked around, she stared at the house. The adobe was clean, as though new. Curtains hung in the windows. At least Carlos held her mother captive in a nice place.

Miles touched her shoulder. With a nod, he led her to the door. The time to see her mother had finally arrived, and Rosa couldn't make her trembling hands work to knock on the door. Miles looked at her, smiled, and knocked. An eternity went by before they heard footsteps. Seconds later, her mother stood in the doorway.

"Mama!"

"Shhh." Miles pushed them inside and shut the door.

Rosa threw herself at her mother and wrapped her arms around her neck. She planted kisses on her mother's cheek before holding her at arms' length to see her face again then pulled her into another hug.

"I missed you so much. Are you all right?"

Mama looked from her to Miles and back again, her shock revealed by her expression. "You. . .you found me."

"Miles did. We owe this reunion to him."

"Miles?"

Rosa slid her arm through his and pulled him next to her. "Miles Fitch. He's from the Alamo. When he found out you were missing, he promised to help me find you." She dropped his arm and hugged her mother once more. "Pack your things. We're leaving."

"Leaving?"

Rosa gave a soft laugh. "Come now, Mama. I know you're stunned, but we may not have much time. If Carlos finds us here, he will try to stop you from leaving. And if that happens, he'll make sure we never see each other again. Hurry."

Mama held a hand to her mouth, her indecision apparent. For the first time, Rosa worried their plan wouldn't work. Why was she hesitating? This was her chance to be free.

"Mama?"

Miles stepped forward. "My parents have a small hut just outside of town. You can both stay there. You'll be safe. I promise."

"Please, Mama. We have to hurry."

"Oh." Mama rubbed her arms as if she were cold. "All right. I suppose I could."

She began gathering some of her clothing and placing them into a basket. Rosa thought she was taking too long and moved to her side.

"Can I help?"

"I'm almost finished."

Rosa looked to Miles for help, but he was peering out the window, checking both directions. She took a step back and eyed Mama. Her mother's lack of excitement gave her pause. They hadn't seen each other in days. Rosa couldn't wait to see her, to spend time with her, to feel her arms again. But Mama wasn't showing any of those things. Maybe it was her fear of Carlos.

"What's wrong, Mama? You seem...I don't know. Scared? Worried?"

Miles touched her shoulder. "We don't have time for this right now, Rosa. We need to make haste. We've been here too long already. You can talk when we get to the other house."

"Of course." Rosa looked from her mother's weathered hands, to the small basket of worn clothes, and then to her worried eyes. "Are you ready?"

Mama scanned the room once more. "Rosa, I—I...yes."

She put her arm around her mother's bent shoulders and squeezed. "It'll be fine. Trust us."

Miles returned to the window and looked around. "All clear. Let's get going."

He opened the door and ushered them outside then motioned for them to follow, placing a finger to his lips, reminding them not to draw attention. Miles led the way, rushing across the open areas then stopping at every corner to make sure all was clear. Rosa kept her mother between them, urging her to keep up with Miles.

"Let me carry your basket, Mama."

She clung to it fiercely. "I have it."

The excitement at finding her mother dimmed at her seeming agitation and reluctance. Rosa bit her tongue. They'd talk when they reached Miles's place. Instead, she focused on where Miles was leading them. She'd have to know how to get back and forth from their new home. Which posed another problem. She didn't have any other clothes than what she wore.

"Where are you taking Carmela?"

The deep, gruff voice made Rosa's mouth go dry and her skin prickle. She'd recognize Carlos's voice anywhere. Before she could turn to face him, Miles placed himself between her and Carlos.

"You again," Carlos spat. "I should have left you in the dirt that night to die. You keep interfering with my family. This needs to stop."

Carlos's frame seemed to swell with each word. Rosa saw his fury and worried for Miles, yet she took a step back and put her arm around her mother. "They asked for my help." Miles's voice was sure and steady. "I'll stay with them until they ask me to leave."

Carlos's eyes went to Mama's. "Carmela?"

She shook her head. "They found me and asked me to go with them."

Rosa protectively wrapped both arms around her mother. "She's staying with me. You'll not separate us again. And I'm not getting you any more information from the Alamo."

Carlos scowled at her then faced Miles. "You told him?"

Miles shifted to block Rosa from her enraged stepfather. "She did. And as she said, she'll not bring you any more information."

A low growl came from Carlos as he lunged at Miles, who stepped aside and thrust the butt of his rifle into Carlos's stomach. Carlos latched on to the rifle, yanked it from Miles, and tossed it aside like a small piece of firewood. Though Miles looked stunned, his stance showed he was ready for battle.

Rosa wanted to scream at them to stop but knew there was nothing she could do at this point. She clung to her mother while she waited and watched, silently cheering Miles.

Carlos went at Miles like an angry bull, ready to stomp him into the ground. The collision between the men left Carlos holding his chest and Miles on the ground. Dust billowed as Miles scooted behind Carlos and kicked the back of his legs, bringing Carlos to his knees. Miles quickly rose and landed two punches near Carlos's temple. The big man, a fallen Goliath, shook his head and pushed to his feet.

They faced off again, fists up, looking much more wary of each other. They circled, throwing punches from time to time, none of them landing. Carlos was stronger, but Miles was faster and slightly taller.

"Stop it!"

Mama's shout drew Miles's attention, allowing Carlos to land a hit. Miles was propelled back three steps but didn't fall. With speed that amazed her, Miles moved toward Carlos and landed three quick punches. Blood oozed from Carlos's nose. Before he could recover, Miles landed more hits to Carlos's chest before ending with another punch to her stepfather's face.

Carlos roared with rage and went for Miles. Rosa's heart clenched. She'd seen that same look on Carlos's face before. As Miles threw more punches, Carlos wrapped him in his arms and squeezed.

Pain radiated from Miles's face as he yelled. Rosa wanted to run and hit Carlos with her own punches, but her mother now held Rosa's arm in a tight grip.

Miles beat on Carlos's face as best he could then smashed his ears several times. Carlos hollered but didn't let go. Miles started poking at Carlos's eyes and was finally released. He spun away and gasped for breath. Carlos rubbed his eyes then headed for Miles again. Miles pulled his knife and pointed it at Carlos. When Carlos didn't stop his advance, Miles sliced it at him a few times.

Carlos stopped and glanced at Mama. Rosa looked at her mother and saw her shake her head.

Carlos faced Miles. "This isn't over. You and I will see each other again."

Carlos shared one last look with his wife and stomped away. Rosa rushed to Miles.

"Go after him. If you don't, he'll come back and take Mama again."

Miles rubbed his back. "No."

"Please, Miles."

He shook his head.

"Why not?"

"Because not all circumstances require death." As she fumed, Miles ignored her, sheathed his knife, and retrieved his rifle. "Let's get to the hut."

In the time it took to get to their new home, Rosa had calmed and realized Miles was right. She needed to keep control of her emotions, just as her mother had controlled hers. She could have lost her husband, seen him killed, and yet she restrained herself. Rosa mumbled a quiet prayer for forgiveness. She'd also have to ask Miles to forgive her.

After a short walk through some trees, they reached the hut and Miles opened the door.. The mud walls and dirty grass-thatched roof made her shudder. Miles glanced around then motioned them inside and lit the lantern.

"I'll round up some food for you. I shouldn't be gone long."

Rosa followed him to the door. What must he think of her? "I'm sorry, Miles. You were right about letting Carlos go."

He stopped and faced her. He looked so tired. Yet he reached out and pushed some loose hair behind her ear before dropping his hand to his side.

"He's been hard on you. I can understand your reaction. But I'm glad you've changed your mind." He blew out a slow breath. "Stay here and you'll be safe. I'll check on you every day and make sure you have whatever you need."

"I need to go to the house and get more clothes."

"I'll get them."

He turned to leave but Rosa stopped him again. "But I still need to do laundry to make some money."

Miles shook his head and looked her in the eyes. "I'll take care of you. You need to stay here."

"I'll not be a prisoner, Miles."

He sighed. "You won't be. I'll be here every day. We'll take walks."

She was about to argue when he placed his fingers on her lips.

"At least wait for me before you wander too far from here."

She smiled. "All right. I can do that."

He nodded, took one last look at her mother, and then opened the door. "I'll be back soon with food."

Rosa closed the door behind him then leaned against it as she turned to her mother. At the look on Mama's face, Rosa's smile slid from hers. The time had come for their talk.

Chapter Twelve

Miles winced as he turned away from the door and paused to rub his side. Deep breaths were painful. Carlos might have cracked one of his ribs. Seemed like he'd done nothing but fight lately. And all in an attempt to help Rosa.

Her mother was no longer a captive, if she ever really was, but was she safe? Maybe Rosa was following in the footsteps of her mother where deception was concerned. As soon as the thought entered his head, he berated himself. Rosa had explained her deception, flawed as it was, and he had no proof that her mother had deceived them. Time would tell, and he aimed to find out the truth if he had to confront Rosa's mother himself.

After a quick look around, he made his way to Rosa's house to gather some of her clothes. Once there, the bench outside looked inviting. He dropped onto it for a quick rest. Between no sleep the night before and the fight with Carlos, a small dog would be able to take him down right now.

"Excuse me."

Miles jumped. He must have dozed off. He looked up to see Rosa's friend.

"Are you all right?"

"I'm fine."

"Where's Rosa? Did you find her mother?"

He nodded. "They're together right now."

"Oh, good. Thank you for finding her."

"Just trying to help Rosa. And come to think of it, maybe you can help her, too. She and her mother will be staying someplace else for a while. She needs clothes. Would you be able to get some items together for her?"

"Sure. Will I be able to visit them?"

"I'll let them decide that."

Ana nodded and entered Rosa's house. While she was inside, Miles searched his memory for where he'd seen her before. He didn't get his answer until she returned with a basket over her arm.

"Ah. That's why you look familiar to me. Your parents run the dry goods store."

She frowned and cocked her head. "Yes, they do. But I don't remember ever seeing you."

"Just over a year ago. It was the last time my parents and I came here for supplies. You were helping an older lady gather the items on her list."

"I've done that many times, yes."

"Good, that's perfect, because Rosa and her mother will need supplies for a while." He stood and grimaced. His body had stiffened while he rested. He dug into his pocket for money and handed it to her. "Beans, flour, sugar, eggs. . .anything else you think they might need."

She took his money and set the basket of clothes on the bench. "Wait here. I'll be back with the supplies as soon as I can."

He returned to his place on the bench and said a quiet prayer, thanking the Lord for His provision.

* * * * *

Neither Rosa nor her mother had moved for several minutes after Miles left. Instead of running to each other for a warm hug, they stared. Mama was the first to look away. She pulled out a chair from the table but clicked her tongue.

"Too dirty here."

Rosa remained against the door. This wasn't the mother she'd known all her life. She looked the same, but that was the extent of the similarities. Gone were the loving hugs, caring questions, and concern for her welfare. The timing of the changes all pointed to one cause. Carlos. She needed to know if she could find her real mother somewhere inside this shell standing before her.

"I thought you'd be happy to see me, Mama."

"I am."

"It hasn't felt like it."

"I'm sorry. You two surprised me."

Mama found a cloth and started wiping the dust from the table and chairs. While Mama cleaned, Rosa replayed the rescue and fight in her head. None of it had gone the way she'd imagined.

Carlos hadn't restrained Mama in any way. The door to the house where she stayed hadn't been locked. Mama was free to open it when they knocked. Several questions clamored to be asked. She gave her mother a long look. They'd all get asked, but she'd start at the beginning.

"Why that particular house? I mean, where did Carlos get it to be able to hold you there? I'm staying at his house, and I'm fairly certain he can't afford two."

Mama paused only a moment in her cleaning. "It's his brother's house. His brother left to go fight for Santa Anna."

That one answer managed to answer so many other questions. But Rosa had a very important one to ask. "If you could have gotten away from that house, Mama, would you have?"

Mama, still leaning over the table, stopped cleaning. She finally heaved a sigh, dropped onto the chair she'd cleaned, and tossed the cloth onto the table.

"I love Carlos, Rosa. I loved your father, too, but he's gone."

Rosa's heart dropped. "And Carlos has taken his place."

"He's taken a place in my heart, just as your father had a place, still has a place. Just a different place now."

Rosa pushed away from the wall and moved to the table. "So what you're telling me is that you could have come to me but didn't. That the note you sent me didn't mean a thing. It was nothing more than a lie, a ruse to get me to obey...to spy for your husband."

"Not a lie. I did miss you and wanted to be with you."

Her throat tight, she sat across from her mother and put her hands over her face, trying to put order to her thoughts. "You weren't really kidnapped, were you?"

Mama reached across the small table and touched her arm. "Look at me, Rosa. Please."

Rosa fought the threatening tears, clasped her hands on the table, and speared Mama with her eyes. "No more lies."

"No. No more lies."

Her mother tried to hold her hand, but Rosa pulled away. Tears appeared in Mama's eyes. Rosa looked away, still fighting her own. The betrayal burned so deep her chest ached. The desire to run away was strong, but the need for an explanation was stronger. At the very least, she'd stay long enough to hear what Mama had to say.

She had to know the answer to the question uppermost on her mind. "Was the fake kidnapping yours or Carlos's idea?"

Mama hesitated. "The kidnapping wasn't fake. At least not at first."

Rosa's mouth dropped open. "He really kidnapped you?"

"That's a harsh word, but yes, I had no idea what he'd planned until it happened. I argued with him for the first couple days, but in all our talking, his explanations started to make sense."

Confusion scrambled her thoughts. "Your husband locked you up against your will, but now you don't have a problem with it because he explained it away?" She lifted her hands then let them fall back to the table. "I still don't understand. You were fine with him keeping us apart and forcing me to get him information, no matter what it took? He told me he didn't care what I had to do to get the answers to his questions. What reason could he possibly give you to make that all right?"

"I didn't know he'd said that. He assured me you were safe, that he'd seen you every day and you were doing well." Mama squirmed in her chair. "Rosa, I know how you can be. You get your hard head from your father. You knew before Carlos took me away that I agreed with his and Santa Anna's position. When I'd considered everything, I stopped fighting him."

"You mean you agreed to it. Knowing it would hurt me, you still agreed to go along with the lie." The tears could no longer be held back and rolled down her cheeks. "How could you?" She swiped at the tears. "How could you allow me to live with the fear that you were being hurt? That I might never see you again?"

She dropped her gaze to the table, shaking her head. "I'm sorry, Rosa."

"If you were sorry, you wouldn't have done it." Unable to sit there and face her mother any longer, she stood. "You're my mother, but I can never trust you again. You say you love me, but how can you do something like that to your own flesh and blood, to someone you claim to love? I would never consider hurting you in such a way. In any way." She paced for several moments then stopped near the door. "I'm leaving. Going back east. Papa has family there. They'll take me in. Help me start a new life."

She started to open the door but hesitated when her mother stood so fast her chair toppled to the floor.

"Stop, Rosa. Please, stop. At least let me talk to you, try to explain before you go."

Moments later Mama's arms came around her. Rosa placed her forehead against the door and sobbed as her mother held her. At her urging, Rosa turned so they could hold each other and cry together.

After several minutes, Mama led her back to the table, but this time, they sat closer, still holding hands and wiping their cheeks and eyes with their shoulders. Rosa sat silently and stared into Mama's eyes through a blur of tears, ready, anxious to hear the explanation that would cause a mother to deceive her daughter.

"There's something I haven't told you about Carlos." Mama hesitated and licked her lips before loosening her grip on Rosa's hand. "I knew Carlos years ago. . .back when I was your age."

Rosa's throat tightened as her mouth went dry. Why was she just now learning this? Mama's secret was just like another lie.

"We were in love. My mama and papa didn't approve of him because he seemed to get into trouble often. They called him a *rufián* and said he'd cause me nothing but heartache. But when they caught us meeting at a friend's house, my papa decided to move to Louisiana to keep us apart." Mama squeezed Rosa's hand. "Though I did fall in love with your father, I think I still held my love of Carlos in my heart. When we ran into each other a couple months ago, well, it was as if we'd never been apart."

Rosa jerked her hand from Mama's. "Which explains why you so quickly forgot about Papa and could so easily choose to deceive me."

"I regretted it the moment Carlos walked out the door, but I decided I might as well take it to its conclusion. If I could turn back time, I'd never hurt you like that again."

"But this doesn't help to convince me why you agreed to it in the first place."

"No, it doesn't. I'll try to do that now and hope you can understand." Mama put her head down and heaved a sigh before looking into Rosa's eyes. "Like Carlos, I want this land to remain part of Mexico."

Rosa tried to speak, but Mama held up a hand and shook her head.

"Let me continue, Rosa. You wanted an explanation." After Rosa nodded, Mama gave her a slight smile. "I know your father came by invitation and with the best of intentions. He and many others were allowed to come to help clear and settle the land where it had sat empty and unused for so long. But there were also rules they were to follow. They were to come by invitation, to become loyal citizens of Mexico, to obey Mexico's laws."

"Papa did that."

"Yes, he did. But many others did not. Thousands continued to cross the border illegally, many of them bringing slaves, which went against Mexico's laws. They were taking over our land. They still are." She touched Rosa's hand. "This is our land. We don't want the immigrants stealing it from us. The only way we can see it ending is to have Santa Anna move them out. By force, if that's what it takes."

She'd heard something similar from Carlos, but at least Mama hadn't called the Americans worthless or rebels. "This still doesn't explain why you lied to me and pretended to be kidnapped to make me find out information from the fort."

"I'm getting to that. I wanted to make sure you understood my position."

"You've made that quite clear over the last several months. Your opinion hasn't changed, and neither has mine."

Mama took a deep breath. "Patience, *mi querida*. Please." She held just one of Rosa's hands, looking at and playing with the fingers. "As you've just stated again, your opinion of the Americans being here hasn't changed. We wanted to know what Santa Anna would be up against, should he come. . .wanted to be able to pass that information on to him. Since you've been so adamant in your position, Carlos thought the kidnapping would be the only way to make sure you brought him information from the Alamo. I ended up agreeing with him. I was wrong, Rosa. I should never have consented to his plan, putting you in harm's way. There were no consequences in the past, so I assumed nothing bad would ever happen. But that shouldn't have mattered. I allowed my love of this land and of Carlos to overshadow my love for you. I'm so sorry."

Rosa sat quiet, trying to run everything through her mind and make some sense of it all. As usual, she came back to one conclusion. Their relationship had become nothing more than one deception after another. And Mama deceived her because they couldn't agree.

"Why do we have to agree on everything, Mama? Why do we have to become enemies because we don't see eye to eye?"

"We're not enemies."

"No? You used trickery to get what you wanted. Carlos slapped me because I didn't want to get him information. Sounds like a battle to me. Just on a much smaller scale than the one that's coming."

"Carlos slapped you? He never told me that."

"Did he ever slap you?"

"No. Never." Tears appeared in Mama's eyes again. "I'm sorry, Rosa. I didn't know."

Rosa nodded. "At least he hasn't hurt you."

"Were you serious, Rosa? Are you really leaving Béxar?"

Rosa shrugged. "I told you before you were. . .kidnapped that I wanted to leave, that I wanted you to leave with me."

"I know. I remember. But this is our home. You love it here. You love this country. You told me as much."

Rosa remained silent. Other than her mother, she had no reason to stay. She didn't want to endure any more battles, not with her mother, and especially not the bloody kind between men.

"Why do you want me here when we can't agree?"

"Like you said, why do we have to agree? Why can't we love each other despite our differences?"

"I do love you. I'll always love you. You're my mother. I just don't know that I can trust you."

The pain from her words was evident on Mama's face.

"Will you allow me the chance to earn back your trust? Please stay, Rosa. I don't know that I could bear you leaving me. Not this way."

She examined her mother's face, the face she'd love all her life. The face of the woman who, until recently, treated her with all the love of a good mother. "Even if we don't agree on everything?"

Mama gave her a trembling smile. "Even if."

Rosa still hesitated. "You hurt me deeply, Mama. Once trust is broken, it's hard to fix."

"But you'll let me try?

"What about Carlos?"

"I'll speak to him. Oh, will I ever be speaking to him."

The two stood and hugged. At the sound of a tap at the door, they pulled apart. Miles walked in, a smile on his face and two baskets in his hands. At that very moment, Rosa knew she was in love with this man.

As she reached to take the baskets from him, Carlos rushed in, shoved Miles from behind, and pointed a gun to his head.

Chapter Thirteen

Rifle tucked under one arm and baskets still in his hands, Miles stood helpless while Carlos pointed a pistol at him. He could kick himself for not being more careful to make sure he wasn't being followed.

With a scowl so severe his dark brows met, Carlos pulled back the hammer of his gun. "Tell me why I shouldn't shoot you right now for stealing my wife."

Miles's heart pounded as his mind scrambled for an answer. He had none.

"Carlos, stop!"

"Stay back, Carmela. I'll make sure this never happens again." Carlos aimed his gun at Miles's face.

"Stop it, Carlos!" Rosa's mother rushed to stand between Carlos and Miles. "Listen to me. He didn't steal me. I agreed to go along with them. You knew that when I nodded at you." She touched his face with one hand while pushing the gun away with the other. "Put that down. You don't need it."

After several moments, Carlos released the hammer and lowered the gun. Miles set the baskets on the table along with his rifle, glad to be rid of the burdens.

"All right." Carlos tucked the gun into his belt. "What now?"

"Now, we go home, live our own life, and allow Rosa to live hers. We talked, and I promised we'd not use her again. We. . .I was wrong to allow it in the first place."

Carlos glanced from Rosa to Miles, then back to his wife. "And the information?"

"We'll find another way."

Rosa stepped up and crossed her arms. "You still have your other spy."

All three turned and stared at Rosa. Unsure of Carlos's reaction, Miles prepared to stop him should he try to quiet Rosa. Before Miles could say a word, Rosa's mother peered up into her husband's face.

"What other spy?" When Carlos continued looking at Rosa, his wife touched his face to draw his attention to her. "What other spy, Carlos?"

"Not here, Carmela." He motioned toward Miles with his head. "Later."

Rosa's mother turned to them, pain and anger gleaming from her eyes. "Come eat with us tonight. Both of you. Come late." She took her husband's hand. "We need time to talk." She looked up at Carlos. "Oh, do we ever need time to talk."

She opened the door and tugged Carlos from the house. Miles waited for them to get a good distance away then turned Rosa to face him.

"So, there really is another spy. Do you know who it is?"

She shook her head. "Carlos just said he had a way of knowing if I was lying. That could only mean he has someone else bringing him information."

Disappointment ate at Miles. If Rosa would have known whoever Carlos was using for information, his search would be over. Now he'd have to follow Carlos's every move to find the traitor. And a meal with him tonight would be the next step in his search. If the man's name didn't come out during the meal, Miles would stay in town and follow Carlos, should he leave the house. In the meantime, he still had to help Rosa.

"Well, you're welcome to stay here, but since the danger is over, would you like to return to your own house?"

She smiled up at him. "I think so. As much as I appreciate the offer of your home, it's enough out of the way that I'd be nervous to stay here by myself. And I can't bring myself to stay with Mama and Carlos again."

"But it's not safe for a young woman to be alone. Your neighbors might frown on you not being properly chaperoned."

Rosa made a face. "As if they've cared or been overly helpful up to now. I'll get a gun. That's the best chaperone right now."

"You know how to use one?"

She gave a vigorous nod. "Papa taught me. He wanted to know I could protect myself. I also think he wanted a son. I reaped the benefits. Those lessons are some of my most favorite memories of our time together."

Still unsure, he didn't figure he'd win this battle at the moment. "All right." He tucked his rifle under his arm again and lifted the baskets from the table. "Let's go."

She tugged at one of the baskets. "I can take one of these."

At first, he resisted but then gave in and allowed her to help. The freedom would give him the ability to keep her safe should anything happen on their walk.

"Thank you." He closed the door behind them then led them into town. "Your mother said you two talked. It appeared you worked things out, especially since she said they wouldn't use you for information again."

Rosa relayed all that took place, her voice low and shaking with emotion at times. She ended by heaving a sigh. "I love my mother, Miles, and I'm glad we'll be together again."

"I hear a 'but' in that statement."

She tried to smile up at him but, except for trembling lips, failed.

"*But* I don't know that I can ever trust her completely again. How can a mother do that to her daughter? I just don't understand." She sniffled. "She really hurt me."

He tucked the rifle under his arm again and wrapped his free arm around her shoulders. He slowed down, forcing her to do the same so he could give her a hug. She pressed her forehead against his shoulder. Unable to imagine her pain, he couldn't resist kissing the top of her head. They remained that way for several moments before he tipped her head back by lifting her chin with his hand.

"You all right?"

This time she did smile as she nodded. "Yes. Thank you, Miles."

They continued their hike into town, but he didn't want to leave the conversation just yet. "You know you have to forgive her for this, don't you?"

She didn't answer at first, staring at the ground while they walked. Then she heaved a sigh. "I know. It might take some time and it won't be easy at first, but I know. I don't think I'll ever forget, though. It might take years for that memory to fade, if ever."

"I understand. Just know that memories may remind us of where we've been, but they don't have to determine where we're going."

Several minutes passed then Rosa took his hand in hers. "You're a good friend, Miles."

"I'm here for you when you need me." To keep his word to John, he had to ask the question he'd been avoiding for fear of the answer. "Would you mind if I called on you from time to time, Rosa, so we can get to know each other better?"

"Only from time to time? I'd been hoping you might come to see me every day." She smiled up at him in a way that made him want to kiss her. "Or at least almost every day."

His heart pounded against his ribs. "I'll do my best. What about tonight?"

"Are you willing to share me with my mother and Carlos? I planned to accept her invitation."

He made a face that had her laughing. "Life is full of sacrifices. I guess sharing time with you will have to be one of them."

As they continued to walk and talk, he stayed alert to everything around them. The open areas between houses and walled properties were getting smaller as they drew closer to the center of town. With houses closer together, there were too many areas for others to hide. He still had to find Starks, and he hoped to get a glimpse of Carlos with his friends, though he had a feeling his wife would keep him occupied with the demand for explanations. When he did get to follow Carlos, he felt certain Starks would be Carlos's spy.

Once they reached Rosa's house, Miles stopped and glanced at the sun, which was low in the sky. "I don't have a lot of time to check in at the fort and get back. If you don't mind, I think I'll sit out here until it's time to go to your mother's."

"You don't have to sit out here. Come inside. With the damp, cool air this evening, you'll get chilled."

He shook his head. "I'd rather be chilled than ruin your good name among your neighbors."

Rosa's mouth dropped open with understanding as she looked around. "I appreciate that, Miles, but like I said—"

"I know what you said, but I'm not going to be the one to cause talk."

She made a face. "What if we leave the door open? We can even pull the table and chairs closer to the door so the prying eyes can see we're just visiting."

Miles grinned. "I think that might work."

He headed inside to unload the baskets then moved the table and chairs as she suggested. Rosa brought two glasses of water and sat to one side of the door where she could be seen. Miles sat across from her. He just stared at her face, suddenly shy of words. She held a resemblance to her mother, but there were also stark differences.

"Tell me about your father."

Her face lit up. "He was such a good man. A man of great faith. I fear I've not gained that trait from him."

"We never stop growing and learning, Rosa."

She smiled. "That's true. There's still hope for me then."

Miles knew at that moment that his attraction for Rosa had bloomed into love. "Always."

Her eyes nearly sparkled. "My father was also a hard worker. He used to work at a shipyard in Louisiana, which is where he met Mama. Her father worked there too. He loved working with his hands. I think that's a big reason he came here. He knew it would take hard work to clear this land and make something of it, but that didn't deter or discourage him in the least. I think it almost inspired him. His face would get peaceful whenever he talked about this place."

Miles smiled even as his heart ached. "He and my father would have been great friends. They sound very much alike."

Rosa put her elbow on the table and propped her chin on her hand as she stared out the door. "In the evenings after we ate, he'd either read to me, tell me stories he made up, or play games with me. When I was little, once in a while, he'd let me play with his hair. I'd comb it every way I could think of. He said it was no wonder he was going bald. I was scraping all the hair out of his scalp." She smiled as her eyes misted. "I miss him."

"Yeah. Me too." He pictured his parents' faces then shook the images away, unwilling to dwell there for fear his anger would show. "I think you inherited your father's work ethic and determination."

She raised a brow. "I haven't noticed that in me. What makes you say that?"

He reached for her club leaning against the door frame and held it up. "Oh, I don't know. Maybe it's because a young lady on her own would go out and find a club for protection while running back and forth from the Alamo to clean the clothes of others." He poked her with one end of the club. "Have you used this on anyone yet?"

"No, but if you keep that up, you might be the first."

He laughed, tempted to persist to see if it would bring about her threatened result. "How do I know you haven't already used it on me? You might have been the one who clubbed me on the head that night."

"You'll just have to take my word for it, though I've come to the conclusion that a thump upside the head would do a world of good for most men."

Laughter burst from him. "Oh, really? And what have we done to deserve such a punishment?"

"Breathe."

The sarcastic drawl of the word had him holding his sore ribs as he laughed. He poked her one more time. "Well, I'll have to do my best to change your opinion of men."

"Good luck, but I look forward to your attempt."

His heart picked up an extra beat at the thought of spending much more time with her. Poor John. He hoped they could remain friends.

"We should probably go. It'll be dark soon."

Rosa's comment made Miles glance outside. "Right. Should I bring the club?"

"Why? Do you think I'll need to use it on you?"

Her sassy grin made his heart skip a beat. "Maybe I should just stick with my rifle."

"Wisdom beyond your years."

His arms ached to pull her close. He settled for offering his elbow. But he had a feeling the day would soon arrive when he wouldn't be able to resist the temptation to hold her in his arms.

Chapter Fourteen

The lighthearted feeling Miles had enjoyed with Rosa ended at the sight of Carlos's scowl when he opened the door to allow them inside. If the scent of food drifting toward him hadn't smelled so good, he'd have been tempted to leave and suffer through the sloppy, tasteless beans at the fort. But then he wouldn't get to spend more time with Rosa or have the chance to follow Carlos later that night. . .if Carlos happened to leave the house. He'd have to be certain not to let Carlos catch him trailing him. Another fight with the man might not end up as well as today. Miles still hurt from their encounter.

Rosa's mother stepped around him. "Never mind Carlos's bad manners. Come in, come in." She grabbed one of his and one of Rosa's arms and pulled them inside. "Have a seat at the table. Everything is almost ready." She shook her finger at Carlos. "You behave."

Her cheery voice didn't hide her red and puffy eyes. Rosa must have also noticed. She followed her mother to the kitchen. Though he'd been invited to sit, Miles waited for instruction from Carlos. The man finally motioned Miles to a chair then sat opposite him. For the second time that evening, Miles struggled for something to say, especially a topic that wouldn't ruffle feathers already disturbed.

"What do you do for a living, Mr. Mendes?"

"Why do you want to know?"

Obviously, a poor choice of topic. He shrugged. "Just trying to find something to talk about."

"Stop it, Carlos." Rosa's mother brought a stack of plates and placed them on the table. "He's a woodworker. Builds furniture and such." She ran her hand across his shoulders. "He's quite good."

For the first time since they'd met, Carlos's expression softened.

"My father used to work with wood until he came. . .here." Miles cleared his throat. "He decided to try his hand at raising grain and cattle."

"He should have stayed with wood."

"Carlos!"

Carlos visibly shrank at the scolding. He rubbed his hand over the smooth wood of the table. "Did he build furniture?"

Finally, a safe topic. "Yes, sir. I think he enjoyed making cradles the most. He liked carving special engravings on them. But he built most kinds of furniture."

Carlos leaned forward. "Engraving? That's something I've never tried but have wanted to see whether I'm any good at it." He tapped the table. "Most of my furniture is plain, like this table."

"But well-built and very sturdy." He battled with himself for several moments then made a decision. "My father kept his carving tools. I don't plan to use them right away. You're welcome to borrow them for a while if you're interested."

Carlos studied him, even narrowed his eyes. "How much?"

Miles shook his head. "No charge. Just use them for a time."

"Oh, Carlos." His wife returned and put her hands on his shoulders.

"Free? You're letting me use them for nothing?"

"Yes, sir. If you want them. I can bring them here tomorrow."

"Why? We're not friends. You must want something."

Miles fought between sadness and frustration. He offered a gift, yet it wasn't well received because of doubt and suspicion. Disappointment crushed the pleasure of being able to do something for another. "No, sir. I want nothing in return."

While Carlos looked confused, his wife beamed as she leaned down and kissed the top of his head.

"He would love to borrow them, Mr. Fitch, wouldn't you, Carlos? We haven't much money and couldn't afford the tools. But it's been his dream."

Carlos never said a word, but his throat worked. He only nodded.

"Well, good then. I'll have them here sometime tomorrow."

Mrs. Mendes wiped tears from her eyes. "Thank you, Mr. Fitch."

"Call me Miles."

She gave him a bright smile. "I'll have the meal on in minutes."

As she shuffled away, Carlos ran his hands over his face then clasped them together on the table.

"Why would you let me borrow them? I almost killed you just hours ago."

Miles shrugged. "But you didn't. And I can't use them right now. You can. My father would be happy to see them being used again."

As if pulling his hand from a puddle of paste, Carlos slowly reached across the table. "Thank you for your generosity. I promise to use them with as much love as your father."

Warmth washed through him as he accepted Carlos's handshake, pushing away his doubts as to whether he'd done the right thing. He glanced toward the women. They both wiped at their eyes before turning back toward the barrel-shaped cookstove. In minutes, the ladies had the meal on the table and were seated.

Rosa arranged her skirt then folded her hands in front of her. "Miles, would you mind blessing the food?"

Their eyes met and he smiled. "Sure." He bowed his head. "Lord, I thank You for bringing us together tonight. May our conversation and actions be a blessing to You and Your name. Thank You for providing this bounty and also for the hands that prepared it. Amen."

"Amen," they all echoed.

Carlos reached for the plate of flatbread, helped himself, and then handed it to Miles. "You're getting a treat tonight. We don't eat like this often, but I enjoy the nights we do."

Miles tried not to react at Carlos's words, though he didn't think the man had ever strung together so many of them at one time. "It smells great."

As the plates and bowls continued to be passed, Miles followed Carlos's example, heaping shredded meat, onions and peppers, beans, and rice onto his flatbread. He rolled it just as Carlos had and took a bite. All sights and sounds disappeared as Miles savored the flavor. He wanted to hold the food in his mouth just to enjoy it for a while, but his stomach demanded to taste it, too. He swallowed and shoved in another mouthful.

When he opened his eyes, it was to find all three at the table staring and smiling. His face heated as he struggled to chew and swallow.

"I apologize, Mrs. Mendes. I mean no disrespect or dishonor to my mother, but I think this is the best tasting food I've ever eaten."

"Thank you, Miles."

Rosa let her fork clatter to the plate. "You said the same thing about my cooking."

Miles's mouth dropped open as his gaze went from Rosa to Mrs. Mendes. "I—I guess you learned a lot from your mother."

Rosa and her mother laughed. "Nice way to get yourself out of that hole."

Carlos wiped his mouth with his sleeve. "You eat like this at the fort?"

The question was loaded and brought the potential of starting another fight or hard feelings. Tension filled the room. Miles decided to ignore the possibility that Carlos was fishing for information and answer as a man who enjoyed eating. He took another, smaller bite and briefly closed his eyes in sheer pleasure.

"We eat well, but nothing that tastes like this. If chickens had eyebrows, even they would raise them at some of the remnants the cook throws out to them."

The three rolled with laughter, and the remainder of the evening was filled with lighthearted fun. Gone were the anger and differences of opinion. Miles couldn't remember the last time he'd enjoyed such a nice evening.

All too soon, Carlos stood. "Excuse me, but I have to meet with someone tonight." He held out his hand to Miles. "It was a good time. Thank you."

Miles stood and accepted the handshake. "I appreciate your hospitality, sir."

As Carlos closed the door behind him, Miles waited in indecision. He finally reached for his hat and rifle. "It's getting late. I should be going, too. Thank you, Mrs. Mendes. It was a great meal and fun evening."

"You're welcome. But Rosa has informed me she will not stay with us. You will walk my Rosa home first, won't you? I don't like her being out at night alone."

"Absolutely." And just like that, his attempt to follow Carlos was thwarted, but he should have known better than to leave without offering to escort Rosa home. "Trust me, it'll be my pleasure."

Rosa stood but didn't move to leave. "Mama, does Carlos have an extra gun here? I'd feel safer if I had a means to protect myself."

"Rosa—"

She lifted her hand to silence her mother. "You know I can use it with accuracy."

"Yes. Your father saw to that."

Mrs. Mendes moved to their bedroom and reappeared with a pistol. "Be careful, Rosa."

Rosa kissed her mother's cheek. "I will. Thank you, Mama." She followed Miles out the door and wrapped her shawl more tightly around her as the breeze ruffled her hair. The moment they were alone, she slipped her hand around his elbow and gave it a squeeze. "You were wonderful tonight. Not only did you offer a gift to a man who almost killed you, but you didn't get upset at his attempt to trick you into giving out information. You truly amazed me."

"I admit I had a difficult time accepting the way you were treated by them, but I gained a sense of peace after some time in prayer. Maybe they were just a little misguided when it came to the way they tried to get things done, but they're good people, Rosa. Just because they don't agree with you and me doesn't necessarily make them wrong or bad."

"No, it doesn't. I'm just now beginning to see that. I guess part of our freedom is the right to have our own opinions. Like Mama said, we should be able to disagree and still treat each other with love and respect."

He pressed her hand to his side, his only way of hugging her. "It's a shame not everyone is as smart as your mother. Which is why we have battles."

The truth of his statement brought reality crashing down upon him. He stopped and turned to face Rosa.

"I don't know if Santa Anna is really coming to fight the men at the Alamo, but if he is, I want you far away from here." He couldn't believe he was asking the woman he loved to leave. "I'll pay your way to someplace safe. I don't want you hurt, Rosa."

In the dim light from several lanterns along the street, he saw Rosa's smile. She reached up and touched his face, igniting a fire on his skin. He couldn't resist and turned his lips into her palm, holding her hand there for several moments before releasing her.

"As much as I want you here, I can't fight Santa Anna's men while worrying about your safety. Promise me you'll leave."

She shook her head. "I can't make that promise. For so long, I've wanted nothing more than to leave Béxar. Now, I only want to stay if you and Mama are here."

His heart soared and crashed at the same time. Fear for her safety would be uppermost on his mind. "Then at least promise me you'll go to my hut outside of town. Maybe it'll be far enough away from the fighting and Santa Anna's men."

"I can promise that."

"Good."

They hadn't gotten far down the street when Rosa added a quiet, "I'll bring my club."

They shared a laugh. He could almost picture a defiant Rosa thumping some overambitious man upside the head, yet he prayed it would never happen.

Chapter Fifteen

Rosa carefully checked the pistol for powder before placing it inside her satchel. She opened the door and peered all along the street. The events of the past few days brought clarity to thoughts of her future. Her life had been altered when Papa was killed. The security he provided had disappeared. But in his wisdom, he'd made certain she could defend herself. At least to some degree. She prayed the day she had to pull out the gun would never come, but if it did, she hoped she could make Papa proud.

The empty street ensured her safety, at least for now. She nearly skipped to Ana Maria's house, her hand still warm from Miles's kiss the night before. She couldn't wait to tell her friend and hoped she'd arrive before Ana and her parents left to open their dry goods store.

For the first time, Rosa had the tiniest inkling why Mama stood behind Carlos, even if she thought what he'd done was wrong. If Mama felt toward Carlos as Rosa did toward Miles, she could understand the tendency to fight for the one you loved. But that still didn't make deceit and betrayal right. Once trust was broken, the mending process could be long, tedious, and possibly painful. That was something she and Mama would have to work on for a long time to come.

As she raised her hand to knock on Ana's door, it opened, and Ana flung herself into Rosa's arms.

"You're safe! I've been so worried." She held Rosa at arms' length. "I know Miles said he'd take care of you, but that didn't stop me from fretting." She wrapped her arm around Rosa's and led them down the street. "Tell me what happened. I want to know everything."

Rosa slowed long enough to turn and wave at Ana's parents, who trailed behind at a much slower pace. Ana's steps were moving as fast as her words.

Ana gave Rosa's arm a tug. "Stop delaying. Speak. And don't leave anything out."

The laughter of pure happiness bubbled out. She held out her right hand, palm turned toward her friend. "He kissed it."

Ana squealed, pulled her to a stop, and peered into her eyes. "Miles? You're serious? Oh, my goodness!" Rosa was yanked into a quick hug. "I'm so happy for you. Wait." Ana held her away again. "You're happy, too, aren't you?"

Rosa nodded, and Ana squealed again before giving another embrace. Then she had them marching down the street. "Why? Why did he kiss your hand?"

"I'm not sure. He was worried about my safety. He was so sweet about it so I put my hand on his cheek. He turned and kissed the palm." Rosa grasped Ana's hand. "Don't you dare tell Mama or Carlos, or even your parents, and don't squeal again, but I think I love him."

Ana groaned instead. "I'm so jealous. Do you think there's a man for me at the Alamo?"

Rosa leaned forward to look into Ana's face. "Don't be silly, Ana. Why would the fort be full of men?"

Ana swatted her arm then giggled. "Stop teasing. I need to go there with you next time. Maybe I'll meet my own Miles."

"I'm going there today. I need money, so I'm going to see if anyone wants me to do their laundry."

"But Miles bought you supplies yesterday."

"I know. I gave half of it to Mama." She spent a few minutes telling Ana everything that happened the day before. The look of horror on Ana's face challenged Rosa's resolve to be strong on her own, but she pushed away the fear. "Mama fixed us a wonderful meal yesterday, so I know she's in need of supplies, too."

"Then I'm going with you. Let me run back and talk to my parents. Wait here. I'll be right back."

Rosa understood Ana's excitement. They'd reached the age of eighteen and hadn't ever come close to the prospect of marriage. With all the fighting going on in the area for the last year or more, marriage seemed the last thing on a man's mind. Her father would have teased that it's because a man could only handle one battle at a time, and a wife was a full-time skirmish. The thought made her smile. She sure missed him.

While Ana bargained with her parents, Rosa took the few steps necessary to pass the house on the corner in order to see down the next street. A vaguely familiar girl headed her way pushing a cart while leading two goats. She struggled with them every time they tried to stop and nibble at the winter grass growing alongside the street. When she got closer, Rosa could see there was a cage filled with chickens in the cart. The sight seemed odd.

Ana rushed back to her. "They're letting me go with you. I can't wait to get there. Let's go."

"I have to go back and get my basket first." She motioned to the girl with the cart. "Who is that? She looks familiar."

After a quick look, Ana smiled. "That's Violet Classon. I introduced you to her at the store about a month ago." She waved. "Let's wait for her. It's strange she'd be leading their goats. I hope she's all right."

Minutes later, Violet reached them, her smile not quite reaching her eyes. Ana pulled her into a brief hug before motioning to the goats and chickens.

"Why do you have those, Violet? Is something wrong?"

Violet lifted one shoulder. "My father decided we needed to leave. He doesn't want to be here for the next battle. He says he can't fight and keep us safe at the same time. I'm supposed to bring these animals to the Alamo. Giving them to the men who'll be fighting is the only way my father feels he can help. We're leaving in the morning."

"Oh, Violet." Ana squeezed Violet's hand. "I'm so sorry. I know how much your father wanted to live here."

"Yes, he did. But now he thinks he can make a living farther east where we won't have to fight for a livelihood."

Ana pulled Rosa closer. "We're on our way to the Alamo right now. You can walk with us."

Rosa held up her hand. "But you have to wait a few minutes. I have to run get my basket so I have something I can carry their dirty laundry in."

Violet motioned to her cart. "You can put them in there."

Rosa looked pointedly at the chicken droppings at the bottom of the cart, her eyebrows high.

Violet smiled. "We'll wait here till you get back."

Rosa rushed to her house thinking that with Violet and her parents leaving, she had her way out of this town, except now she didn't want to leave. She paused at the door with basket in hand. For weeks she'd been praying for a chance to leave, and here it lay at her feet. Was this God's answer, giving her a sign to leave? Surely not. She was finally looking forward to a bright future. Well, except for the upcoming battle and the fact that Miles planned to be one of the men fighting.

Pushing that thought from her mind, she hurried back to Ana and Violet, and the three of them began what was sure to be a fun outing. They had to help Violet get the cart and goats up the hill to the Alamo. They all were out of breath by the time they arrived at the fort. Rosa led the way toward the gate, prepared to head straight for the barracks to find work.

"Hold it right there, ladies."

Rosa stopped at the demand. Ana and Violet hovered right behind her as a man with feathers sticking out of his hat stepped into their path.

"You can't go any farther."

"What? Why? I come here all the time."

"Not anymore. Not unless Mr. Fitch escorts you the entire time. Wait right here. I'll see if I can find him."

Rosa exchanged a look with Ana. "All right."

More time with Miles wouldn't be bad at all. Even Ana bumped her from behind at the news. But why? What had changed? The only answer that came to mind was that Miles had told his superiors about her spying. She understood his loyalty to the defenders of the Alamo, but what about his loyalty toward her? Maybe their relationship wasn't as close as she'd thought. Was she about to be banned like her mother?

* * * * *

Miles stood at the corner of the barracks eyeing the different groups of men huddled together motioning toward others. Murmuring could be heard but nothing clearly. The only thing clear was the tension in the air.

Peacock strode toward him, his feathers bobbing with each step. He motioned behind him with his thumb. "Your lady and her friends are here. The colonels said they weren't allowed inside unless you were with them."

Miles nodded. "That's right." He pushed away from the wall to follow Peacock back to the gate. "What's wrong with the men, Peacock? They act like they don't like each other."

"You haven't heard? Colonel Neill left. Travis is in charge, and

Bowie doesn't like it. Since they don't see eye to eye on everything, neither do the men."

Miles looked around as he walked. His and John's dispute was minor compared to this one. How Crockett was going to fix this clash, he didn't know, but it had to be mended. The men needed to fight against their enemy, not each other.

He was about to greet Rosa and her friends but motioned for them to wait. "Peacock, how long have you been posted at the gate?"

"Started yesterday. Why?"

"You seen Starks?"

Peacock smiled and shook his head. "That man has more people looking for him."

"What do you mean?"

"All the colonels told us to let them know if he showed, and now you're asking. What's he done?"

Miles lifted a shoulder. "Not sure. I just want to make sure I don't have any trouble with him while the ladies are here."

That was true. He just didn't tell it all. He joined the girls. "Ladies, you've just brightened a drab day." He nodded to Rosa and Ana then smiled at their friend. "I'm Miles Fitch."

"Violet Classon. My father sent me with these animals. We're heading east tomorrow. He wants to leave the goats and chickens here hoping you can use them."

"I'm sure the cook can use the milk and eggs and will be pleased to have them. Follow me. We'll put them with the other animals. I'll let the cook know."

He took over pulling the cart and led them across the compound, through the opening leading toward the chapel, and into the stockyard. At least he thought the girls had followed. Instead, they'd stopped in front of the chapel and appeared to be examining the building. He motioned for one of the men to take the goats and chickens then pushed the cart back to the girls and tried to figure out what held their interest.

"Is something wrong?"

Rosa reached out and ran her hand over one of the columns. "Isn't it beautiful? Just look at all the work, the ornamentation and carvings."

He looked again. "What?"

Rosa glared at him. "Are all men blind to beauty?"

He took a step closer and examined her face. "No. I know beauty when I see it."

As she gave him a shy smile, her face turned rosy. "You mentioned getting a tour of this place. Is today a good day? My friends would like to see it as much as I would."

He looked around. The men were still in groups. Maybe the ladies wouldn't notice the tension. "Sure. It'll be a short tour, if that's all right. Then I'll walk the three of you back to town."

"I'll enjoy any amount of time we can spend here. I think we all will."

The look she gave Ana seemed to have special meaning. When they didn't explain, he motioned to the chapel.

"The chapel didn't get finished, meaning there's no roof. There are rooms inside, but for now, the majority of the inside is filled with dirt for a cannon ramp. They tell me this whole compound was built as a Spanish mission around one hundred years ago."

The fact that their powder magazines were housed inside didn't need to be mentioned. He pointed to the north on his left.

"That area there is our stock pens." He looked at Violet. "That's where I put your animals. Now let's go over here."

He led them back through the opening behind them and into the center of the compound. He motioned to the building along the east wall. "That's the long barracks, where most of the men here get some rest. The door there at the end by the opening we just walked through is the hospital. The first building south of there is the kitchen. Most of the buildings along the south and west walls are more barracks, along with some storerooms and workrooms." He shrugged. "That's about it."

Rosa's mouth dropped open. "You were serious when you said this would be a short tour."

He smiled but was ready to have them out of the fort and on their way to town. There were too many men with too much tension. Anything could happen while the ladies were here. "There really isn't that much to show. What you see is all there is."

"Well, the chapel is my favorite building. It looks like a lot of love went into its construction."

Ana spent little time looking at the buildings. The men held most of her attention, which made him nervous. The time had come to get them back to town.

"Are you ready to go?"

"Oh." Rosa looked at Ana. "Almost. I had planned to see if any of the men had laundry for me. Is that all right?"

"Sure. Why don't you wait here while I check with them?"

He gave the ladies one last look, doubting he should leave them alone for even a minute, and moved from group to group. A few of the men nodded and headed to the barracks. While he waited for Rosa to gather the clothing, he dumped a bucket of water in Violet's cart and used a broom to wipe out the chicken refuse.

With all three ladies finally rounded up and ready, Miles was about to grab the cart handle when John Prine headed their way, his long strides eating up the ground between them.

"Fitch, hold on a minute."

Miles tensed, ready to do battle. From the corner of his eye, he saw Rosa do the same. What could he possibly want other than to cause trouble?

At his arrival, John clapped Miles on the back but never took his eyes from the girls. "Thanks for waiting." He tipped his hat to the ladies. "Who are your friends?"

Miles clenched his jaw for a moment wishing he could be on his way. "This is Ana Maria. Her parents own the dry goods store in town, and she works there with them."

John smiled and extended his hand for hers. He clasped it briefly, bowing low enough to almost kiss the back of her hand. "I think I'll have to make a trip into town soon. Hard to believe I've missed out on such bounty." He turned to Violet. "And who do we have here?"

Miles wanted to cuff the man upside the head for being so obvious. "This is Violet Classon. Her father has given the Alamo his goats and chickens as a way of helping the men here. They're heading east in the morning."

John gave Violet the same treatment as Ana. "Be sure to thank your father for me, Miss Classon. We appreciate help of all kinds, and his is most generous." He touched his hat again. "Since Fitch has neglected to introduce me, I'll do so myself. I'm John Prine. Very pleased to make your acquaintance."

John had yet to acknowledge Rosa. Time to test where things stood.

He motioned to Rosa. "And you remember Miss Carter, of course."

John glanced at her with a slight nod. "Of course." He turned back to Ana and Violet. "Ladies, is there anything more I can do for you, or has Fitch adequately taken care of your needs?"

Miles didn't know whether to laugh or hit the man. John's slight of Rosa was much too obvious, and he hoped she wouldn't be hurt or offended. But Ana and Violet seemed completely unaware of the tension, so enamored were they with John's attention. Their faces colored as they giggled.

Ana took a step toward John and touched his arm. "You're most kind, but Miles has seen to our needs. He even gave us a brief tour of the fort."

John's eyes went to his with a slight frown. "He did. Very good. I'm assuming you were about to leave."

"Yes." Ana hooked her arm in John's. "Would you walk with us to the gate?"

"It would be my pleasure." He extended his other elbow to Violet. "Shall we?" He looked over his shoulder. "You'll get the cart, Fitch?"

"It would be my pleasure, Prine." Miles extended his arm to Rosa as he made a face. "I guess we servants had better hurry along. Wouldn't want to keep the master waiting."

Rosa laughed. "He does seem to be in rare form today."

"You're not hurt that he all but ignored you?"

"Not at all."

They walked past John and the girls, allowing her friends time and privacy to say their goodbyes. Once past, Rosa squeezed his arm.

"You seemed in a hurry. Is everything all right? Was it because of John?"

"Not John, no. I think the men are getting a little restless. Too much time of not enough to do. Waiting isn't something men do well. I didn't want anything to happen while you were there."

"That makes sense." She looked back then stopped. "Wait."

Miles turned to see Ana still at the gate talking to John while Violet chatted with Peacock. "What're they doing?"

Rosa made a face. "Ana had hoped to meet a nice man like you here today. I never dreamed she'd meet John."

"That's not the way to meet a man."

"Why? Does she have to get into trouble and wait for whichever man comes to her rescue? That's how I met you."

He tried not to smile and failed. "That's not what I meant. She shouldn't force a meeting. She should wait for something to just, well, happen."

"Oh, really. And how is something going to happen when she never comes here? If she just waits around, she may never meet the right man."

This conversation wasn't getting him anywhere, especially not farther away from the fort. If the girls had their heart set on meeting someone special, he might never get them away from here.

"Will it help if I spread the word that she works at the dry good store? She may get more men visiting her than she bargained for and may not want that now that she's met John, but it beats standing in the midst of all these men who enjoy gawking and may be getting the wrong ideas. Plus she'll have her parents around to help protect her."

"That's not a bad idea. Let me see what I can do to help move things along."

In minutes, he had all three ladies headed back to town. He hoped they didn't make a habit of visiting the Alamo. His nerves might not be able to withstand their onslaught of feminine notions.

Chapter Sixteen

Rosa had thoroughly enjoyed the past week. When Miles wasn't taking his turn standing post inside the Alamo, he spent a great deal of his time entertaining her. The walks they took to watch the sun go down were her most favorite times with him. There was no doubt in her mind she'd fallen in love with him, and she was fairly certain that he, too, was in love. If only he'd say the words. But because he wouldn't be able to see her tonight, she'd have to wait at least one more day.

"Cheer up, Rosa. You'll see Miles tomorrow." Mama's teasing brought a smile.

"And it can't get here soon enough."

"No proposal of marriage yet?"

Rosa stood from her chair at the table and joined her mother in the kitchen. "What makes you think he's anywhere close to wanting marriage?"

"Oh, I don't know. Maybe it's the way he spends every spare minute at your side. Or the way he looks at you with longing in his eyes."

"Stop, Mama. You're making the ache in my heart worse."

Mama laughed and put her arm around her shoulders. "That's the way it's supposed to feel, mi querida. Then you know for sure it's love."

"You felt like this with Papa?" The slightest hint of guilt pinched her heart for asking such a question.

Mama's eyes softened as she gazed out the window. "Ah, yes. I remember nearly wanting to strangle him for taking so long to declare his love. I think I loved him the instant I saw him, so tall and strong and confident. I couldn't understand why he hadn't felt the same way and proposed the moment he saw me."

Rosa bumped her mother with her hip and laughter spilled from them. She couldn't remember the last time they'd had so much fun together. Mama had been working hard to mend the break of trust between them, even going as far as confiding that the reason Carlos disappeared almost every night was to learn and pass along more information. Plus, Mama and Carlos had been good to their word not to pester her for information, even after learning Miles had given her a tour of the Alamo. Each visit was enjoyable and lighthearted. Tonight looked to be no different.

They were about finished preparing the meal when Carlos walked in wearing a wide grin while holding something behind his back. He edged around the room, keeping his back to the wall, making his way to the bedroom.

"It smells great, ladies. We about ready to eat?"

Mama crossed her arms. "Not until you show me what you have."

"Have? I have nothing."

Mama's brows rose. "And your belly will have nothing, too." She started toward him. "What have you been up to, Carlos? What are you hiding from me?"

He stopped, leaned his back against the wall, and held up his hands. "See? I have nothing."

Hands again behind his back, he kept inching toward the bedroom. Mama rushed at him and wrapped her arms around him. An odd feeling washed through Rosa. This was the first time she'd seen this side of Mama's relationship with Carlos, and her love for him was obvious. She ached for the loss of her father but also enjoyed seeing her mother happy again.

"What is that? It feels wooden."

Mama looked up into Carlos's face and received a kiss before he revealed the surprise. He turned the wooden plank toward Mama, who sucked in a breath.

"Oh, Carlos." Mama ran her hand over the plank. "It's beautiful." Mama took it from his and turned it toward Rosa. "Look at it, Rosa."

Rosa moved closer and understood her mother's reaction. Carlos had turned a piece of wood into a lovely carved sign that said, "Carmela's Kitchen." He'd also carved and painted beautiful flowers on each side of the words.

She smiled at Carlos. "You did a great job, Carlos."

"Thank you, Rosa." He put his arm around Mama. "She brings out the best in me."

For the first time since they'd met, Rosa no longer hated Carlos. He'd been good to her mother, made her happy, took good care of her. She took the final step to show her approval and gave him a hug.

* * * * *

Miles crouched in his usual hiding place down the street from Carlos's house. He felt a pinch of guilt for allowing Rosa to think he had to stand guard at the Alamo tonight. But after a talk with Bowie and Crockett, he knew he needed to try harder to find Starks or whoever else might be spying for the enemy.

The two colonels had gotten another man from the fort to work at the cantina where Miles saw Starks, and he learned information was still being leaked. Miles had allowed his feelings for Rosa to get in the way of his search for the spy. He had let down his fellow fighters. It was time to make it up to them.

He shifted to keep his legs from going numb. He'd lost track of time when the door to Carlos's house opened. Rosa and Carlos left the house. Miles trailed them all the way to Rosa's house, using trees and buildings as cover. Carlos bid her good night then headed west, past the cantina where Miles was hit on the head, and down a few more streets before he disappeared into a ragged building, more of a hut, where a light was already burning.

In minutes, Carlos appeared near the window, obviously talking with someone. Curious as to the other man's identity, Miles made his way from one structure to the next, trying to get into a better position to see inside. He eased around the far side of another building, still too far from the place where Carlos went inside, trying to remain quiet and unseen.

Just as Miles was about to move around the final corner, he heard a gun cocked right behind him. He stopped and put his hands out.

"Drop the rifle!"

Miles laid it on the ground.

"Down on your knees."

"Look, I'm just—"

"Get down on your knees!"

As he dropped to his knees, Miles finally placed the voice. "Starks?"

The man barked a laugh then kicked Miles in the side. Miles coughed several times from the pain. He could feel Starks's breath next to his ear.

"You're gonna be begging me to kill you before I finally grant you your wish."

A second later, Starks smashed his fist into Miles's ear. Miles fell to his belly only to have Starks jump on top of him. Blow after blow, Starks pounded his fists onto Miles's head and torso. With ears ringing and the taste of blood in his mouth, he couldn't roll over to fight back.

"Stop right there!"

In the dim lantern light, Miles saw Starks reach for his gun and point it in the direction of the voice. Miles kicked at Starks's arm. The gun went off, followed by another blast. Starks grunted and fell to the ground next to him.

Miles pushed to his knees and looked for the other gunman. John stepped into the light. "You looked like you could use some help."

While trying to catch his breath, Miles wiped blood from his face and nodded. "Thanks, John."

"I think I need to thank you, too. He was about to fire on me." He knelt next to Starks. "I know him. Isn't he the man who attacked Rosa?"

"Yes."

"What're you two doing out here?"

Miles felt for a pulse and found one, though it was slow and weak. "I've been looking for him, but he found me first."

Starks groaned and coughed then cursed. "You were supposed to die, not me."

There was a rattle to his breathing. Miles hoped he lived long enough to give up some information.

"Who you been talking to, Starks?"

He started to laugh, but it turned into a strangled cough. "You think I'm gonna tell you anything?"

He coughed and gagged then spat. He mumbled something else, but Miles couldn't hear him. He leaned closer and saw the grin on Starks's face.

"I'll tell you this much. You got the wrong man. The one you're after is still out there. I was just the messenger."

He laughed again then his body tightened in a spasm before he went limp. Miles felt for his pulse again and found none.

"He dead?"

Miles nodded. "Yeah."

"What was that all about? All that wrong man talk?"

He blew out a long breath. "Long story." He looked at the hut where Carlos had entered. The light was out; the place probably empty after the gunfire. He shook his head. Missed his chance again. "Help me carry him to the fort, will you?"

John eyed him a moment then nodded. "Sure. Grab the rifles and his pistol. I'll carry him."

John tugged on Starks's arm while Miles helped lift the body over John's shoulder. He shifted the body a couple times, and then they began the long walk to the fort.

"What're you doing out here, Prine?"

He chuckled. "I was here to see Ana. She's fun to be around. Not as serious as Rosa."

"Oh?"

"Yeah, well, as I was leaving I thought I saw you. You were acting odd so I decided to follow you. Good thing I did."

"I agree. Thanks again."

Struggling to hold all the weapons and breathing heavily from his beating, Miles forced one foot in front of the other. He'd gained plenty of information tonight, but not what he was after. John was no longer interested in Rosa. That pleased him to no end. And now he knew of another place to watch for Carlos. But they still had a traitor in the Alamo.

Bowie and Crockett wouldn't be pleased at all to know that bit of bad news. And since John was in on the events tonight, if Travis didn't know about the traitor before, he would certainly learn about it soon. The tension inside the Alamo was about to grow.

Chapter Seventeen

Lieutenant Colonel William Travis paced in his quarters, hands clasped behind his back. Orange, pink, and purple rays from the sunrise streamed through his door and window. This was the first time Miles had dealt with the man, the first time they'd been this close. His youth surprised him. Travis couldn't be more than five or six years older, which made Miles wonder if that was the reason for the distance, the conflict between him and Bowie, who had to be at least ten years older than Travis. Probably more. Yet Travis had a certain air about him. Not really arrogance, though he could easily be mistaken for that very thing. Maybe confidence was the word Miles sought.

He finally came to a stop in front of Miles. "You're telling me that man out there, that *dead* man, is not the traitor."

"I'm telling you he's not the *only* traitor. He told me he was just the messenger, that the other man is still out there."

For a few moments, no one made a sound except for Bowie, who couldn't seem to stop the cough racking his body. He sat hunched, holding his cape tightly around his shoulders as though he thought of it as a shield. Crockett sat on the corner of Travis's table, slightly swinging one leg. He kept his eyes on Miles but remained silent. John, who was now part of the secret about a traitor because of what had happened the night before, fidgeted, checked his hands, and adjusted his clothing too many times to count. He stood against the wall and looked anywhere but at the men in the room.

Travis rubbed his chin. "He didn't give you a name?"

"No. In fact, he seemed quite pleased to tell me there was another man, that he wasn't the one I should have been looking for."

"So it could be anyone inside the fort. Maybe even one of my officers." Travis moved to the window and scanned the compound as if he could spot the culprit. "I just sent Jim Bonham off with a message asking for reinforcements. What are the chances this traitor is aware of that too, and he is passing along that news, letting Santa Anna's army know we need more men?"

"At this point, does it matter?"

Crockett finally spoke, but his words had Travis spinning on his heel.

"Why *wouldn't* it matter?"

Crockett lifted one shoulder. "I'm guessing Santa Anna already has his men on the move, as many of them as he could muster. Do you think he really cares how many men are in here? He's coming to fight regardless if we have two hundred or two thousand." He held up a hand to stave off Travis's next comment. "Yes, I agree it's best to keep our advantages, or disadvantages, to ourselves, but I think by now it matters very little."

A frown creased Travis's brow. "He might be weeks away. He could easily send for more men if he thinks it's necessary."

"He could." Crockett shrugged again. "Whatever he does or doesn't do won't affect where we stand right now. We don't know where he is or how much longer it'll be before he gets here. We'll just keep doing what we're doing until he arrives. We'll just have to be much more careful about what takes place here until then."

Crockett turned to Miles. "During all of your investigating, did you come up with anything at all that might help you know who the traitor is?"

"I have another place to watch. I'm fairly certain that the meetings taking place there will reveal who he is."

Crockett nodded. "Get it done. Lose sleep if you have to, but find that man."

"Yes, sir."

As Miles and John left the room, the door closed behind them. Miles wished he could have stayed to be a part of their meeting. He could learn a lot from those three men.

"What're you doing next?"

John's question made Miles slow his steps. He looked toward the kitchen. "Obviously I'm not sleeping." He gave a wry grin. "But I'm hungry. I'll see if the cook has anything left. Then I guess I'd better get to town."

"I'll walk with you. I told Ana I'd check on her this morning."

Miles gave him a sidelong glance. "You two seem to have gotten pretty close in a short period of time." He weighed his next question before taking a chance. "Whatever happened with Rosa?"

"Nothing happened. Or should I say, you happened. So I moved on to Ana."

"You don't seem too mad about it."

He lifted a hand and let it fall again. "No, not really. I was at first, I guess. But I like Ana. She talks a lot, but she's. . .cheery. Lively. Like she doesn't have so many problems weighing her down. Rosa seemed upset all the time."

"She wasn't getting along with her mother for a while. They've worked it out."

"Good."

John didn't appear all that interested, so Miles let the conversation die. The two men tucked into some leftover biscuits and gravy then made their way out the gate. They hadn't gotten far when two men on horseback rode out of the fort, splashed across the San Antonio River, and galloped off to the south. Miles and John shared a look, brows raised. Miles was certain the riders were the result of the meeting in Travis's quarters. They continued into town, parting ways at the edge. The first place Miles wanted to check was the small hut where he'd trailed Carlos. If at all possible, he'd take a look inside.

* * * * *

Rosa strolled the aisles of the dry goods store with Ana beside her chattering on about John and his great attributes. The girl floated on air with more than a little bliss, and Rosa caught herself glancing at Ana's feet. Ana grabbed and shook Rosa's arm, nearly making her drop the small bag of flour in her hand.

"You're not listening, Rosa. I said I think he might want to marry me."

"That's wonderful, Ana." She pulled her friend into a brief hug. If only she could say the same about Miles, but he had yet to give any indication he thought their relationship was headed that direction. Why were men so difficult? "I'm happy for you."

She placed the flour in her basket and continued down the aisle, praying John wouldn't hurt Ana, who had assured Rosa that he had been a perfect gentleman. Little did Ana know he had been the same way with her, right up until the end. But after the way their relationship ended, maybe John had learned from the mistakes and had changed. Still, maybe she should warn her friend.

"Just be careful, Ana. He—"

Ana's squeal brought Rosa's attention to the door. John had just arrived. After taking Ana's mother's hand in his and kissing its back, he shook hands with her father. Ana was the last to receive his attention, and he also kissed the back of her hand but kept it clasped in his.

Wishing she were anywhere else, Rosa made her way to the front to purchase her goods. "Good morning, John."

"Miss Carter."

Rosa almost smiled. So, this was how things were to be between them. His indifference was actually a relief, though she fought a twinge of jealousy that Ana seemed to see more of John than Rosa did of Miles. The thought begged her to ask, "Is Miles standing watch again this morning?"

"No, he's. . .ah. . .busy with something else."

Odd. John acted as though he thought better of his first answer. She pushed for a clearer response. "Is he busy here in town?"

He peeled off his hat, scratched his head, and then turned the hat in his hands. "He might have mentioned something like that."

Why was John so nervous? "Was he coming by my house?"

"Possibly. In fact, I wouldn't doubt that at all."

She turned to Ana's parents and showed them the items inside the basket. "How much?"

She placed the coins on the counter and rushed from the store. She hadn't seen Miles at all yesterday. She planned to be waiting for him should he stop by today. If her mother hadn't been waiting for the supplies from the store, Rosa would have gone straight home. Instead, she planned only a quick stop before rushing home.

As she was about to knock, the door opened. Carlos stepped out, leading her mother by the hand.

"Rosa. Good timing. Your mother wants to see the rocking chair I just finished. Come with us. I used your friend's tools on part of it. "

While she searched for an excuse to go home, her mother took the basket from her, set it inside, and then tucked her free hand around Rosa's elbow.

"Come along, Rosa. Then you can tell your Miles all about the chair and the wonderful job Carlos does with the carving tools."

Mama managed to say the one thing that could convince her to join them. Besides that, she hadn't been to Carlos's shop since they'd first met. In such poor condition, Rosa wondered how the hut still stood. But Carlos said he'd been working on it. Curiosity drove her to join them. She just wouldn't stay long and quickened her steps to speed things along, right up until Mama tugged at her arm.

"Slow down, Rosa. What's the hurry?"

"Nothing. Nothing at all. Sorry."

She tried to relax, measuring her steps to match her mother's. It seemed they'd been walking forever.

"Carmela!"

One of Mama's friends waved her over. Mama squeezed her hand and patted Carlos on the chest.

"I haven't seen her in over a week. Let me go say hello. I won't be long. I promise."

Not another delay! They were almost there. Couldn't Mama have waited to greet her friend after seeing the chair? Rosa paced then walked to the street that led to Carlos's shop. Carlos trailed her.

"Is something wrong, Rosa? You're acting nervous."

"No. Nothing's wrong. Really. I just have things to do at home."

She peeked behind Carlos to see if her mother was coming. Carlos did the same. With her mother still busy chatting, Rosa took the last few steps to see around the corner and gasped. Miles was coming out of the shop. Sneaking would be a better description. The moment he saw her, his back went ramrod straight. She motioned behind her to indicate Carlos then waved Miles away. He nodded his understanding and raced off.

The crunching of Carlos's footsteps indicated he was approaching. "Would you like me to show you the chair now so you can go? I can show Carmela later."

Rosa backed up then rushed around the corner and bumped into Carlos. He grasped her arms to keep her from falling.

"Are you all right? Did something happen over there?"

"No, not at all. I just don't want to leave Mama behind." She tucked her arm through his and led him away from the shop. "Let's see if we can hurry her along."

The sooner the better. Miles had some explaining to do, and she didn't plan on sleeping nor allowing him to rest until he told her everything.

Chapter Eighteen

Rosa spotted Miles waiting on the bench outside of her house in his usual position. . .feet stretched out in front of him with his arms acting as pillows for his head. How could he be so relaxed? He had wandered through a hut that wasn't his. No doubt it was to spy, and she'd had more than her fill of conspiring against one another.

Several emotions had warred inside her on the walk home, anger being the strongest in the battle, but disappointment came in at a close second. The spying was supposed to be over. At least that's what she'd been led to believe. Miles had better have a good explanation for sneaking out of Carlos's shop. If he didn't. . . ?

She came to a stop right in front of Miles, crossed her arms, and refused to say a word. He was the one who had to do the talking. And he'd better start soon. Her patience dangled on a string the size of a spider's thread.

"Thank you for your help back there. It would have been bad if Carlos had seen me."

That was it? A thank-you? No explanation? She tapped her foot in an attempt to keep from erupting. It wasn't working.

"That's all you have to say? You were in Carlos's shop uninvited. Why? What possible reason could you have to be in there? He told you he builds furniture."

Miles stood and reached to touch her. She took a step back. He wasn't getting out of this mess by trying to be nice.

He motioned to the bench. "Can we at least sit while I try to explain?"

"I don't think I can. I'm too upset to sit."

"Maybe because it's too hard for you to kick me when you're sitting?"

His question and the adorable teasing look on his face hit his intended target and doused the fire. She was still annoyed with him, and she still expected an explanation, but she couldn't stay mad. She fought a smile but her lips twitched.

"That's better. I don't like it when you're angry with me."

She frowned as she shook her finger at him. "You're still in trouble."

"I know."

He motioned to the bench again. This time she accepted but sat on the end, as far from him as possible, crossing her arms once more. He may have put out the fire, but it still smoldered. Thankfully he didn't attempt to touch her as he sat.

"Why, Miles?"

He propped his ankle on his knee. "I tried to come up with reasons I could give you but in the end decided the truth was best."

"It is."

He hesitated, rubbing at a smudge on the leg of his buckskins. "I'm still trying to find out who the traitor is at the fort."

"Well, it's not Carlos."

"I know. But I'm certain Carlos knows who it is. If I follow him around, I have a good chance of finding out."

"And following him around means entering his shop without permission?"

He took a deep breath. "I realize going in there wasn't the best of ideas, but I'd hoped I'd find something, a note, message, anything that might reveal the identity of the traitor."

"Did you find something?"

"No. But I at least had to check to make sure." He paused. "What I did find is that Carlos made a rocking chair and did a great job carving on it. My father would have been pleased."

She looked at his face, trying to decide if he was sincere or still trying to soften her ire. By his expression, his sentiments seemed heartfelt.

"Carlos would appreciate hearing that, but now you can't say anything or he'd know you saw it." She'd come to like Carlos and wanted to protect him, especially for her mother's sake. "Are you going to get Carlos into trouble, Miles?"

"No. Not at all." He turned on the bench to face her. "Even if he really is working with the traitor, it's not Carlos I'm after. He's only doing what he thinks is right, just as I am. I only want to stop the spy from spreading information." He attempted to touch her hand but pulled back before making contact. "I give you my word."

"All right. I believe you." She had only one more question, and then she'd be ready to forget the whole thing and have fun. "How did you know that's where Carlos worked? I never brought you by there or told you about it."

He made a face. "I know you thought I was standing watch last night. I let you believe that, but actually I was following Carlos. His shop is where we ended up."

"But what made you think you might find information about the traitor there?"

He rubbed his hands on his thighs and no longer looked at her.

"What happened last night, Miles?"

He shifted his position on the bench. "A man was killed outside that shop. The same man who attacked you at the Alamo so many days ago. Seems like a lifetime now. But I suspected him of being the traitor."

She touched the bruises on his face. She'd noticed them earlier but was too upset to mention them. "Were you the one who killed him? You've got more bruises."

"Not me. He did attack me, but John shot him to protect both of us."

"John? When did he get involved?"

"Last night. He saw me sneaking around and followed me. I'm glad he did. Starks caught me off guard. He had me down." Miles took her hand in his. "So, are you still mad or are we back to being friends?"

"I'm not mad. Not anymore."

His features relaxed, even managed a smile. "I was sure you'd question what happened today, but I never thought you'd be so angry. I didn't think you liked Carlos."

She leaned her head against the house and thought back to the last several days spent with Mama and Carlos. The memories brought a smile.

"I used to detest him, but I don't now." She faced Miles, her smile widening. "I've spent a lot of time with him and Mama since she and I had our talk, more at her insistence than anything. Mama's trying hard to make amends. But I've noticed in our time together that they really do love each other. I've seen how happy he makes her. He's good to her. That's what made me try harder to like him. I don't want to see anything bad happen to him for Mama's sake."

"I understand. And I'm glad. It's good for family to get along. And I'll do whatever I can to make sure nothing happens to him."

"Good." She took both his hands in hers. "And now that all the confusion's been cleared up, what are your plans for the day? Are you busy, or do we get to spend some time together? We didn't get to see each other yesterday."

"I think I can manage a few hours." He stood and pulled her to her feet. "What would you like to do?"

"A walk? And maybe eat something I didn't have to cook?"

"Great idea. What's your mother fixing?"

She gasped and swatted his arm. "That's not what I meant!"

He laughed. "It was worth a try."

She narrowed her eyes and shook her finger at him. He grasped it and tugged it to his lips, sending a shiver through her.

* * * * *

Miles strolled through the woods with Rosa at his side thinking if she didn't stop looking at him with those soft, adoring eyes, he'd have to kiss more than her finger. Maybe if they talked more. . .

"You seem much more relaxed than before. Maybe happier is a better word. Is it because you have your mother back and don't have to spy anymore?"

"That definitely has a lot to do with it. Coming to an understanding with Mama and Carlos has made life much more enjoyable. But I have to give you credit, too."

"Me? How did I help?"

"How did you not?" She clasped his hand in hers and walked much closer, almost hugging his arm. "You not only were the means of me getting Mama back, which has had so many benefits, but you've been spending time with me."

He puffed out his chest and walked with a swagger. "Ah, yes. I do have a certain charm, an appeal to women in distress."

She laughed and swatted his chest, which caused him to cough and tuck it back in. "Stop. And yes, you do have a charming way about you. But hopefully it's reserved just for me."

He gave a slight bow. "I'm at your service alone, my dear."

"And such a gentleman."

He liked how her face colored along with her shy expression. Before he could act on it, she stopped their walk with a tug to his hand, her face suddenly serious.

"But one of the biggest ways you've helped me is with your example. You've been through your own struggles, your own tragedy, and yet your faith has remained strong."

"A strong faith is its own struggle. I still struggle. It's something we have to work at all the time. It doesn't just happen."

"I know. At least I know it now. My father's faith was always strong. I wanted to be like him, but I failed. I blamed God for all the bad things that happened, never once laying claim to my own bad choices. But then I met you, and you remind me so much of my father, which reminded me to strengthen my faith. So, yes, you deserve some recognition for my happiness."

He tucked some of her stray strands of hair behind her ear then cupped her cheek. "I think you need to give yourself some credit. It takes a wise person to see where they're weak and get to work on building strength in that area."

"It happens even faster with a good teacher."

She was incredibly beautiful. And the way she was looking at him. What was he waiting for? He was about to kiss her when she shrugged.

"So I guess I'd better go find one."

She started to laugh and tried to run away, but he caught her hand. He gripped it tighter and pulled her close. Her sweet breath washed across his face as she continued laughing.

"Always full of mischief."

She grinned. "Always."

He allowed his rifle to slip to the ground then cupped her cheeks again. "What would you say if I told you I wanted to kiss you, Rosa?"

"I'd say it's about time."

Without need of further invitation, he tasted her lips once, twice, pausing a mere moment before a third and last kiss. He needed to stop before he did something he'd regret. He took a step back.

"I could use a lifetime of those."

"I'll see what I can do."

"I like that answer."

He shoved his hands into his pockets to keep from touching her again and felt the necklace that little girl talked him into buying. He pulled it out and held it up. Rosa gasped and ran her fingers over the beads.

"This is beautiful. Where'd you get it?"

"From a pretty girl."

Rosa's startled eyes stabbed his. "Oh?"

He smiled. "Yes. She was all of about five years old with an angelic face with eyes that could talk a man into buying every piece of jewelry she offers. I stopped at one."

She made a face. "You're much too easy."

"Probably. But it gave me the excuse to get you something."

"Thank you, Miles."

He held it open, and she ducked her head, allowing him to put it on her. He ran his hands down her arms trying to decide if he should steal one more kiss. The battle didn't last long, especially because of her look of expectation. Then he forced himself to step back again.

After collecting his rifle, he grasped her hand, still craving her touch. But when he heard a stick snap off to the side of them, he tugged her behind him as he stepped in front of her, and leveled his rifle toward the sound. He blinked and looked again.

"That you, Morrell?"

William Morrell moved away from a tree. "It's me."

"You almost got yourself shot."

"So did you. I thought you were those deer I've been tracking. Buckskin and noise. Not a good combination when there's a hunter around."

The two shook hands. "Why're you hunting?"

"The cook wanted meat. I love to hunt and heard there were deer around. I volunteered to see what I could do."

Morrell glanced at Rosa, and Miles stepped aside. "I'm sorry. Miss Rosa Carter, this is William Morrell, one of the men at the Alamo."

Morrell tipped the rim of his hat. "We met once, briefly, but it's nice to see you again."

The memory of the night Starks broke into Rosa's house came rushing back to him. "Of course. You got me out of Rosa's house before her stepfather shot me."

Morrell smiled. "That's the night. Where ya headed? Back to the fort?"

"Not just yet. We plan to get something to eat first."

"You too, huh. I think everyone's sick of the food at the fort. Guess I'd better get going after those deer so we'll have some good grub tonight." He tipped his hat one more time. "Be careful. Wouldn't want either one of you getting shot."

Once more, Miles clasped Rosa's hand in his, glad to be alone again. He led them to the cantina where he ate the night Starks broke into Rosa's house. The last thing he wanted was to leave Rosa's side to go back to work, but he still had a job to do. He was determined to find the traitor tonight so he could spend more time with Rosa until the time he was called to fight Santa Anna's army. In the coming days, he wanted to have a talk with her about their future.

Chapter Nineteen

Nothing. Miles sat outside Carlos's wood shop most of the night and nothing had happened. Not even Carlos had showed. He pushed away the thought that maybe Rosa had warned him. She wouldn't do that. Not after the day they shared and his promise that Carlos wouldn't get into trouble.

He pushed to his feet and stretched the stiffness from his legs and back before heading to check on Rosa and then on to the fort. He rubbed at his eyes, which seemed to hold an entire bucket of sand.

If it weren't for Crockett's orders, he'd try to get some sleep. Instead, he'd grab a bite to eat and get back to his search for the traitor. He glanced at the overcast sky. If he waited much longer, a downpour would soon wash the sand from his eyes.

As he made his way to Rosa's house, a few raindrops fell, soon followed by a torrent. He took cover under an oak tree and hoped the rainstorm wouldn't last long. The cloudburst brought along cooler weather. With his clothes soon soaked, he shivered and prayed the sun would follow. He lost track of time, uncertain of how long he sat under the tree watching puddles form and run off from the street. He contemplated whether or not he should make a dash for Rosa's house. At least he'd have a chance to dry off, and he couldn't get any more drenched. With a sudden decision, he pushed from the ground and ran down the street.

Before he made it to Rosa's house, the rain slackened to a drizzle. As he slowed to a walk, the sound of two men arguing grabbed his attention. Carlos stood toe to toe with William Morrell, both yelling at each other in Spanish. Miles ducked behind a hut and peered around the corner. Carlos glanced each direction then grabbed William's arm and pulled him from the center of the street. Miles rushed to the other side of the hut for a better look.

William seemed to be the aggressor, poking his finger against Carlos's chest before giving him a shove at whatever Carlos had said. Miles shook his head. Carlos was bigger and stronger. William better watch for a swinging fist.

Carlos must have had enough. He grabbed Morrell by the shirtfront, hollered something in his face, and then thrust William away from him as though disgusted. With Carlos's back turned, William yanked his pistol from his belt. Before he could pull the trigger, Carlos spun around and hit William in the face with a blow so hard, Morrell reeled back before landing in the mud with a splash. Carlos pointed his finger at him, shouted one more thing, and then stomped away.

As he watched Morrell rub his jaw before pushing to his feet, Miles wished he knew more Spanish. He'd love to know what that fight was about. Instead of heading for the fort, William wandered northwest, away from the Alamo and toward the woods. Miles considered following but decided to forego a stop at Rosa's house and return to the fort, giving him a chance to talk to Crockett about Morrell being the traitor, as well as a chance to get some food in his belly.

Half an hour later, Crockett squinted at Miles. "Morrell? Are you sure? He seemed to be a good man. Dependable."

"Does that mean you told him everything?"

Crockett stood, took a few steps, and then propped his fists on his hips. "Not me and not everything but probably too much." He rubbed the back of his neck as he paced. "Unbelievable." He dropped onto his chair. "All right. Find him and try to bring him back. I don't think there's enough time for him to do us much harm, but I don't want a man like that fighting beside us. I'll tell the men at the gate to watch for him." He blew out a breath and shook his head. "Good work, Fitch."

"Do you really think any information he passed along hurt our chances here?"

Crockett stared out his window. "I don't know, Miles. The enemy knowing any details about our condition is never a good thing. But if I were Santa Anna coming to rid the land of what he believes to be rebels and immigrants trying to take over his country, I'd come with every man and weapon I could."

Miles blew out a breath, his chest suddenly heavy. "Right." He started for the door then paused. Since he'd arrived, he had the feeling that something wasn't quite right, like Crockett was keeping something from him. "How's Bowie?"

"Worse. He doesn't get out and about much anymore. For the most part, Travis has taken over complete command of all the men now, even Bowie's volunteers, though if you were to ask Bowie, he's still in control of his men."

"I'll pray he gets better. He's a good man. He'd be good in a fight."

"You got that right."

He hesitated one more time. "Anything else I need to know?"

Crockett looked at him long and hard. "We've heard rumors that Santa Anna is getting close. Travis put a man in the San Fernando church bell tower to look for signs and sent two men out to scout the area."

"You think they're that close?"

Crockett lifted a shoulder. "Better careful than careless. Regardless, you stay focused. Unless you hear otherwise, find Morrell and then report back here."

"Yes, sir."

Miles stopped by the kitchen, shoved a chunk of meat into a large piece of bread, and took a bite. Venison. Morrell must have found the deer he was after. At that thought, doubts assailed him. William cared for the men here at the fort. Would he, *could* he actually become a traitor against the very same men he would fight with against Santa Anna? The argument with Carlos might not have had anything to do with giving him information about the Alamo.

He shook his head. The only way to know for certain was to find him. He hurried to town and began his search, wishing he would have followed Morrell instead of going to the Alamo. But Crockett needed to know so he could warn the other men to watch for him.

Hours later, after walking every street in town and wanting nothing more than to rest, he knocked on Rosa's door. With no sign of Morrell or Carlos, he wanted to sit for a bit before starting again. Rosa's company was just what he needed to revive his energy.

"You looking for me?"

He turned and smiled. "I am. What're you doing out and about so early?"

"I like walking with Ana and her parents on their way to the store. Otherwise she's so busy, we don't get to spend much time together. And now that she and John are close, walking with her to work is almost the only time we have."

"She and John are close now, huh? That didn't take long."

"I know. She told me the other day that she thinks John wants to marry her."

He raised his brows. "Pretty serious."

"Sounds like it." She crooked her finger at him as she moved to the door. "Have you eaten?"

"Not since I left the Alamo. You offering?"

She opened the door and motioned him inside. "I don't have much, but you're welcome to what I have."

"Just a chance to sit for a while would help a lot. That and your bread."

"Then your prayers are answered because I have a chair and bread. Have a seat." She moved to the kitchen. "So, you've been doing a lot of walking? Why?"

"Looking for that man from the Alamo that we saw yesterday. I have a message for him, but I can't find him."

"Maybe you need to go to the woods and act like a deer again."

He laughed. "Maybe so. Might have to try that next."

They enjoyed a quick, simple meal, but most of all, they enjoyed their time together. As she fingered the necklace he gave her, she kept looking at him with what seemed to be some sort of expectation. His gut told him she wanted marriage. And if he were honest, so did he. But with the upcoming battle, he wasn't ready to promise anything.

He pushed his plate away and tapped the table. "I should get back out there."

"You look tired."

He nodded. "There's always time for sleep but there's only so many hours in a day. I've been given a job. I'll get some sleep when I get it done."

"Then you'd better hurry or you'll be walking in your sleep." She followed him to the door. "Be careful, Miles."

He stopped and looked into the face he loved. He caressed her cheek then leaned down for a kiss. "When this is all over, there's something I want to talk to you about."

"Oh?"

He smiled. That one little word held a cartload of hope. "Pray it's over soon."

"I will. You've got my word on that."

He didn't want to leave. "I have to take my turn standing at a post tomorrow but look for me the day after, probably the afternoon. We'll go for another walk. I'll even take you back to that little cantina."

"Sounds like the perfect day."

He gave her a mock salute and began his trudge through town. He was coming to love this town as much as he loved his land. What he enjoyed most was seeing the children playing outside, hearing their laughter and squeals of delight, which most times brought a smile to their mother's faces as they watched their antics. Now more than ever, he hoped he'd have a family to raise. He tried to picture their faces. They all looked like Rosa.

He ended his search with a trek through the woods where he last saw Morrell. With no success and darkness in a hurry to arrive, he headed back to Carlos's wood shop and hunkered down for another long night.

Rays from the rising sun bounced off a window and stabbed him in the eyes the moment he opened them. He pushed to his feet and berated himself for falling asleep. He glanced down each street then strode to the wood shop and peeked in the window. Still empty. Maybe he hadn't missed anything during the night. He did his usual jaunt around the town and didn't see Morrell. But he couldn't look any longer. He was expected at the Alamo.

They pointed him up to the southwest corner again, and he was pleased to see Hector would be on watch with him. The two shook hands before he turned to look over the town. He enjoyed being up high, giving him a better view of the land. The sunshine hitting on the adobe homes and walls made the town nearly glow. Everything looked fresh and new.

"You've been busy, my friend. All the time I see you running back and forth from the fort to town. You need to slow down and get some rest or you'll be no good for that pretty señorita of yours."

Miles smiled. "I may already be no good for her, and lack of rest doesn't have anything to do with it."

Hector laughed and clapped him on the back. "You all right, señor."

Miles scanned the walls of the Alamo, noting the number of men standing watch, more of them along the south and west walls than the north and east. He took a long look at the men milling in the compound. One group sat on the ground playing cards. "There seems to be a lot more men now."

"Sí. They've been arriving the last several days. A group of over thirty rode in a few days ago."

"Great. We need every man we can get."

"I agree. That's why I don't understand why you killed Starks." When Miles looked at him, Hector nodded. "Sí, I heard. We all have."

"Then you heard wrong because I wasn't the one who killed him, though I was there when it happened. It was a situation of kill or be killed. Starks wasn't a good man. I don't think I would have wanted him at my back when the fighting started."

"We didn't hear that part."

"It's all right. I'll shoulder the blame. I would have pulled the trigger had I been in the same position." He motioned to the men again. "It's good to see so many. Any idea of the number?"

Hector lifted a shoulder. "I'm guessing over two hundred. Some have come; others have asked to leave to get their families safely away from Béxar."

Miles scanned the plains and woods to the south. All appeared quiet. "Any word on Santa Anna? Has he started this way?"

"I haven't heard. I never leave the fort, and Travis isn't talking. Not to us anyway." Hector leaned on the wall, bringing him closer to Miles. "But you've talked to him."

Miles smiled and shook his head. "Not much gets past anyone around here, does it?"

"Not much, señor. As you can see, it's a small place."

He glanced around again. "It may be small, but it sure has a lot of wall space to defend."

"Sí, and about enough men to stand several feet apart from each other. Too many feet apart."

"Yeah, I thought that, too." He took a breath and said a short prayer as he let it out. "We still have time. More men will come." *Please Lord, let more men come.*

Chapter Twenty

As Rosa waited for Miles to arrive, she switched back and forth between checking the window and cleaning the house. She already had to clean the window twice to remove her nose prints. If he took much longer, she'd have to start cleaning the entire house for the second time. Never mind the fact that it wasn't afternoon yet.

Expecting Miles wasn't the only thing that continually brought her to the window. Over the last few days, families had been leaving town, but today, it seemed like a mass exodus. She'd never seen so much activity. She'd have to check with Mama later to see if she'd heard anything about Santa Anna's arrival that would cause so many people to leave all at once.

She returned to wiping away spiderwebs from the corners of the house, wondering how much longer before Miles would show. When the knock finally came, it made her jump then brought a smile. She rushed to the door and yanked it open. Miles looked better every time she saw him. More rested this time, too.

"I was starting to wonder if you'd remembered."

His eyes widened. "Is it even afternoon yet?"

She laughed and motioned him inside. "I was ready as soon as I rose this morning."

He mimicked her by motioning her outside. "Then let's get started."

Once she'd grabbed her shawl and wrapped it around her shoulders, he offered his elbow.

"Which way this time?"

"North. Maybe we'll see those deer your friend mentioned. Then we can go west to check your parents' place."

"Check it for what?"

She shrugged. "I just want to make sure I can remember how to get there."

He tugged her to a stop and peered into her eyes. "Is that really the only reason?"

She made a face. "I've noticed a lot of people leaving lately. Makes me wonder if Santa Anna and his men are close. If so, I may take you up on your offer to stay there while they're here."

"I hope you do. I think you'll be safer farther from town."

They continued through town and would soon pass the dry goods store. Miles slowed her one more time. "Maybe I should pick up some supplies to keep at my place. I don't want you to have to come out of hiding unless absolutely necessary."

"But I don't even know if I'll need to use it yet."

"I'd feel better if I knew you had everything you'll need."

He was probably worrying for nothing, but if it helped him feel better, she'd agree. "All right. Plus it gives us a chance to see Ana again."

Once inside the store, Rosa, Ana, and Miles meandered along the shelves doing more talking than shopping. After Miles placed some dried beef into the basket, he looked bored. Or maybe it was impatience, almost uneasiness, but he smiled in all the right places. It was time to purchase the supplies and be on their way before she completely lost his attention.

She led them to the front so Ana could total the items. "Will you be seeing John today?"

"I don't know. I didn't get to see him yesterday."

"Really? I thought you two spent time together every day."

"We have, up until yesterday. I don't know what happened. Maybe he'll come by today and let me know if something's wrong."

"Hope so." Rosa leaned close to Ana so no one else could hear. "Let me know if you need to talk." She raised her voice again. "I'll bring back this basket tomorrow."

"Thank you."

Miles reached inside the basket and removed the dried beef, tucking the strips into the leather pouch at his side. They left the store and started down the street. Rosa held the basket in one hand, her other safely tucked in Miles's.

"You looked a little anxious in there. Is that what buying supplies does to you?"

Miles smiled. "Not usually." He motioned around. "Have you noticed all the activity in town? People milling or moving everywhere. And I've never seen the store so busy. I figure they're getting what they need for the trip out of here."

"I've noticed. They've been moving out all day, and they all look nervous. Do you know anything about it?"

"I haven't been told much of anything. Maybe they're as ready for this battle to be over as all the men in the fort. Waiting for the unknown is never easy."

She smiled. "That's true."

They turned down another street and hadn't taken more than a few steps when Miles's arm was jerked from her hand. Someone had hit him from behind, sending him tumbling away from her. His rifle skittered across the dirt and rocks out of his reach.

"Miles!"

Before she could run to his side, someone grabbed her from behind. Miles pushed to his feet but appeared unsteady. He touched the back of his head then looked at his bloody hand. She tried to pull away from her captor, but a man's arm came around her and jerked her against him. She grabbed his arm to break his grip. The blade of a knife flashed in front of her before it was pressed against her neck. She wanted to scream but was afraid she'd get cut from the movement.

"Stay back, Fitch, or I'll kill her."

Miles stopped his advance. "What're you doing, Morrell? You know you can't get away."

Morrell laughed in her ear. "I can do whatever I want. I've got the girl."

Miles's fists clenched. "You hurt her and you're a dead man."

"I won't hurt her unless you make me. Just stay there and let us walk away."

"That's not happening. You can leave, but she stays."

Miles met her gaze. He looked like he wanted to leap across the distance and kill the man with his bare hands. He reached for his knife but hadn't yet pulled it from the sheath. Rosa wanted to shake her head at him but was afraid any motion would slit her throat. She tried to convey her feelings through her eyes. But just in case, she tried to reason with her captor.

"Please, let me go."

"Won't happen, sweetheart. You belong to me. I earned you, and I'm not leaving without you."

Confusion at his words muddled her thoughts. She tried to focus. "I don't understand. How did you earn me?"

"Ask Carlos. Better yet, I'll tell you myself once we get away from here."

He started to back up, pulling her with him. She couldn't fight if she wanted to live.

* * * * *

Miles held out his hand, hoping just the movement would stop Morrell from trying to leave. "Wait, William." He swallowed hard, his mind scrambling for something to say. "Why Rosa?"

Morrell sneered. "She's mine. I keep what's mine."

That made no sense. Miles looked at Rosa. She not only looked terrified, but she also appeared just as confused.

"How is she yours?"

"I'm done talking. I should have killed you that night behind the cantina instead of just raising a lump on your head. Then it wouldn't have come to this." He spat on the ground. "You want to know anything more, go see Carlos. It's time for me to go, and Rosa's coming with me."

"No, Morrell. She's staying. There's no way I'm letting you leave with her."

"You really want to make that threat when I have a knife at her throat?"

Miles couldn't move. Any attempt on his part to stop him and Rosa would be hurt or killed. He'd never been so helpless in his life.

"That's what I thought. Just stay where you are and everyone will be fine."

"Morrell!"

Miles looked toward the voice. John stood at the end of the street with his gun pointed. Morrell swung Rosa that direction, his knife still at her throat. Miles saw his chance. He pulled his knife from the sheath. A gunshot blasted before he could take a step.

William Morrell's body jolted then crumpled, taking Rosa to the ground with him. Miles looked at John, but the gunshot didn't come from him. Miles turned the direction of the gunfire. Carlos stood opposite him, the pistol still in his hand, the barrel smoking.

Miles ran the few yards to get to Rosa. He rolled Morrell's body off of her. Blood ran down her throat. Miles scooped her into his arms. She struggled to get up.

"I'm fine."

He held her tight against him so she'd stay down. "You're bleeding. He cut your neck."

John joined them. Carlos wasn't far behind. He dropped to his knees.

"I'm so sorry, Rosa."

"I don't understand, Carlos. He said I was his because he earned me."

Carlos shook his head as tears rolled down his cheeks. He ripped a sleeve from his shirt and placed it at her neck. Miles took over, pressing the cloth against the cut to stop the flow of blood. He prepared to lift her.

"Let's get you to your mother so she can fix this cut."

Rosa stopped the attempt to leave by grabbing Carlos's arm. "I won't go until I know why that man thought I belonged to him."

Carlos ran his fingers through his hair. "I never thought it would come to this. I told him the other day the deal was off, that I'd come up with some money to pay him."

"What deal?"

Carlos glanced at Miles and John before finally looking at her. "He wanted you in exchange for information about the Alamo." He shook his head. "I was so stupid, but I agreed. I'm sorry, Rosa. I. . .I was desperate and made a foolish mistake." He clasped her hand. "I can only pray that one day you can forgive me."

Several emotions raced across Rosa's face. Miles remembered that exchange between the two men. He swung between

Always Remembered

astonishment and anger that the man would use his stepdaughter in such a way. He couldn't begin to imagine what Rosa was feeling. But he would help her deal with them later. They needed to go.

"We need to get the bleeding stopped, Rosa. Let me take you to your mother."

"All right."

Miles lifted her into his arms. He glanced at John. "Thank you for your help."

"I need to talk to you."

"All right. Just let me take care of Rosa first."

"I don't think it can wait, Miles."

Miles hesitated in indecision. Carlos tapped his shoulder.

"Let me take her."

Miles looked at Rosa. She nodded, and he handed her over. "I'll be there shortly." His heart ripped in half as Carlos took his girl away. He looked at John. "What's so important?"

"Travis is calling all men in. He wants all of us back at the fort." He nodded toward Rosa. "And all residents of the town will no longer be allowed access."

In the next instant, the bell started ringing from the San Fernando church tower.

Chapter Twenty-One

Miles craned his neck to look at the tower. They were too far away to see the man inside, but he had to be yanking the rope with all his might. Miles looked at John, whose face was a mixture of fear and resignation. The day had come.

John clapped him on the shoulder. "I'll take care of Morrell's body."

"Thanks. I've got to check on Rosa. I'll get to the fort as soon as I can."

"Right. Just hurry."

Miles helped John get the body over his shoulder, and then he scooped up the contents of the basket and his rifle. In minutes, and completely out of breath, he pounded on Carlos's door.

The door opened. A broken Carlos stood in the opening, tears streaming down his face. Miles pushed past him, dropped the basket near the table, and ran to Rosa's side. Her eyes were closed. He put his hand on Carmela's back.

"How is she?"

Rosa opened her eyes. "I heard the bell. Is Santa Anna here?"

"I don't know. I can't stay long, but I wanted to check on you. How do you feel?"

Rosa looked at her mother. Carmela grasped one of Rosa's hands and one of his.

"It was just a cut. Not too deep. She'll be fine."

Miles let out the breath he felt he'd held since Morrell first placed his knife against Rosa's throat. "Good. I'm so glad."

He removed his hand from Carmela's and took Rosa's in his as he knelt next to her. "I've got to get to the Alamo. All fighters have been told to return. But I'll try to get here whenever I can to check on you and your mother. Just remember, you're welcome to stay at my house. In fact, I hope you do. You'll be safer away from the fighting. But if not, I insist you stay with Carlos and your mother. It's much too dangerous for you to be alone now. Just a pistol isn't enough protection any longer."

He leaned close and kissed her forehead. Then he rose and faced Carlos. As much as he hated leaving Rosa in his hands, he had no other choice. He struggled for words but none came. He decided to leave without saying anything.

Carlos reached for his arm as he moved into his path, blocking him from the door. "I would like to apologize to you, and I hope one day you can forgive me."

Miles couldn't speak. Anger clouded his judgment as to whether or not Carlos was sincere. He very well could be one of Hector's two-headed snakes.

Carlos didn't wait for a response. "For years, I've thought of all immigrants as selfish, greedy people. I thought of them as evil thieves, sneaking in and stealing our land. But over the last week, I've learned I was wrong. You and Rosa have put a face on the people I've seen only through a blur of anger and hatred. You two have shown me that we are all the same. We are merely people looking to make our way through this life the best way we can." His throat worked as his eyes filled. "I am so sorry for what I've done, especially to Rosa. I became the very kind of person I despised and am filled with shame. I pray you two can forgive me."

Miles's throat tightened as his anger evaporated. He held out his hand. Carlos grasped it then pulled Miles toward him and thumped him on the back a couple of times before releasing him.

Miles managed a smile. "Thank you for that." He motioned with his head toward Rosa. "Take good care of her for me."

"Nothing will happen to her. You have my word."

Miles nodded. Though Carlos's word meant little, at this point, his hands were tied. He took one last look at Rosa, his heart tearing in half. "I've got to go."

"I know. Be careful, Miles."

"I will."

Miles ran along the outskirts of town to get back to the Alamo. He didn't know how close Santa Anna's men were, and he didn't want to be seen or caught by any of them. At the San Antonio River, he searched the land for any sign of the Mexican army. Seeing none, he ran across the bridge and up the hill to the Alamo. As he approached the gate, he heard someone above him holler to open the gate then had to step aside as a man on horseback rode out at a gallop.

Once inside, he glanced around then looked up at the eighteen-pounder cannon. The corner was crowded with men, as was the entire west wall. With limited space along the walls, he climbed up onto the walkway above the low barracks on the south wall. It, too, was crowded, but he found a small spot to stand on the far side and tried to see past all the heads in his way as he hoped the roof over the barracks would hold.

"See anything? Is Santa Anna out there?" He desperately wanted to see the man responsible for his parents' death. "Where's the army?"

The man closest to him gave him a glance but immediately returned to looking for the enemy. "The man in the bell tower said he saw some movement. Even thought he saw a flash or two."

Hector moved to stand beside him and joined the conversation. "The second set of riders Travis sent out came back saying Santa Anna's army wasn't far away."

Other than some murmuring, for the most part the men were quiet, almost as if holding their breath as they waited for the first sign of the Mexican army. Miles glanced around the walls of the fort. Several men were positioned at the cannons on the north and east wall, probably told to stand guard in case Santa Anna tried to circle around and come in from behind. He nodded at Peacock, who stood beside the cannon at the palisade. After acknowledging him, he too craned his neck in search of the Mexican army.

Men scurried around outside the fort, rounding up as many cattle as they could and herding them inside the stock pens. A handful of men ran from town pulling carts. Miles eyed the goods in the cart as they pulled them inside. Some contained corn while others held what appeared to be blacksmithing materials. Not far behind, some men from the Alamo carried children and tugged on their wives' hands, hurrying them along while urging the older children to run. They all entered the fort and were led into the chapel. Miles had mixed feelings. The Alamo had thick walls and a lot of artillery, but it would also be the target of the Mexican army. Just how safe would the families be?

A few men were digging a hole. Miles bumped Hector and pointed. "What are they doing?"

"Digging a new well. With the river nearby, they shouldn't have to dig too deep. But we'll need the water should we get surrounded."

The majority of the men stood on every available space at the west and south walls. Miles stepped back and checked to see the position of Travis and Crockett. They both stood at the southwest corner next to the big cannon. Bowie stood with them, surprising Miles. He hoped that meant the leader of the volunteers was feeling better. He caught John's eye, who was positioned near the cannon, and nodded. John returned the nod then directed his attention back to the direction they expected to see Santa Anna arrive.

They didn't wait long. Voices from the men along the walls rose as the army emerged from the trees and rode into town. Men on horseback arrived first, followed by swarms of more men, all wearing dark blue uniforms, giving them a fearsome and impressive appearance. Several carried the red, white, and green Mexican flag. The parade of men marching into town seemed to never end. Some split off from the main group and headed south, taking up positions around the Alamo. Cannons were rolled into place along the banks of the San Antonio River.

Miles continued to watch the stream of troops advancing into town and toward the Alamo. His breathing became shallow as he tried to estimate the number of men Santa Anna brought for the battle. If the leader of the Mexican army wished to intimidate the Alamo defenders by the sheer number of troops, it worked. At least for Miles.

He leaned toward Hector. "We don't have nearly enough men."

"Sí." Hector's voice was low, quiet. "I was afraid of this. Santa Anna means to win this battle and win it with a great statement."

As they spoke, Travis strode down the cannon ramp and disappeared into his quarters. Miles waited a few minutes for him to return, but Travis didn't return. Just as Miles questioned the leadership ability of Travis, he reappeared and called out the names of two men. He handed them each a folded piece of paper, shook their hands, and then returned to his position near the southwest cannon. The two men who'd received their orders ran to the stock pens. Minutes later, they both rode out of the Alamo and galloped east.

Miles and Hector shared a look before they continued to observe as the Mexican army marched in and around town bringing more cannons with them. Miles prayed Carlos had moved the ladies out to his house. Terrible thoughts went through his mind at what the troops might do to the residents as they took over the town.

When a bright red flag appeared at the San Fernando church bell tower, the men fell silent for a moment before their voices buzzed again.

Miles elbowed Hector. "What's that mean?"

"No quarter." Hector's expression was grave. "He'll take no prisoners."

Miles's heart skipped a beat then thudded hard. In the previous weeks, the upcoming fight seemed a distant possibility. Now, the impending battle had suddenly become very real.

A bugle blared, followed by a man from the Mexican army slowly riding toward them on horseback. Miles peered up at Colonel Travis for a reaction. Travis observed for a short time as the men surrounding him stared. Minutes later, Travis gave a command, and the men around him swung into action as they prepared the cannon. When ready, they looked at Travis and received a nod.

Miles felt the vibration from the blast of the eighteen-pounder under his feet. Fear for Rosa's safety forced him to watch where the cannonball landed. He breathed a sigh of relief when it hit far from Carlos's home. The relief ended when he remembered the little girl who sold him the necklace and the little boy with the puppy. During all his trips to Béxar, the many families living along the street had grown familiar. Used to seeing them selling their wares or visiting with fellow neighbors while the children played in the streets, he feared for their lives and said a prayer for their safety.

A good many of the men laughed, clapped each other on the back, or shook hands, their way of congratulating Travis for his response to Santa Anna's presence. The men had been waiting weeks for this fight and seemed relieved to see some kind of action being taken.

Four blasts, only seconds apart, sounded from the banks of the river, silencing the earlier cheers. By instinct, Miles ducked his head, as did many of the men along the walls. The small cannonballs hit inside the fort but landed without striking man or building. More cheers went up with no resulting damage or injuries.

Miles and Hector exchanged a look. Miles blew out the breath he'd been holding. "I told Crockett I'd help guard the palisade. Guess I'd better get down there."

"I'll come too. Not sure where I'm supposed to fight. That's as good a place as any."

Like them, groups of men dispersed and took up positions along all the walls, though the defense remained heaviest along the south and west walls. Shortly after Miles and Hector took up a position along the palisade beside the Tennessee volunteers, Crockett arrived, gaining the attention of the men who'd be fighting with him.

"As you can see, men, we have a tremendous battle ahead of us. They outnumber us by a great margin. We must do our best to defend this fort until reinforcements arrive."

"Will they be arriving, sir?"

Crockett eyed the young man who'd asked the question; then he paced in front of them. "Travis has sent out dispatches asking for more men. We expect they'll arrive in two or three days."

Cannon fire from the Mexican army began again, causing them all to peer over the palisade wall. Most of the cannonballs hit the west wall. Miles imagined the damage the heavy balls were causing to the limestone.

The constant booming was unnerving. Crockett must have noticed the men's alarm. He walked along the wall, talking to and shaking the hands of each man, offering as much encouragement as he could muster.

Miles gladly accepted Crockett's handshake and clap on the shoulder. "I heard about Morrell. Good work, Fitch. You found the traitor, and we owe you a debt of thanks." He remained next to Miles as they looked out at the Mexican army. "How's your girl?"

"Morrell cut her throat, but it wasn't deep. She'll be fine."

"Good. Did you get her out of town?"

Miles looked at his feet. "No, sir. But she is with her mother and stepfather. They promised to keep her safe."

Crockett paused. "Doesn't make you feel any better, does it?"

"No, sir. They haven't been all that trustworthy, but there's really nothing more I can do other than leave her in God's hands."

"I understand your desire to take care of her yourself, but I'm glad to have your help here. We need good men like you. Just say a prayer and let the good Lord take care of her."

Miles forced a smile. "Yes, sir. I'm happy to be here. I'd like nothing better than to help rid this country of men like Santa Anna."

"Hold on to that thought, Fitch." He moved on to Hector and they shook. "Keep an eye on him, Hector. He's gonna be a great fighter for us."

Hector smiled. "Yes, sir."

As Crockett continued down the line of men, Miles and Hector faced the Mexican army again. Miles prayed the reinforcements would soon arrive and help them end this battle. The death of Santa Anna meant he and all the other defenders could get on with their lives. Yet doubts plagued him as he wondered how they would win from inside a fort where they fought more on the defensive than the offensive. He hoped the colonels leading the men had come up with a plan that would put Santa Anna on the run.

188

Chapter Twenty-Two

At the roar of the first cannon blast, Rosa sat up in bed then scrambled to her feet, her thoughts only of Miles's safety. As she said a quick prayer for him, she hurried to the window and peered out. Her mother wasn't far behind.

"You shouldn't be up yet, Rosa."

"I'm fine, Mama. Like you said, it was a shallow cut."

"But you lost a lot of blood."

"I won't stay here long." She tried every angle from the window. "I can't see anything from here except that red flag hanging at the San Fernando church bell tower."

Mama gasped and moved away from the window. Rosa turned in time to see the look exchanged between Mama and Carlos.

"What?" She grasped Mama's arm. "What does that red flag mean, Mama?"

Carlos strode the few steps to the window and stared. "It's the symbol of no quarter."

Rosa frowned in confusion, though by the tone of Carlos's voice, the flag meant danger. "What's that mean?"

Mama pulled her close. "It means that if the men in the Alamo don't surrender, they'll all die. They'll keep no prisoners."

Rosa couldn't breathe as she stared at Mama. Miles's face came to mind right before white spots appeared. She swayed and her knees felt weak.

"Carlos, catch her!"

Before she hit the ground, Carlos had her in his arms and carried her back to the bed. Another cannon blasted, followed seconds later by another, then two more. Carlos returned to his position at the window. Rosa couldn't stop the tears from falling. She tried to sit up.

"I'll go help Miles. I can load the guns, keep him fed. . . something! I've got to do something to help. I can't just sit here while Miles could get hurt."

Mama sat on the side of the bed, effectively blocking Rosa from being able to rise and leave. "You can't help him, Rosa. No doubt the Mexican army is between us and the Alamo by now." She tucked Rosa's hair away from her face then caressed her cheek. "And you know Miles wouldn't want you in there with him but would rather you stay back here where it's safer. He said as much before he left."

More tears rolled down Rosa's temples. "I fear for him, Mama. Nothing can happen to him." She sniffed and thought it was time to confess her feelings. "I love him, Mama."

Her mother smiled. "I know, mi querida. I could see it in your eyes when you looked at him."

The two held each other until Carlos interrupted. "You two stay here. Keep the door latched. I'm going to go closer and see what's happening. Maybe I can find my brother and he can let me know of their plans."

Mama pulled from Rosa's arms and followed her husband to the door. "Be careful, Carlos." She shook her finger at him. "You be sure to come back to me."

He grabbed her finger, pulled her close, and kissed her long and hard. "I'll be back. Just make sure you latch this door."

While Mama was busy at the door, Rosa pushed from the bed and took up a stance at the window again. Lying in bed only made her worry worse. Mama turned from the door and clicked her tongue.

"I guess scolding you won't make you get back in bed, will it?" When Rosa made a face, Mama shook her head. "I didn't think so. But I don't know why you want to stand there when you can't see anything." She pushed a chair next to Rosa. "At least promise me you'll sit and rest once in a while."

"I can do that."

The cannons began blasting again. Rosa counted to at least ten, many times twice that, between each explosion. She pictured the Alamo compound in her mind and wondered where Miles was standing and prayed it was as far away as he could possibly get from where the cannonballs landed.

Since standing still was almost as tiresome as lying in bed, Rosa helped Mama put together a meal, though she wondered who would eat it since she had no appetite and doubted Mama was even a little hungry. From time to time, Rosa returned to the window, the red flag drawing her attention every time.

Hours passed and the food had grown cold by the time they heard a knock on their door. Mama and Rosa looked at each other, waiting to hear Carlos's voice.

"Let me in, Carmela."

With a sigh of relief, Mama opened the door. He quickly turned and latched it again. His action brought more fear to Rosa. If Carlos was scared, they might be in trouble.

"What's happening out there, Carlos?"

Mama asked the question before Rosa could form the words. She almost feared the answer but wanted to know.

"I found my brother. It took some time, and many of the men threatened me harm until they knew I wasn't the enemy." He glanced at Rosa then continued. "Santa Anna has taken up residence and set up his command post at the main plaza by the San Fernando Church."

"And all the cannon fire?" Rosa had to know who was firing. "That's from Santa Anna?"

"Sí. He ordered the men to weaken the walls of the Alamo. They will continue blasting until told to stop."

All the explosions already had Rosa on edge. She couldn't imagine day after day of all this noise, which made her wonder how many days she'd have to hear it before Santa Anna thought it was time to attack. She imagined a lot of that decision depended on how many men were in the army. Carlos should have the answer to that since he'd been wandering around the town. But would he tell her?

"How many men does Santa Anna have?"

Carlos looked from her to Mama. His throat worked, and he motioned for her to sit. She shook her head, already knowing she wouldn't like the answer.

"How many?"

"A lot. He has many, many men, Rosa. His army far outnumbers the men in the Alamo."

Each word was a nail driven deep into her heart. For the first time in her life, she understood a man's need to hit something, to strike out in order to relieve the tension and frustration of helplessness. Most women resorted to crying as a means of relief, but even that wouldn't help her feel better. She felt trapped and wanted out. She rushed toward the door, but Carlos arrived at the same time and held it shut.

"Don't go out there, Rosa. It's too dangerous. Santa Anna's men are everywhere. My brother said a group of men will be going through the town looking for food and will take it by force if necessary in order to feed all the troops." He turned to Mama. "Where's our flag? My brother told me to hang it on the door as a sign to his men not to bother us."

Mama peered up into his face. "Why would they listen to your brother?"

"Because he's been promoted to an officer."

Mama nodded and ran to a chest next to their bed and pulled out the flag. Carlos located a hammer and some nails. He pointed at each of them.

"Stay inside. This won't take long."

As Carlos nailed the flag to the door, the pounding matched the cannon blasts. Rosa wanted to press her hands to her ears to keep from hearing all the noise, but she doubted she could extinguish all the sound. When she was about to ask her mother if they could go to Miles's house to get farther from the racket, she heard men's voices outside the door.

She leaned closer but couldn't make out the words. She moved to the window for a look at the visitor. The sun hung low in the sky, making it difficult to see clearly, but the man, whose face looked much like Carlos, wore a magnificent uniform of heavy, dark blue cloth. Gold buttons, along with many trimmings, ran from his neck to his waist. A shoulder belt crossed his chest. His *chacó*, the dark headdress sitting high atop his head, was adorned with many accoutrements, the red pompom at the top shaking as he spoke. The horse next to him snorted and stomped one leg.

The man caught her watching, stopped talking, and stared. Then he gestured toward her while muttering to Carlos, who turned for a look. They talked another minute before shaking hands. The man in uniform looked at her one more time, nodded, then mounted the horse and rode off.

Carlos entered and eyed her. Her gaze never wavered. She belonged here."Was that your brother?"

Carlos didn't respond.

"What did he have to say?"

Again, he gave no answer except to deepen his scowl. "That was very rude, Rosa. It is disrespectful to listen to another's conversation."

"I didn't hear a word, but right now, with Miles's life in danger, being well-mannered isn't a priority. If I can find a way to help the defenders of the Alamo, I will do just that."

"It is too late for that. Prayer is all that is left."

Doubts about her stepfather gave birth to anger. "Have you turned your back on Miles again now that Santa Anna and his army are here?"

"I have not turned my back on Miles. In fact, my brother accused me of treason when I showed compassion toward the men at the Alamo."

Shame brought on remorse. "I'm sorry, Carlos."

He nodded and turned to her mother. "We will stay here tonight. Then, if you'll feel safer, I'll take you and Rosa to Miles's house."

Part of Rosa wanted to go to Miles's place, yet she also wanted to stay close to the fighting so she would know when the battle had begun. . .or ended. If she remained, she might get a chance to sneak out and see what was happening and possibly watch as Santa Anna's army was crushed.

At that last thought, she looked out the window again, listening. The cannon fire had ended. Surely the battle wasn't over. She turned to Carlos for an explanation.

"They are just stopping for the night. They'll begin firing on the Alamo walls again in the morning."

The cannons might have fallen silent, but it was as if one had just landed on her heart. Sleep would be impossible knowing Miles was still in danger. She prayed he'd get some rest to be ready for the upcoming battle.

Chapter Twenty-Three

The cannons fell silent at the same time Miles could no longer see the sun. He'd never enjoyed quiet more. The steady boom of the cannons had unnerved him more than he'd realized. None of the men could rest for the need to be alert to the cannonballs the Mexican army lobbed over the wall instead of into the wall. They never knew when they'd need to duck or dive out of the way.

While some of the men drifted off, no doubt to find food, Miles sank to the ground, seeking a short rest. Others continued to keep watch. Crockett spoke with Travis a short time then wandered along the palisade, once again checking in with his men. He approached Miles.

"You hanging in there, Fitch?"

"Yes, sir. The cannons get tiresome, and I'm glad of the silence, but I'm ready for anything."

"Good." He turned to walk away but paused. "I plan to check the damage to the wall. You interested?"

Miles pushed to his feet. "Just tell me when you're ready."

"After dark. I don't want to give them an easy target."

"I can understand that. I plan to live through this battle."

Crockett grinned and clapped him on the back. "Me too. Go grab something to eat then come find me."

"Yes, sir."

He strode off toward the kitchen though he wasn't all that hungry. But if today was any indication, it would be a good idea for everyone to get something in their bellies when they had the chance.

After accepting a plate of beans and johnnycakes, Miles found an empty spot against a wall and sat with the plan to get as much rest as he could. He nursed the food, as did many of the other men. The man next to him all but licked his plate clean, yet he still didn't rise but set the plate on the ground next to him.

"Where you standing post?"

Miles glanced at him and figured the young man with a scruffy beard to be one of the new arrivals since he'd not seen him before today. "The palisade. You?"

"West wall, right about the middle."

"You saw a lot of action."

"More like a lot of ducking. After all the blasting, I'll be ready for the order to fire. Cause a little noise of our own."

Miles smiled. "I can understand that. It'll be nice to give instead of receive for a while."

The man blew out a long breath. "Well, guess I'd better get back. There's more men up there who need a break." He held out his hand, which Miles accepted. "Good luck to you, young man. Get as many as you can."

"I'll try."

The comment hit his gut hard. He'd never shot at a man before, let alone killed one. He'd told himself all he had to do was picture the enemies who killed his parents and pulling the trigger would be easy. Now that the chance had come to avenge his parents' deaths, he hoped he could fight as expected—be a man worthy of his calling.

Darkness fell quickly. He carried his empty plate to the kitchen, thanked the men for the meal, and then went in search of Crockett. He found him next to the gate near Bowie's quarters. The silence lent a somber feel to the air.

Miles moved next to Crockett. "Everything all right?"

"He's gotten worse." Crockett motioned with his head toward Bowie's room. "Travis is in there talking to him now."

"I saw Bowie up by the eighteen-pounder today. I thought that meant he was better."

"No. He just didn't want to miss out on Santa Anna's arrival." Crockett gestured with a wave for him to follow, and they walked out the gate. "I doubt he'll ever get up again," he said in a quiet voice meant only for him. "Bowie's too weak to get out of that bed, has a fever, and can't seem to get a good breath. He won't be able to help us fight."

"That's a shame. He's a great leader."

"That he is. But I imagine he's handing his role as leader of his men into Travis's hands. That's probably making him feel sick too." He stopped at the edge of the southwest corner just under the eighteen-pounder cannon and peered into the night at the houses in La Villita. "All right, those buildings look dark. Let's see if we can examine this wall without them sending a cannonball our way. I'm not too concerned about rifle fire. We're out of range."

"That's comforting. A cannonball to the gut is much better than a musket ball."

Crockett chuckled. "You're all right, Fitch." He peered around the corner. "No time like the present. Let's go."

They scooted around the corner and ran their hands over the walls, Crockett down low and Miles up high. They tripped a few times over the cannonballs lying on the ground.

They were almost to the north wall when Crockett stopped. "This isn't bad at all. There are chips and dents but not much structural damage. How about you?"

"Same. They must be too far away for their small cannons to make a significant impact."

"I'm thinking you're right. Let's get back."

Before they reached the corner, a cannon boomed. Crockett took off at a run with Miles on his heels. The cannonball smacked the wall not far behind them as they rounded the corner.

Once inside, a puffing Crockett clapped him on the back. "Nothing like a little sniff of death to get the blood boiling, huh?"

"I could live without that kind of excitement."

Crockett laughed. "I'm with ya." He motioned behind him with his thumb. "I'm going to check in with Travis, let him know what we found. Head back to the palisade. I'll be there shortly to set up watches."

The cannons began their bombardment again, though slower than earlier. Miles returned to his place at the palisade and found Hector standing at the wall, his rifle across his arms as he held his plate of beans and johnnycakes. His expression was thoughtful as he stared out at the huts and houses of La Villita.

Miles leaned on the palisade next to him. "I'll keep watch, Hector. Sit and enjoy your meal."

Hector grimaced. "I've always liked frijoles, but these are getting tiresome."

Miles couldn't help but laugh. "I think every man in here feels the same."

Crockett arrived shortly. "All right, men. We're gonna set up watches. Half of you can try to get some rest for part of the night then switch out. We have to have someone watching at all times. Santa Anna may have his men try to sneak closer so their shots can be more accurate. . .and deadly. Ya'll decide who goes first. Sleep if you can, but if not, at least get some rest."

After Crockett left, Hector turned to Miles. "You rest first. I'm still trying to pack these frijoles down my throat."

Miles smiled. "They any better now that they're cold?"

A shudder raced down Hector's beefy frame.

Miles laughed. "Never mind. Don't answer that." He reached inside his leather pouch and pulled out a strip of the dried beef he'd purchased earlier that day. "Here. See if that helps those beans go down."

Hector grinned as he accepted the gift. "Bless you, señor."

Miles hunkered down and hoped he'd be able to get some sleep. He had a feeling rest would be in short supply until this battle was over. Thoughts of Rosa and how she fared the barrage of cannon fire rolled through his mind. He pictured the different ways to get into town, wondering if he'd be able to manage a quick trip to see her without getting caught. He could only imagine what the Mexican troops would do to an Alamo defender. He prayed they wouldn't find or bother Rosa and her mother.

Much too soon, Hector jostled him with his foot. "It's about midnight, señor. My turn for sleep."

Miles rubbed the dryness from his eyes and took up his position at the palisade while Hector all but dropped to the ground. In what seemed to be less than a full minute, soft snores drifted from the sleeping man. Miles wished he could fall asleep that fast, but that hadn't happened since he'd heard about his parents' death. His father had once told him that falling asleep fast came from a clear conscience. He wondered what his father would say to him if he knew Miles had trouble sleeping.

As rays from the rising sun lightened the sky, activity beyond La Villita, approaching as well as inside San Antonio de Béxar, grabbed his attention. He poked the arm of the fellow next to him, who'd propped himself between two of the logs of the wall so he could snooze. When the man came to life, Miles pointed at the town. Moments later, the man was fully awake. Murmurs could be heard along the walls as others became alert to the movements.

A company of cavalry had ridden into town to the accompaniment of the Mexican army continuing their barrage, showering the Alamo with shells and shot. Still at a half-mile distance, the cannonading did no more damage than the day before. As the day wore on, three different divisions of infantry arrived, increasing the Mexican forces as well as their number of cannons. In response, Travis sent off a courier with yet another letter asking for reinforcements.

Hector rested his arms on the logs of the palisade. He shook his head. "As if Santa Anna needed more men and artillery. I'm afraid he aims to win and make a statement doing it."

"What are you thinking, Hector? That we can't win?"

Hector gave him a long look then stared out at the Mexican army again. "I'm only saying that we need many more men. . .soon."

"Crockett said three days. We just have to hold off that army for a couple more."

Peacock joined them, his feathers bobbing in the evening wind. "You really think we can hold off an army that size if they all come at us at once? Especially for two or three days?"

Miles and Hector exchanged a glance. Miles hitched a shoulder. "Won't know until we have to do just that. Let's just pray it doesn't come down to that."

Peacock nodded. "Anyone heard how many men we're expecting to show?"

Hector shook his head. "Don't know, but with all the dispatches Travis has sent out, I think we can expect a lot."

A cannonball landed behind them and slammed against the palisade between their feet. Hector turned and looked toward the direction it came as a handful of men stared, their mouths open.

Peacock spat into the dirt. "That's gonna make sleep a lot harder."

Hector rubbed his whiskered cheek. "Either they got a bigger cannon or they're closer. Don't like either choice."

Miles peered out at the setting sun. "You reckon they're about out of cannonballs so they can quit their barrage?" He examined Hector and Peacock's faces. "Yeah, I didn't think so either."

Though the cannonading slowed, it continued through the night, keeping the men up and watchful. Miles had to appreciate Santa Anna's method of battle. Keep the enemy from getting rest and his army would fight men in a weakened and weary state. He prayed the Lord was on the side of the defenders.

Chapter Twenty-Four

With a new club in hand, taken from Mama's wood stack, Rosa carefully lifted the latch on the door, turned the knob, and slipped outside. Carlos and her mother would have stopped her from leaving the house if they knew, but Carlos left the day before and hadn't returned, and she never said a word to Mama about her plans.

She waited until almost sunrise before making a move. She didn't know how anyone managed to get any sleep with all the cannon blasts. And since that might mean the men in the Mexican army were busy, in her mind, it was the best time to see what was happening, and hopefully find a way to help the men inside the Alamo. If only she could run back to the other house for her pistol, but doing so would be much too dangerous since it was much closer to Santa Anna's headquarters.

She headed north, trying to stay far away from the river, where she figured the men would be positioned. At the very least, she might get to see Ana and make sure she and her parents were safe. The best that could happen was that she would learn some information that could help Miles and his fellow defenders. She didn't want to think about how she would get the information to him. She'd worry about that if it happened.

Rosa avoided any building with a burning lantern, staying in the shadows as much as possible. The open areas made her nervous. She hiked her skirts and ran as fast as she could. When she reached the north edge of town, she veered east, using the trees and bushes to hide her progress. As the first group of uniformed men came into view, the pink and orange glow of the rising sun had just become visible.

With a prayer she wouldn't be seen, she scooted up to the next tree to get a better view of the Alamo and where Santa Anna had his men located, crouching low so she'd blend in with the bushes. She peered through the murky dawn light and caught her breath at the sheer number of troops and cannons. She lost track of how long she'd been watching, but it was long enough for her legs to go numb. She stood and rubbed her thighs while stomping her feet to get her blood flowing again.

"Do you know how much danger you're in being out here by yourself?"

Rosa gasped and spun around. Ana's father stood behind her with his hand on the handle of a pistol tucked into his belt. She put her hand over her heart, its rhythm starting again but at a much faster beat.

"Oh, Mr. Mendoza. Thank goodness it's you."

"What are you doing out here, Rosa?"

"I just wanted to see this for myself. I hate being locked up in the house and not knowing anything."

"Then ask questions, or at least ask for an escort. You can't wander around out here on your own." He pointed at her club. "Not even with that. It won't help you. Not with this many dangerous men around."

She glanced at her club. Deep down she knew it was a false sense of security, yet it somehow gave her courage. Now, Mr. Mendoza's scolding took that away. "I'm sorry. I'll go back."

He peered down the road behind him then looked at her. He hesitated. "Hold on. I'll walk with you."

Curiosity made her pause. He grasped her elbow and propelled her toward Mama's house. Wagon wheels crunching against the ground made them both stop and turn. Carlos sat atop the large wagon flicking the reins as he rolled up the trail toward them. Rosa jerked her arm away from Mr. Mendoza's grasp and stared.

The boards of the wagon creaked when he hit a hole. Carlos slapped the reins against the mules' hips and hollered to get them moving. The front wheel rolled out only to have the back one drop in, and Carlos did the process all over again. Once the wagon was free, Carlos looked up. When he spotted her, he yanked back on the reins.

"Rosa? Why are you out here?"

"I could ask you the same thing."

Carlos scowled at Mr. Mendoza. "Why is she here?"

"She was standing over there watching the army when I got here. I was trying to get her home."

Suspicion motivated Rosa to walk to the wagon and look inside. Sacks of gunpowder and crates of artillery filled the back end along with bags of corn and beans. Carlos jumped down from the seat and stood between her and the wagon.

She glared at him. "All those kind and caring words you spoke to Miles were lies. All along you planned to help the Mexican forces kill him and the other defenders of the Alamo."

She'd never been so angry. The desire to hit him raced through her, but she knew it wouldn't do any good. Instead she turned to Mr. Mendoza.

"How long have you been helping him? Did he just talk you into this recently or have you been a part of this all along?"

He didn't answer but looked at Carlos, who stared at Rosa before lifting a shoulder.

"Where do you think we've been storing everything?" Carlos asked matter-of-factly. "Mendoza has the means to order everything and plenty of room behind his store to stockpile the supplies."

Rosa gaped at Ana's father. "How could you?"

"I'm a Mexican citizen, Rosa. Why wouldn't I try to help our cause?"

"Does Ana know what you've been doing, or have you deceived her the same way Carlos has me?"

His gaze dropped to the ground. Carlos crossed his arms.

"Of course she knows, Rosa. She works there."

Rosa's heart dropped to her feet. Her friend, or the person she thought was a friend, had been as deceptive as her mother and stepfather. The thought so weakened her knees, she leaned on the wagon to keep from falling. She played the last couple of weeks through her mind and then speared Mr. Mendoza with a hard gaze.

"So, when she asked to go to the Alamo with me, that wasn't to look for a man but to seek out information to get those men killed. Is that right?"

The storeowner, shoulders rigid, looked proud of his daughter. "She did well for such a short amount of time. She would have learned more if your man friend would have given a better tour."

Bitterness rose until she could taste it. "And her friendship with John? That was just to use him for information?"

"It was at first. But she really did start to love him. I warned her against getting close. There was only one way for that relationship to end."

The betrayal burned a hole in her heart. Thinking Ana was a friend, she'd confided much to her, and it had been used against her and the men at the Alamo.

"Don't think poorly of her, Rosa. She did what she did because I asked for her help. She loves you like a sister. I know she'll want to keep your friendship when all this is over."

Mr. Mendoza looked sincere, but then so did Carlos when he'd apologized to Miles. They were just as good at pretense as they were at betrayal. She'd had enough of all of them. She'd go to her mother's home, gather her things, and stay at Miles's house.

Before she could take a step, the first gunshot echoed over the town, followed by many more. Carlos grabbed her arm with one hand and motioned to Mr. Mendoza with the other.

"Get the wagon to your store. I'll be there after I get Rosa home."

He didn't wait for comment or argument and all but dragged Rosa down the street. She beat on his arm trying to force him to release her.

"Turn me loose!"

He slowed only long enough to get a better grip. "I'm taking you to your mother whether you like it or not. I can't believe you left her alone to fend for herself. She needs you there to help her stay safe. Sneaking off was selfish."

Her anger flared into an explosion. "If you want her to be safe, then you stay with her! She's your wife and you're her man. If anyone has been selfish, it's you for leaving your wife alone for so long. And all because you want to make sure the Mexican army has enough artillery to kill Miles."

That comment stopped him. "I don't want Miles killed. I promise you I don't. But there's nothing I can do to save him if he insists on fighting with the Alamo defenders. I gave my word I'd acquire artillery for the Mexican forces. I'm not going back on my word for Miles. Your mother knows and understands this."

"Of course she does. She wants Santa Anna to win as badly as you do." She jerked her arm and was surprised she'd gotten free. She stopped and pointed her finger at Carlos when he reached for her again. "I won't stay with you and Mama any longer. When we get back to the house, I'm packing my things and going to Miles's place." She put her hands on her hips. "I wish I had my gun."

"To shoot me?"

"No. To help Miles shoot the men of the Mexican army."

She was stunned to see Carlos smile.

"I believe you'd do just that."

"I would."

"Then I'd best make sure you never get your hands on that gun." He motioned for her to follow. "Come. Walk with me to your mother's. Then I'll see you safely to Miles's house."

As she walked beside Carlos, she shook her head. He was the most confusing man she'd ever met.

* * * * *

The men at the southwest corner by the eighteen-pounder spotted them first. Mexican infantry were working their way toward the south wall of the Alamo, using the huts and homes of La Villita as cover. At their shout, Miles peered over the palisade. Movement from the river to the village could be seen. Hundreds of uniformed men forded the river and ran toward them.

Miles glanced around for Crockett but didn't see him. Peacock was at one of the cannons. Hector stood beside him, his gun pointed toward the village.

"I sure hope everyone has abandoned La Villita. Much as I hate to ruin people's homes, we should have torn down all those *jacales*. Not much we can do about the adobe buildings, but those huts will give Santa Anna's men too much of an advantage."

Miles nodded his agreement. This battle would be difficult enough without aiding the enemy.

Crockett strode up behind them. "Ready your guns, men. It looks like the battle has finally begun. We'll do this like we've been doing the watches. Half of you shoot then step away while you reload and let the other half shoot so we can have someone firing at all times.

Make every shot count." He marched along the palisade checking to make sure everyone was ready. "Fire on my command."

Though the morning dawned cool and comfortable, Miles broke out in a sweat. The time had come, and though his nerves were jumbled, he was ready.

Lord, make me sure and steady.

Miles balanced the barrel of his rifle between two logs of the palisade, half-cocked the hammer, and lifted the frizzen to check his powder. The rifle was ready. He fully cocked the hammer and aimed down the sights, picked out a man, and waited for Crockett's command.

The Mexican army closed in, some within fifty yards of the south wall. Miles could hear his heartbeat in his ears, and it had increased speed.

Breathe. Just relax and breathe.

He could hear his father's voice as he taught Miles to shoot his first deer. He was almost as tense then as he was now. He kept talking to himself, trying to calm down and slow his breathing, as he waited for orders to shoot.

"Fire!"

Chapter Twenty-Five

Crockett's command animated the men, and the first shots went off. Miles waited until he had a sure shot, said a prayer, and pulled the trigger. His man went down. He stepped back from the palisade and tried to reload. His shaking hands took longer than usual to pour gunpowder from his powder horn into his barrel.

"Calm down, son." Crockett stood right behind him. "You're doing fine. Just get it reloaded for another shot."

He sounded very much like Miles's father. Miles took a calming breath and tipped a small amount of powder down his barrel. He pulled a lead ball and a small piece of cloth from his side pouch, wrapped the ball, and pushed it into his barrel, tamping it down with the ramrod. After adding a tiny amount of gunpowder to the flash pan, he stepped up to the palisade for another shot. There were Mexican infantry everywhere. He dropped another man and stepped back again.

As he reloaded, he could hear Crockett shouting out encouragement to the men, keeping them working fast and steady. Crockett stopped, aimed, and fired on the enemy. By Crockett's smile, he'd either hit his target or he enjoyed the fact that the battle had begun. Off to his right, the men on the roof of the low barracks were firing their rifles down on the Mexicans. Travis ordered the cannons to fire. They discharged grapeshot and canister, scattering and killing some of the Mexican forces. Pride swelled in Miles's chest at how fiercely the Alamo defenders were fighting against the odds.

He returned to the wall and looked for another infantryman. He took his aim on one and fired. As minutes turned into an hour, Miles lost track of how many times he'd repeatedly fired and reloaded. The Mexican army had become good at staying hidden behind the huts, stepping into the open only long enough to fire on the Alamo. Miles searched for another target and spotted a man's leg.

He bumped Hector. "See that second hut back along this side? There's a man's leg sticking out. I'm going to shoot it. If that man steps into the open because he's been hit, shoot him. Ready?"

"Sí."

Miles took careful aim and fired. A second later, most of the man's body appeared as he grabbed his leg. Hector shot, dropping the man. Miles and Hector nodded and smiled.

Crockett approached and clapped them on the back. "Good shooting, men. Keep it up."

Even with all the shots going off and shouts of encouragement from Crockett, Miles didn't think they were making much of an impact on all the men heading their way. Where a dozen had fallen, a hundred more were on their way to replace the dead. When Miles returned to the wall from reloading, he noticed two of their own men with torches sneaking away from the fortification of earth, rocks, and tree trunks protecting the Alamo gates.

Though they were being fired upon by the Mexican army, the two men continued toward La Villita and set fire to the thatched roofs of several huts closest to the Alamo, effectively destroying many of the infantry's hiding places and forcing them to retreat.

Miles and Hector shared a look before firing on the withdrawing men. The shooting continued as did the burning of huts. Another hour later, most of the Mexican infantry had returned to the far side of La Villita, with many running all the way to Béxar. The skirmish was over.

The defenders cheered, especially when the torch men returned to the fort unharmed. They'd only managed to set fire to a quarter of the huts, but their efforts played a large role in sending the enemy running and scattering.

Miles shook hands with Hector and all the men around him. They were few in number compared to the Mexican forces, but they'd put up a great fight. Miles was proud to be counted among them.

Crockett strode along the line of men, clapping them on the back and shaking hands. "I thought that was to be the main battle, but it appears Santa Anna had something else in mind. He tried to set up a battery of cannons and howitzers, but we helped change his mind. Congratulations, men. That was great work."

While Miles and a handful of other men remained at the palisade to keep watch in case of another assault, the others hurried to find something to eat. After all the excitement of the morning, the afternoon seemed to drag on as they went about adding shot, gun powder, and artillery to all the cannons and riflemen. The sight of the quickly diminishing stores sent a shock of alarm through Miles. He could only pray that when the reinforcements arrived, they'd also bring more artillery supplies.

As night fell, a norther blew in, chilling the men to their bones. Many of them, not dressed warmly enough, shivered uncontrollably. Only a few fires were lit for warmth to conserve firewood.

Travis walked among the men. "I need volunteers to go out and burn the rest of La Villita's huts. Any of you willing, come see me."

Travis stood at the gate and waited. Less than a dozen men approached him. Miles handed his rifle to Hector.

"Will you hold this for me? I'm going to volunteer."

"Sí."

As he reached the group of men, John joined them, shaking Miles's hand as he walked past. Each of them was handed a torch.

"The Mexicans will see your progress, so be careful. Burn all the huts if you can, but get as many as possible. Good luck, men."

Each of them dashed out of the fortification in front of the gate one at a time for fear leaving in a group would get them all killed. Miles raced hard over the uneven ground, praying he wouldn't get shot. He stopped at the first mud hut to catch his breath. John bumped into him as he did the same. The man leading the foray stopped next to them.

"You two are fast. How about you head toward the river and start burning those farthest from here?"

Miles wasn't eager to get that close to the Mexican army and their rifles, but he volunteered for the job and intended to do his best. "All right."

He looked at John and received a nod. They ran past the huts already burned and headed for those closer to the river. Before lighting any of the homes, he kicked the door open and checked for residents. He couldn't live with himself if he harmed any of the villagers.

The straw huts burned to the ground in a burst of flames. The mud huts lost only their roofs, but when Miles leaned against one burned earlier that day to rest for a moment, the house all but crumbled to the ground. As much as he hated burning down the homes of families, each blazing hut made him feel that much safer, giving the Mexican army fewer places to hide.

Cannon bursts and rifle fire sent them running for cover, forcing them to leave only the huts farthest from the fort. John caught up to Miles.

"Let's get back to the fort. Toss your torch on an unburned hut and grab as much firewood as you can carry."

Back inside the Alamo, Miles dumped his armload of wood right where he stood, rested his hands on his knees, and sucked in great breaths of air. As his breathing and heart rate returned to normal, he noticed some men pointing and mumbling. He moved to John's side.

"What's wrong?"

"Evidently not everyone returned."

Murmurs raced among the men, some stating the men had been shot, while others feared they'd deserted. Miles avoided forming an opinion, since neither option was pleasant. One thing was certain. Between the running and the fires, for the time being, he wasn't cold.

He retrieved his rifle from Hector then climbed onto the roof of the low barracks. Instead of peering into the dark toward the burning homes of La Villita, he stared toward the north edge of Béxar. As of yet, they hadn't fired that direction, but he still worried about Rosa.

Crockett moved next to him. "Thinking about your girl?"

"I am, as well as wondering if there's a way to get over there to check on her."

"I half-expected you not to come back right away after burning La Villita so you could do just that. I'm glad you didn't. Santa Anna has his men stretched all along the river, even past our north wall. I didn't want to worry about you getting caught. I doubt they would have welcomed you with open arms."

"Sure they would have. Then they'd have tortured me right before they put a musket ball between my eyes."

Crockett laughed. "You sure have a unique way of looking at things, son. When this thing is over, you'll have to show me your land. I think I might want to be your neighbor."

Crockett returned to the palisade, leaving Miles to stare at his home in peace. But peace wouldn't come, and he doubted he'd ever feel it again until this battle was over and Rosa was by his side. He finally understood why some of the men brought their families into the Alamo when Santa Anna arrived.

* * * * *

Rosa couldn't stop shivering. She put on another layer of clothing then tossed one more stick of firewood into Miles's small stove. Why didn't she think to grab something warmer than her shawl while she packed her clothes? But with her mother following her around, grasping and clinging to her while begging her to stay, Rosa's main thought was to get out as quickly as possible. She refused to feel guilty. She had no doubt Mama knew what Carlos and the Mendoza family had been doing. She'd promised no more lies, but as far as Rosa was concerned, their secret was very much a lie.

If she managed to survive this frigid night, she'd have to spend most of the next day gathering more firewood. She prayed the men at the fort were staying warm, especially Miles. But in all her trips to the fort, she didn't recall seeing many stacks of wood other than those used for the cookstove. She could only hope the norther wouldn't last long.

The covers on the bed called her name. She climbed in and pulled them up to her chin. A second later, the dust from the quilt caused her to sneeze. She'd have to clean this place if she intended to stay. And stay she would.

She'd been lulled into renewing her trust of her mother and Carlos, only to have it thrown back in her face. Oh, how she'd love to get her hands on that wagon of artillery. She had a feeling the men at the Alamo could have used those supplies much more than the Mexican army. Especially after all the rifle and cannon fire she heard this morning. At the sight of smoke boiling into the sky, fear for the defenders made her want to run to the river to find the cause. Common sense kept her in place.

As she tried to come up with a way to help Miles and his friends, sleep eluded her, even after trying both sides and her stomach. She threw off the covers, lit the lantern, and placed a pot of water on the stove to heat. If she couldn't sleep, she could at least stay warm by cleaning.

While the water heated, she found a straw broom in a corner and began pushing the loose dirt toward the door. She understood that since Miles and his parents only stayed here a few times a year, there was no need for a wood floor. But if she allowed herself to picture her and Miles as husband and wife, she'd try talking him into covering the dirt with wooden planks.

With that thought, she dropped onto a chair and wept as her mind filled with doubts that she'd ever see Miles again. The blast of a cannon punctuated her fears, and her long night got longer. She'd never been more alone in all her life.

* * * * *

Miles finished his plate of hash and headed to the stock pen without a word to anyone. He paused long enough to check his horse then crossed into the next pen and hurried to the lowest part of the north wall. He'd just gotten a leg over the top when he heard someone cough.

"Don't do it, son." Crockett moved in front of a torch as he made his way toward Miles. "I can't stop you from going, but I advise you don't."

"I can make it. I just want to make sure Rosa's safe."

"I understand, and I've no doubt you can make it there. You might even make it back without getting caught or at least seen." Crockett leaned against the wall. "But what's your gut tell you, Fitch? You told me you left her in good hands, so will your foray into Béxar do anything more than set your mind at ease? Will it change anything for that young lady? Because on this end of things, all your leaving will do is possibly make us lose a good man or cause doubts in the minds of many as to whether or not they can trust you, wondering if you're sneaking off to give information to Santa Anna's men."

"You know I wouldn't do that."

"Yes, sir, I do know that. I trust you completely. But I'm only one man, one voice. A lot of these men think highly of you. Are you sure you want to do something to cause them doubt?" Crockett pushed away from the wall and started walking away. "It's up to you, son. Be sure you're right. Then go ahead."

Miles sat at the top of the wall for another minute then dropped inside the stock pen of the Alamo. Two men entered and saddled horses. Only one reason anyone would get ready to ride. Travis was sending out more letters.

"I'm putting Rosa in your hands, Lord. Take good care of her." He paused and waited for the men to mount up and ride out of the pen. "Take care of them too, Lord. Let them bring more men."

He returned to the palisade and received a nod from Crockett. He slid to the ground in an attempt to stay warm and get some rest, knowing full well sleep wouldn't come.

Chapter Twenty-Six

Miles tucked his chin and pulled his cape a little higher up his neck trying to keep the north wind at bay. He didn't remember ever being so cold. If it hadn't been his turn to keep watch, he'd have curled up as close to the fire as he could without getting burned. He wished he'd have kept his torch. Even a small fire was better than none. Perhaps the rising sun would bring warmth and a ray of hope.

As the fingers of dawn stretched across the land, Miles stood a little straighter. He squinted and then blocked the sunrise with his left hand. He swallowed hard at the sight and bumped the man next to him. "You see that? Where's Crockett?"

"What's wrong?"

Miles pointed from the remains of La Villita all across the south and to the east. "Look at that. The Mexican infantry crossed the river during the night and set up a battery all along the south and east. Look at all the cannons."

The man pursed his lips and nodded. "They were busy last night."

"I felt safe with them on the other side of the river. Now they're entrenched close enough to cause us big trouble."

Hector pushed from the ground, looking more than a little stiff. He rubbed his eyes and peered over the palisade. "Sí, that is bad. If we're not careful, they'll continue to work themselves closer each night."

Crockett strode up behind them. "I was afraid of that. In the days and nights to come, they'll work their way all around until we're surrounded. Just pray that more men get here soon. In the meantime, we need more firewood. Anyone want to stretch their legs and try to find some on the east side? Step up if you like hot meals. Some of you can round up all the cannonballs lying around and stack them. We can reuse them. Just make sure there's enough of you left here to keep watch."

Hector shook his head and hunkered close to the logs of the palisade. Miles didn't blame him. Toting firewood and watching for shooters wasn't easy work. Neither was hauling cannonballs, especially for someone his age. Miles joined the group exiting the fort, anything to get warm. But unlike last night, he took his rifle with him. He wouldn't be able to carry as much wood, but at least he could put the men in the Mexican army on the run.

Miles and all the other men wandered toward the hills and trees east of the Alamo, but none of them had found much of anything that could be described as firewood. A gunshot from the trees made them all duck and fall to the ground. Miles scanned the trees for the shooter and found more than one. Several infantrymen were scattered out, each taking aim. Gunfire exploded.

A cannon, then another, blasted from behind them. The cannonballs flew over their heads and landed in and near the trees. The Mexicans ducked behind the trees, and the Alamo men had a chance to run. Miles rose to his feet and raced for the fort. More cannons exploded as they retreated empty-handed.

Still panting, he took up his position next to Hector. "Well, that was a good idea." He shook his head as he leaned on the logs of the palisade. "I'm not fond of being used as a target. I think I'll stay inside these walls from now on."

Hector chuckled. "It took you two times to figure that out? I thought you were smarter than that, señor."

Miles made a face then smiled. "Thanks, Hector."

Hector laughed harder. "The young are slow learners."

Miles forced a scowl. "And the old are poor teachers."

Hector hooted then shook his head. "And the young always have to have the last word."

Miles opened his mouth to argue then clamped it shut. Hector clapped him on the back. "Ah, there is hope for you yet."

Crockett strode up beside them. "Sounds like you two are having fun. Any movement out there?"

"No, sir. None yet."

"Good. Only shoot the ones you're sure you can hit. How're you two doing with powder and balls?"

Hector shook his pouch. "I'm good."

Miles nodded. "Me too. I refilled after the fight yesterday, but it didn't look like there was much left."

"Yeah, we're running low, so make every shot count." Crockett blew out a long breath. "Travis ordered everyone to cut back on cannon fire since those take more powder. But we still want the riflemen to shoot if they have a shot."

"We sure will," Miles assured, but worry wormed its way into his heart. Did they have any chance against this onslaught? They were outnumbered, and their supplies were low.

Crockett nodded and continued down the line to spread the word.

Hector raised his brows. "Never thought I'd see Crockett worried."

If that were true, they all had much to worry about. Miles shook his head. "Only about the supplies, Hector. Crockett knows we can fight. We proved that yesterday."

Shouts and shooting to the east grabbed their attention. Miles ran to the chapel doors. "What's happening?"

"They're trying to block or divert the ditch that brings water to us."

Miles glanced at Hector then back at the men on the wall. "Did you stop them?"

"Working on it."

Miles left them to their task and returned to his post. "Never thought I'd have to worry about needing water."

"Sí." Hector poked his thumb behind them. "Look. They have the men working on digging the well again. They must be worried."

As Miles watched the handful of men dig deeper in the hole, he did some fretting of his own. The men could go on for a time without food, but water was essential. Santa Anna seemed well-versed in the effective strategies of warfare.

* * * * *

Rosa strolled from tree to tree, picking out the pieces of wood that would best fit in Miles's small stove. She had no means of chopping them smaller, so she had to be selective. In no way did she want to freeze as she did the night before, and the day hadn't warmed up much. The north wind saw to that.

With her arms full, she returned to the hut, dropped off the wood, and then grabbed the bucket from the kitchen. Collecting wood was the easy part of her day, but she also needed water, and she didn't look forward to the task. Retrieving water from the river or the well in town was much too risky, so that left the creek to the west. She wasn't exactly sure where to find the creek, but she refused to return to the hut without water.

As she followed a narrow path that appeared to be used only by deer and other animals, the knowledge that sometime soon she'd need to visit the dry goods store filled her with dread. Supplies were running low, and since she couldn't hunt and had no garden, the store was her only option. The idea of seeing Ana and her parents was far from pleasant. She hadn't seen Ana since Santa Anna had arrived in Béxar, and at the moment, she wasn't sure which of the two of them she'd be more displeased to confront.

The path Rosa followed disappeared under a clump of bushes. She pushed through and almost fell into the creek. She couldn't help but smile as she dipped her hand into the water. Clear and cold, the creek whirled in a small pool at the end of the path before turning away as it continued downstream to the south. She walked upstream a few feet and dipped the bucket. She'd have to make several more trips to have enough water for food and bathing, but she didn't mind. The walk was pretty and the trips would help fill her day.

Voices and bawling cattle not too far off forced Rosa to back away from the creek and seek shelter. A large fallen tree to her right would have to suffice since she didn't have much time. Toting her bucket so it wouldn't be seen, she walked as fast as she could around the upturned roots and hunkered down low.

In minutes, two wagons, a herd of cattle, and a small group of pigs appeared at the water's edge, driven there by at least ten uniformed men on foot and four on horseback. She gasped when she recognized Carlos as one of the wagon drivers. There was only one reason Carlos would be with the Mexican army, and that thought filled her with contempt. For a man who professed not to want Miles killed, he appeared to be doing everything he could to that very end.

As the cattle and pigs wandered into the creek to drink their fill, the men spread out farther upstream to fill their water skins. Rosa ducked lower, almost lying on her belly, to keep from being seen. Two of the men were so close she was afraid they'd hear her breathing. She prayed they wouldn't see her footprints along her side of the creek. Their chatter hadn't stopped since they'd reached the edge of the water.

"Gaona had better hurry with the supplies. All this corn and livestock we took from those ranches will help, but they won't last long."

Rosa almost gasped at their admission of stealing. She prayed whoever Gaona was *would* hurry. There was no telling how far the

Mexican army would go in order to feed so many men. She had no doubt they'd shoot the innocent residents to get what they wanted.

"Hurry. We need to get this food to our men in Béxar."

Rosa hoped they did hurry to Béxar. The sooner they left, the sooner she could get back to Miles's house. She peered through the tree branches, watching the men and livestock start to move. As Carlos climbed onto the wagon seat and grabbed the reins, he looked her direction. Though he made no indication he'd seen her, something told her he was aware of her presence. His gaze made her feel colder than the frigid air. After this scare, she'd have to work up the courage to make more trips for water, but she'd do it anyway. She refused to let a group of lawless men make her live in fear.

Chapter Twenty-Seven

The constant movement and work done by the Mexican army to move closer to the Alamo kept Miles and the other defenders on the alert at all times. For the last two days, rest was a luxury few of them enjoyed. Miles only shot when he was certain he'd hit his target.

Despite everyone's efforts, the Mexican forces had not only managed to cut off their water supply, but they'd moved just out of range of their rifle fire. Miles knew discouragement had become their greatest enemy. To make matters worse, a steady barrage of Mexican artillery had started again, falling in and around the Alamo.

Peacock leaned on the cannon near Miles, staring at the Mexican work force digging ditches around the Alamo. "It's been six days. I thought the reinforcements would have arrived by now."

Miles peered down his rifle's sights at one of the infantrymen. "I'm sure it took some planning, getting men and artillery together. They'll probably be here in the next day or two." He doubted Peacock believed his words any more than he believed them himself.

"They'd better. Won't be long and we might be hurting for water. Those cattle won't last all that long either."

Miles looked over his shoulder at Peacock and smiled. "You're the only man I know who likes eating more than I do."

Peacock patted his belly. "I take care of it; it takes care of me."

Several men around them laughed. One came up and joined them, leaning against the palisade. "I would have thought you'd look better than you do what with all the care you take of that bottomless bucket."

Peacock licked his finger and ran it along his mustache. "Didn't know you'd been looking, Smith."

Miles joined in the laughter, glad the mood had lightened. Then he looked down his rifle once again. One of Santa Anna's workmen had risen up as he dug his part of the ditch. Miles slowly let out his breath and pulled the trigger. The man's body went rigid then fell limp to the ground.

Peacock whistled. "Nice shot, Fitch."

Smith turned to him, his brows raised. "That ought to keep them back for a while."

"Or turn them into moles."

"Remind me not to make you mad." Smith lifted his rifle. "I think that earned you a break, Fitch. I'll watch for a while."

Miles nodded. "Thanks. I'll take you up on that."

He strode into the chapel and up the cannon ramp to the highest point. His gaze involuntarily moved toward town. Hundreds of troops were entrenched along the San Antonio River while hundreds more camped in Béxar. He stared toward his parents' home and then toward Carlos's place. Though he couldn't see troops in that area, he still feared they'd taken over the town enough that Rosa was in danger. He prayed Carlos kept his word and Rosa was safe.

He scanned the territory, starting at the river and moving west, looking for the best way to get through the line of Mexican forces. They had the Alamo surrounded, but there were areas weaker than others where couriers could sneak through, especially at night.

"You still looking for a chance to check on your girl?"

Miles merely glanced at Crockett, still examining the area to the east. "No, sir. I'm just wondering how many more riders can get through that line. Travis has been sending out dispatches almost every day. He sent another yesterday. And since no reinforcements have arrived, one has to wonder if any of those riders has gotten through.

If I were a betting man, I'd say this first line isn't the only one those couriers would have to worry about. Santa Anna appears to be a bright fighter. I've no doubt he has more men farther down those roads."

Crockett nodded. "I'd say you're right, and that you've been giving this a lot of thought. Any reason why, other than you're hoping more defenders will soon arrive?"

Miles stared out at the Mexican line while rubbing his thumb on the worn wood of his rifle. After a few moments of thought, he decided to reveal his idea. "I think I can get through. I learned a lot from the Tonkawa Indians, and I think I can get to Gonzales, or wherever we need to go, to get some help."

"So, you think no men are coming?"

"Do you?"

Crockett peered into the distance before answering. "Yes, I do. Not sure how many, but I believe we have help on the way."

"Then you need to pass that along to the men. Their spirits are getting low."

Crockett eyed him. "And yours, by the sound of it." He nodded. "I'll see what I can do. And I'll talk to Travis about sending you out. In fact, you can come with me. Maybe speaking in your own defense might get through to him."

"All right." Miles followed on his heels.

They found Travis coming out of his quarters and fell into step beside him. Miles let Crockett broach the subject.

"You remember Fitch, don't you, Colonel?"

Travis glanced at him. "I do. Is there a problem?"

"No. But he asked if he could be the next courier you send out. He spent time with an Indian tribe and knows how to get around the enemy."

Travis stopped and gave Miles his attention. "You're saying the others haven't gotten through that line?"

"I don't know, sir. Some might have—but we've yet to see reinforcements."

He nodded. "Then we should have help soon. And if I send out any more letters, I have my men to handle the task of seeing them through. Besides, I've seen you shoot. I'd like to keep you around. But thanks for the offer."

He strode away. Crockett hitched a shoulder. "He's a good leader, Fitch. Smart and competent for such a young man. If he trusts his men, so will I. But like he said, your offer is appreciated."

As the cannons from the Mexican forces continued to blast, Miles was left standing alone in the middle of the compound, the feeling of helplessness his only companion.

* * * * *

As Rosa made her way to the dry goods store, each step felt heavier than the last. Not knowing exactly what to expect from Ana and her parents didn't make the trip any easier. She didn't know which she preferred. . .cold and unfriendly or contrite and an attempt to make amends. All she knew for certain was she wouldn't be making the trip if it weren't necessary.

Rosa left the edge of the trees and started down the street to the store. Before she reached the doorway, she stopped and took a deep breath then stepped inside. The breath she took left in a gush. Mama stood at the counter with Ana and her mother.

"Rosa!" Mama rushed to her and wrapped her in a hug. "It's so good to see you." When Rosa wrested out of her embrace, Mama took a step back. "When will you stop this foolishness and come home?"

"I'm not about to live in your house just to watch you and Carlos undermine the efforts of the men at the Alamo."

"We're not doing anything to help Santa Anna's men."

"No? Then why was Carlos driving the wagon full of food stolen from nearby ranches?"

"How did you—" She had the courtesy to look down, even ashamed. "They needed to eat."

Rosa barely registered her mother's mumbled, contrite words. "Yes, well, don't we all? But not all of us steal to eat. That's why I'm here." She moved away from her mother then stopped, her mouth open. The shelves were bare. "What happened? Where's the food and—"

Ana's mother joined them. "The army went through town and confiscated all the food they could find. They have a lot of men to feed."

Rosa examined each face—the people she thought she knew. "And so everyone else needs to starve? And these are the men you protect against those at the Alamo? I don't believe it." There was nothing more here for her. She turned to leave as quickly as her feet could carry her.

"Wait, Rosa. I have food for you. Come home with me. You don't have to stay if you don't want to, but at least let me give you some supplies. You and Miles helped us more than once. Let me help you."

Rosa stopped near the door. She wanted to decline, but she needed food for her very survival. She turned back but stood rooted near the door. "I'll take food if you have it." She came closer to the counter and turned at a tap on her shoulder.

Ana stood behind her with a mixed expression of fear and hope. "Can we talk, Rosa?"

She saw her *friend* in a whole other light—as an enemy of the Alamo, and mostly, an enemy of Miles. "There's nothing for us to talk about, is there, Ana? Everything you've said to me in the last few weeks has been lies. Why would I believe you now?"

Ana shook her head. "They weren't lies. Not. . .all of it."

"So now I have to decipher all our conversations and try to weed out the lies from the truth, is that it? What kind of friendship—"

Mama touched her arm. "Give her a chance, Rosa. Nothing she did was intended to hurt you."

Rosa recoiled at her mother's touch and looked into Ana's eyes. "I do have one question. You know Mama and Carlos forced me to spy for information, that I wouldn't have done it otherwise. Were you coerced into assisting your parents, or did you help all on your own?"

"I—was hesitant at first, but then I helped whenever they asked."

Rosa's heart twisted in her chest. "And John? Did you also use him as I did?"

"At first, yes. But the more he came around, the more I liked him. . .loved him." Ana took a step closer. "I never meant for him to get hurt. And I especially never meant to hurt you. You're my best friend, Rosa, and I don't want to lose you."

"And that's why you tried so hard to find me." Sarcasm dripped from her voice. "So you could explain."

Her mouth dropped open twice. "I was afraid."

"Of what?"

"That I really had lost my best friend."

"I'm not your best friend, Ana. Best friends don't betray one another." Rosa turned on her heel and headed toward the door once more.

She never made it outside before Ana grasped her arm and turned her around. "Other than not telling you what I was doing, what did I do to you, Rosa? What did I do to make you want to throw away a beautiful friendship?"

"Beautiful? You lied! I trusted you, and you lied." Rosa looked toward the woman who raised her. "Same as my mother."

"Please. . ." Ana held fast to her arm. "I hate that I couldn't tell you what I was up to, but how did that hurt you personally? Why should we let what I believe to be right about the war affect us. . .affect what we mean to each other?"

Rosa stepped back. "Are you serious, Ana? You want me to forget the man I love, his safety, for our so-called friendship?"

Ana's expression fell, and Mama put her hand on top of Ana's still holding Rosa's arm. "You and I talked about this, my daughter. We both said we don't have to agree on everything to still love one another. Why is your friendship with Ana any different?"

Rosa backed away from their touch. "Because you all portrayed one thing and acted another. Such pretense can't be trusted. Love shouldn't come with a list of exceptions."

Mama stared into her face with tears in her eyes. "What made your heart so hard, Rosa? What has killed your love?"

"You! *All* of you. . .made my heart so hard." Rosa's heart shattered as her tears flowed. "My love isn't dead, Mama. Only my trust."

Mama pulled her into her arms and held her tight. "Is it better to be alone than to try to rebuild the trust? It can never happen if you build and maintain a wall." Mama stroked her hair. "We love you so much, Rosa. We never set out to hurt you. It happened and we're so sorry. But don't let us lose you because of it." She kissed Rosa's cheek then stepped back to look in her eyes. "Is there a chance you'll ever get past this?"

Rosa looked at the faces she loved—and once trusted. "I gave you a chance to rebuild the trust, and all I got in return was more deception."

"You consider not telling you everything deception?"

"Yes. Wouldn't you?"

Mama frowned. "I'm not sure I can agree. We were doing what we knew was right for our people. Not letting you know was for your own good, so you wouldn't be hurt or upset."

"But I am hurt and upset."

"But it wasn't intended. We wanted to protect you." Mama squeezed her arms. "We love you, Rosa. Nothing we did was meant to hurt you."

What Mama said was true. They didn't set out to hurt her. Only to work toward something they believed was right, which was opposite of her own belief. So who was wrong? She wiped her eyes.

Mama tried again. "Love can heal all things if we let it."

Ana reached out to her and squeezed her arm. "And I do love you, Rosa. I've never had a friend like you. I don't want to lose you."

"None of us do, Rosa. Come back to us. Please."

She took one step away. "I never stopped loving you. But all wounds take time to heal. That's what I'm asking you for. . .time."

She looked at her mother and received a nod. As they walked out together so Rosa could get some food, Rosa prayed for God's healing ointment on each relationship because she knew she couldn't do it on her own.

* * * * *

At the sound of a fiddle, Miles backed away from the palisade for a look. Crockett stood atop the roof of the low barracks, his back to the Mexican troops as he played for the Alamo defenders. Miles peered out at those entrenched a couple hundred yards away to see if any of them would try to shoot Crockett in the back. Instead, it appeared they were enjoying the music as much as the defenders.

With grins on their faces, many of the men whooped their approval. Some whistled along while others clapped and stomped their feet to the beat. Even Travis smiled and tapped his toes.

While Travis was a good and capable leader, Crockett had a way with the men. A certain rapport. And he'd found the one thing that could lift the spirits of the defenders. Music.

When Crockett turned his way and their eyes met, Miles gave him a smile and nod. Then he touched his fingers to the rim of his hat in a salute.

Chapter Twenty-Eight

Miles wasn't sure if Crockett's fiddle playing lulled the Mexican forces into a calmer disposition, or maybe they were just tired, but other than meager attempts to draw closer to the Alamo, the next day was quiet. Even the cold weather gave way to milder temperatures. Though nothing had really changed for them, the men's mood had improved, and Miles was grateful for the small blessing.

But as the sun dropped lower in the sky, activity outside the Alamo increased as a man on horseback rode around the Alamo. A hum of voices traveled around the fort as the men commented the rider was probably checking to see not only how the Mexican forces were doing but also the defense of the Alamo.

Crockett motioned to one of his men. "Show him how well we're defending the fort."

The man ran up the cannon ramp, took careful aim, and shot the man from atop his horse. A cheer went up as others congratulated the sharpshooter. The festive atmosphere lasted until dark. Then quiet fell as the stars glimmered their soothing light.

As Hector settled down for some rest, peace fell over Miles as he started his watch. They'd shown Santa Anna and his army that the defenders of the Alamo weren't to be taken lightly. And though that army continued trying to inch their way closer, the accuracy of the riflemen in the fort kept them at bay. And if the artillery held out until reinforcements arrived, they just might be able to win this battle.

His thoughts turned to Rosa. Was she still staying with her mother and Carlos? Were they still getting along? What was she doing to fill her days now that she couldn't come to the Alamo looking for work? So many questions and no answers. He missed their walks and conversations. Her wit was quick and sharp, giving him many fits of laughter. He smiled now at the memory. He wouldn't allow himself to dwell on the kisses or he'd drive himself mad. But just the fringe of the memories chased away any desire to sleep, so he allowed Hector to rest longer.

Hours later, in the dead of night, voices from outside the fort caught his attention. He scooted closer toward the gate, avoiding all the men lying on the ground. At first he thought maybe it was their snores that had broken the silence, but then more discussion at the gate began again, rousing many of the sleepers. Travis arrived and finally gave the command to open the gate, while a cluster of riflemen stood at the ready. Miles lowered his rifle, ready to shoot just in case.

Moments later a large group of men rode into the compound. The man in the lead wheeled his horse around.

"I'm George Kimball from the Gonzales Ranging Company. We're here to help."

Raucous shouts went up as the men were welcomed. The men celebrated with handshakes and backslapping as Travis and Kimball conferred. They strode up the ramp to one of the twelve-pounder cannons. Minutes later, the men scrambled to ready the firing of the cannon. Travis gave the order and the cannon boomed.

Miles raced up the ladder to the roof of the low barracks to see where the cannonball landed, but he was too late.

"Where'd it go?"

"In the main plaza."

Nowhere near Rosa. He breathed easier. Then the cannon blasted again. Silence fell as the men waited for the ball to land. It hit a large building at the main plaza. Someone shouted it was Santa Anna's headquarters while another declared he hoped the leader was in the building when the cannonball hit. Again, there were more shouts of elation, and the revelry began.

Someone bumped Miles from behind, and then a grinning Crockett moved beside him and motioned to the newcomers. "Feel better now, Fitch?"

"I do. And I'll feel even better when more groups like that arrive." He looked Crockett up and down. "I figured you'd have your fiddle out here to help celebrate."

"Oh, I don't know, Fitch. All those shouts and the sound of the laughter is the best music I've heard in a long time."

Miles smiled and nodded as they both moved toward the Gonzales group to welcome them and their help.

For the next two days, the newcomers received a taste of what the defenders had been enduring as the heavy cannonading continued. Miles could see the constant barrage was getting to them much like it had for the defenders when the siege first started. Though he could never get used to the blasts and wished it would end, he'd become accustomed to the steady explosions.

When Miles heard the command to open the gate, his heart beat a little faster as he expected more reinforcements. One lone rider entered, a white cloth tied to his hat. He spent a moment looking around then rode directly to Travis before dismounting. The two, surrounded by curious defenders, talked for several long minutes.

Miles only watched until the faces and shoulders of the men fell. He spotted John Prine and singled him out.

"This doesn't look good. Who is that and what'd he say?"

"That's Bonham, one of Travis's couriers. He just told us that the Goliad group led by Fannin isn't coming."

The breath left Miles as his chest felt tight. "How many were there that were supposed to come?"

John made a face. "Word was probably over three hundred in that bunch."

Miles's mouth went dry. He looked John in the eyes. "Are there any more on their way, John, or is this it?"

He lifted a shoulder. "The men from Gonzales said more were coming. How many, I have no idea." They both watched Travis disappear into his quarters. "No doubt he's writing more letters asking for more help." John shook his head. "I'm starting to wonder how many of the dispatches are actually getting through."

"I know. I've wondered the same. I even told Travis I'd be a courier for him. He turned me down, said he needs my shooting here."

"You really think you could get through?"

Miles stared at Bonham, taking his time before answering. "He made it through." He shifted his rifle. "I spent a good amount of time with an Indian tribe and learned a lot from them, including how to sneak around without being heard or noticed. Given the chance, I'd sure try out some of what I learned."

"Did you tell Travis that?"

"No. He said he had his men to do the running."

John nodded. "I'll see if I can't slip your name into a conversation. Never know. It might make an impact."

They shook and then John strolled off the direction of Travis's quarters. Miles returned to his place at the palisade, his spirits sagging. They sank even lower when, that afternoon, more Mexican troops arrived in Béxar. Miles couldn't begin to count the number, but he guessed at close to a thousand. This time, all the loud celebration came on the part of Santa Anna's men. But as they enjoyed their festivities, Travis sent out yet another man with more letters. Miles assumed either John hadn't gotten a chance to talk to Travis or his comments fell on deaf ears. Once again he fought off the feeling of helplessness.

* * * * *

At the sound of cheering, Rosa headed across the room toward the door. She'd hardly moved the latch when her mother's voice stopped her.

"You know you can't go out there, Rosa. It's too dangerous."

"I just want to see what all the yelling is about."

"There are too many of Santa Anna's troops wandering around town. You won't be safe."

Rosa sighed and shoved the latch back in place. "I'm in a cage."

She paced around the table, something she'd done so many times since Mama had talked her into staying with her and Carlos she feared she'd have a trail worn in the wood floor before the battle was over.

"You feel trapped? At least we have food and are comfortable."

"Don't you want to get out and take a walk, visit friends, *something* other than sit in here? At least when I was at Miles's place, I could get out of the house once in a while."

She saw the pain on her mother's face and wished she'd have bit her tongue instead of voicing her thoughts.

"I'm sorry, Mama. I'm grateful for the safety and food. I really am. I'm just not used to being locked up like this."

She moved to the window and stared out. Better to deal with the tedium in silence than complain and deal with regret.

Carlos strode around the corner of a neighbor's house. Rosa scooted to the door, shoved the latch, and opened the door for him.

"What's happening? Why all the noise?"

Carlos shared a look with his wife and then licked his lips. "More of Santa Anna's troops arrived."

Rosa's mouth went dry. He already had so many. Too many for the Alamo defenders to fight. "How many?"

Carlos hesitated then shrugged. "I'm not sure. A lot. I'm guessing close to a thousand."

Rosa's knees weakened, and she started to shake. She moved to the table and dropped onto a chair near her mother. With her head in her hands and tears leaving tiny pools on the table, she started to pray for Miles and his friends.

Chapter Twenty-Nine

Miles sensed the growing tension. Soon after Travis sent off his latest messages with another courier, a steady bombardment began on the Alamo's north wall. Word spread around the fort that the wall wouldn't take much more, that it had started to crumble. Travis placed more men along the line, hoping to dissuade the heavy battering by shooting some of the Mexican men. Miles waited to hear the cannon blasts slow down, but the steady booming continued. By nightfall part of the wall collapsed.

More news passed around the fort that a man named Jameson had asked the men to help reinforce the wall with rock and lumber under cover of darkness. Miles volunteered and headed that direction. John stopped him.

"Travis wants to speak with you. Follow me."

They entered Travis's quarters. "Are you still willing to be a courier?"

Miles's heart picked up speed. "Yes, sir."

Travis nodded. "Good. I'm sending you and a couple others out at different times. Bonham returned this morning with the report that Fannin wasn't coming. I want the three of you to try to find a way through the Mexican line and make your way toward Goliad. If Fannin happens to be on his way with his men, help them make haste to get here." He handed Miles a folded note. "If he's still in Goliad, give him that message and then do your best to convince him how much we need their help. Describe what the men are going through. Say whatever it takes to move them toward us."

Miles pocketed the message. "Yes, sir."

Travis held out his hand. "Godspeed, Fitch."

They shook. "Thank you, sir."

Miles all but ran to the stock pens and saddled his horse. The poor beast hadn't been ridden in weeks. Miles hoped the horse could make the ride. He led the horse out of the pen and across the compound toward the gate. Hector stood in his path, his hand outstretched.

"Good luck, son. I pray you have good success."

Miles grasped his hand in a tight grip. "Thanks, Hector. See you in a couple of days. Keep things under control till I get back."

"I will do my best."

Once the men had opened the gate for him, he led his horse through the defensive breastwork and across the bridge over the ditch before climbing onto the saddle.

He reached down and patted the horse's neck. "All right, Spike. We've got a job to do. Ride hard, old man."

From all the hours standing at the palisade, Miles could see his route in his mind. He couldn't head straight for the Goliad road. The Mexican army would have it too well guarded, probably in more than one area. He'd have to angle around it then cut back once he was certain he'd passed the troops.

"Lord, guide my path. Lead me through the enemy." He remembered something his mother had once read him from the Bible. "Deliver me from those who pursue me."

He took a deep breath then heeled Spike into a trot. Once they rounded the breastwork, Miles pointed his horse southeast where the Mexican army was the weakest and urged him into a gallop. The closer he drew to the Mexican entrenchment, the faster he urged his horse.

A shout then another reached his ears. He hunkered low over the saddle, held on tight, and continued to heel his horse. About the time he expected a rifle shot, the big cannon from the Alamo boomed.

Miles grinned, knowing the explosion would distract the Mexican forces, maybe just long enough to get him through the line. Rifles around and behind him blasted, but he stayed low and kept going.

Minutes later, the rifles fell silent. He'd made it past the first line. He slowed down to catch his breath and get his bearings. After altering his direction, he continued on at a slower pace, unwilling to have the enemy know his location because of galloping hooves.

More rifle fire went off, but the sound came from behind. He guessed the other men Travis sent out were on their way and prayed for their safety.

Miles rode at a trot for half an hour, weaving in and out of trees and bushes, and then veered toward the Goliad road. He dismounted, ground tied his horse, and ran to the road. He looked both directions and didn't see a thing. Though he knew there could still be Mexican troops along the way, he decided to use the road so he could ride faster. He returned to his horse and froze at the snap of a twig to his right. He pulled his knife and prepared for a fight.

"Have you forgotten all we taught you, old friend?"

Miles's breath left him in a gust, and he laughed as he replaced his knife in the sheath. "I've never known a Tonkawa to break a twig."

His Tonkawa friend moved out of the shadows into the glow of the rising moon wearing his usual long loincloth and buckskin leggings. His breastplate was mostly hidden by a piece of buffalo hide. He'd added more plumage to his horned headpiece since Miles last saw him. He carried a small branch in his hand, which he broke again before tossing the pieces to the ground. They grasped each other's forearms in greeting.

"Good to see you, Turtle."

"You also, Mice."

Miles laughed. "Still haven't mastered the *l*?"

"I am sure it will come right about the time you pronounce my name correctly."

"That's what I thought. What're you doing here?"

"I heard about the battle. I came to see if you needed help. I've been watching from a distance. Never thought I would see you again."

Miles climbed onto his saddle, and Turtle swung onto his mount. "I'd love to sit and talk, Turtle, but I've got to get to Goliad as fast as I can. We need reinforcements."

"Yes, you do. I'll ride with you, my friend."

"Thank you."

The two rode hard side by side for a while and then slowed to a trot to let the horses catch their wind before galloping again. They continued switching all throughout the night and the next day without running across any of Santa Anna's men.

During one of their trots, Miles moved his horse closer to Turtle. "How's your family?"

"Good. All is well."

"You married yet?"

Turtle laughed. "No. Then I will have to be. . .what you say?"

"Responsible?"

"Yes. I am not ready to answer to a woman."

This time Miles laughed. "I doubt it's all that bad or men wouldn't keep getting married."

"You sound like a man in love." They rode in silence and then Turtle laughed again. "It is so. Tell me about her. Besides that she is beautiful."

Miles smiled. "She is that. And she's funny, fun to be around, smart."

"Is nice to hold?"

Miles grinned. "Yes. Very. She has a nice friend. I could introduce you."

"No, thank you. I will be the first in my generation to show wisdom."

They both laughed at that. Miles had missed spending time with his friend and was glad Turtle had sought him out.

"You kill any of your enemy?"

Miles shrugged. This wasn't a conversation he wanted to discuss. "A few."

He heeled his horse back into a gallop so they couldn't talk any longer. The horses had a rest, and he wanted to get to Goliad so he could get back to the Alamo. With the sun not far from setting and a couple of miles outside of Goliad, Miles reined in his horse. Turtle drew up next to him.

"Why stop now? We are almost there."

"I know. That's why I stopped. I don't know these people, and they don't know me. I'm not sure how they'll react to seeing you. Maybe you should wait here."

Turtle glanced toward Goliad then at Miles. "I will wait."

Miles reached to shake his hand. "I appreciate your company, old friend."

He heeled his horse toward town and arrived on the outskirts of Fort Defiance minutes later. The fort looked stronger and in much better condition than the Alamo. He hollered for them to open the doors.

"Who are you?"

"Miles Fitch from the Alamo. I have a message from Lieutenant Colonel Travis for Colonel Fannin."

The gate scraped open, allowing him entry. He dismounted and looked around.

"Where will I find Fannin?"

One of the men pointed to the far side of the fort where a group of men clustered. "What's happening at the Alamo? They still holding off Santa Anna?"

"They were, up to when I left. They're good men who need reinforcements." Miles was about to find Fannin but turned back. "Why haven't you left yet? I know Fannin's received letters before now."

The man jerked his thumb toward the group. "Ask Fannin. We're obeying our commander. If it were up to me, I'd be there already, defending the Alamo."

Miles eyed his uniform. "What about the volunteers? I could lead them back there."

"The volunteers are also obeying Fannin's command."

Miles heaved a sigh and nodded then led his horse across the compound. "I'm looking for Colonel Fannin."

A man stepped forward from the group. "That's me. Who might you be?"

"I'm Miles Fitch from the Alamo with a message from Travis."

He pulled the letter from his pocket then handed it over. Fannin opened the letter then turned to let a torch give him more light. He quickly read the message before tucking the paper inside the pocket of his uniform.

"We're not able to help."

The refusal hit Miles in the gut. "But sir, the Mexican forces have the Alamo completely surrounded with thousands of men. We only have a couple hundred. We need more men, and we need help soon. I'm not sure how much longer we can hold out. We're low on artillery, and their cannons have already collapsed part of one wall. We need—"

"If it's that bad then I doubt our three or four hundred will be of much help."

"I disagree, sir. You and your men could be the deciding factor in our winning the battle. The few men we have there have held off that multitude for over a week."

Fannin pulled back his shoulders and shook his head. "We can't go. We must stay here and defend the southern corridor."

"But Colonel—"

"You can put your horse with all the others. You'll stay here and help us protect this fort. Your one gun won't help those Alamo defenders now." He turned and pointed to one of his men. "Show him where he can tend to his horse and where he can get some food and rest."

Fannin didn't wait for a reply but strode away. When he was out of earshot, the men surrounded Miles.

"Tell us what's happening there."

Anger boiled inside, but it wasn't toward these men. He bit back a sharp reply and took a breath to gain control. "What's happening is that the Mexican forces are chipping away at the walls of the Alamo. And in our efforts to stave off their attack, our supplies are dwindling. We need help and soon. Why hasn't Fannin led you men there? Is this fort in such a vital position that he couldn't take some time to help us defeat Santa Anna? Getting that man and his army out of the territory would keep you from having to fight him here."

"We tried to get there."

Miles craned his neck. "When?"

"About a week ago. We didn't get far. Between wagons breaking, oxen wandering off, and most of the men with poor gear, seemed like we had nothing but trouble. Fannin called off the march. Bonham was here not long ago doing the same thing you're doing. . .trying to get Fannin to the Alamo. He didn't succeed either."

"You think there's no hope for getting him to change his mind?"

The men all looked at each other then shook their heads. "You wasted your time."

Another man leaned close. "We had several men disappear one night not long ago. There's talk they were on their way to the Alamo. You didn't run across a group on the road?"

"No, but I avoided the road for a while in case Santa Anna had his men there to stop the couriers and any men trying to get to us. There were two other men who left when I did. Maybe one of them found your group."

The first man stood and held out his hand. "I'm Phillips. Come on. I'll show you where you can bunk."

Miles grabbed the reins to his horse. "I'm not staying. I'm going back to help."

Phillips stopped. "No offense, but I have to agree with Fannin on this. Your one gun won't make much difference."

"Maybe not, but I've got friends in there. I said I'd be back, and I aim to do just that."

"I doubt Fannin will let them open the gate for you."

"I'll find a way. I'm not staying."

He paused. "I understand. Then at least get some food in your belly first. I doubt you took time to eat on the way here."

"I didn't. My horse could use some feed and water too." He followed Phillips but also wanted something for Turtle. "Could I get enough for the ride back?"

"That won't be a problem." He stopped at a doorway where the scent of cooking meat drifted out. "You're still assuming Fannin will let you go."

"Are you planning to tell him I'm leaving?" When Phillips hesitated, Miles knew he needed to take a chance and attempt to convince him. "Do you have friends here, Phillips?"

"Yes."

"Would you leave them to fight such a battle as we have coming, even if it were to save your own skin?"

Phillips stared at the ground. "No, sir, I guess I couldn't do that to them. And I wouldn't want them to do that to me."

"So you'll help me get out?"

He looked around then nodded. "Sure. Let me know when you're ready to leave." He pointed over his shoulder. "One of the cooks will fix you up. Give me your horse and I'll get him fed. We'll be right over there."

"Thanks, Phillips. Don't let him gorge. I need him to run again."

Miles tucked into the stew and biscuits like he hadn't eaten in a week. He wrapped and stuffed two biscuits into his side pouch and found the cook again.

"Anything besides stew I can take back with me?"

The cook pointed at a covered pot. "Dried some beef awhile back. Aim to use it tomorrow. Grab what you need."

"Thanks." He tucked the beef in with the biscuits. "Any idea what day this is?"

The cook shrugged and looked at another who shook his head. "March fourth. Lost track of time with all the fighting, huh?"

"You could say that. Thank you."

Dark had settled in for the night. With only torchlight guiding his steps, he went in search of his horse. Since he couldn't get any of the men to join him, it was time to head back.

He found Phillips and his horse and extended his hand. "Thanks for your help, Phillips."

They shook hands and headed for the gate. Miles spotted Fannin at a table inside one of the rooms of the barracks and hoped the man wouldn't look up. The soldiers at the gate were just about to open up when a shout went up.

"Hold up there. Keep those doors shut. I gave orders that he wasn't leaving."

Miles turned, his temper burning. "I'm not under your orders."

"You are when you're in this fort."

"You afraid of the report I'll bring back to Travis?"

"Keep talking, young man, and you'll end up in our stockade unable to help anyone. This is for your own good." He pointed to his men at the gate. "Lock it up."

Miles clenched his fists but relaxed them again. This was one mess he couldn't fight his way out of and win.

Chapter Thirty

Rosa grasped Carlos's arm before he could walk out the door. "Please, Carlos. We're about to go mad locked up in this house. You get to go out and about, but we're trapped in here."

Carlos looked at his wife, who nodded. "We've been in here for days on end. A quick visit with the Mendozas would be a blessing." She moved to his side and grasped his other arm. "If you walk with us, we'll be safe. Let us visit an hour or two; then come back and walk us home. Right, Rosa?"

"Right. Getting out for a while might save our sanity, which, in turn, might save your life."

Mama laughed. "Maybe not your life but possibly your hair."

Carlos finally smiled. "In that case, get ready. I'd like to leave soon."

Mama pulled him low and kissed his cheek then ran off and returned with her shawl. Rosa took hers from the hook by the door and wrapped it around her shoulders.

"Was that soon enough?"

He chuckled. "So fast, I'd almost think you had this planned for a while."

Rosa and her mother exchanged a smile then followed him out the door. He motioned for them to wait while he checked the next street then waved them on. They continued the same procedure all the way to the Mendoza house. Only once did Carlos make them wait for Mexican soldiers to pass. Rosa thought that odd since there had been so many in Béxar, making her wonder where they'd all gone.

They knocked on the door of the Mendoza home and waited quite awhile for someone to answer.

"Who is it?"

"Carmela and Rosa."

The door flew open. "Come in! Come in!" Mrs. Mendoza moved back to let them enter. "I'm so glad you came. We've missed seeing our friends."

Carlos didn't enter but waved and walked off. The ladies hugged and sat at the table. Ana fetched two more cups and poured the coffee as she eyed Rosa as though trying to get an idea of where their friendship stood. Rosa still wouldn't trust them, but she'd decided to try to give the relationship a chance to heal.

"What have you been doing to fill your time? I'm assuming you're locked up in your house like we are in ours."

Rosa nodded. "We are, and we've run out of things to do. We've read everything in the house at least twice. I've even resorted to refolding my clothes."

The Mendoza women laughed. Mama patted the table.

"She's serious. We had to get out before she started trying to count the hairs on my head."

They shared more laughter. Ana fingered her coffee cup. "We understand completely. We started on a new quilt just to keep ourselves sane. I don't know how many times the constant booming of those cannons made me prick my finger." She held it up as proof.

Mama grasped it for a better look. "Maybe we can help. I'd at least like to see what you've done."

They spent more than an hour working together on the quilt while chatting about anything they could think of that had nothing to do with the fighting going on around them. Carlos knocked on the door much too soon for their liking, but the afternoon was a blessing, and it gave Rosa and her mother an idea to fill their hours.

* * * * *

Miles had already walked the perimeter of the fort twice, seeking a way out, but in order to get his horse out with him, he had to use the gate. Fury at his situation ate a hole inside his stomach. He paced in front of the chapel trying to come up with a solution until he feared wearing out his footwear or leaving a trench.

Most of Fannin's men had bunked down for the night hours ago. Only a handful of soldiers kept watch along the walls. But unless he could convince the gatekeepers to ignore Fannin's order, he wouldn't get back to the Alamo anytime soon.

The moon chose that moment to peek over the fort's wall. That meant morning was only a few hours away. He could always escape over the wall and ride double with Turtle back to the Alamo, but that meant leaving his horse behind. Trying to get through the enemy line without a horse would probably end in his death, and he'd be of no help to anyone. . .unless Turtle let him borrow his horse. With frustration riding him hard, he wandered over to check on his horse and possibly say goodbye.

"Wish you had wings, old boy. That would sure make life easier right now."

"If you've resorted to talking to your horse, you're in worse shape than I thought."

Miles breathed a sigh of relief that his visitor wasn't Fannin. "I *am* in bad shape, Phillips. I've got to get out of here."

"I figured as much. I've talked to our man at the gate. He said he'd let you out if you took him with you. He wants to help."

Miles grinned. "Done. Thank you, Phillips."

He rushed to get his horse saddled while Phillips saddled one for the other man. Then he started for the gate when Phillips stopped him.

"Let's go along the far wall. Don't want Fannin catching us or we'll both end up in the stockade."

The man at the gate already had the doors open. Miles didn't stop until he was outside, unwilling to be caught inside and trapped again. Phillips handed the new man the reins to the horse.

"Fitch, this is Matthews."

Miles grasped his hand. "Good to have you with me, Matthews. Thanks for your help."

"I've wanted to get to the Alamo since the first dispatch arrived. I don't know why Fannin isn't going, but I'm tired of waiting."

"Then let's get going." Miles turned to Phillips. "I appreciate all you've done. Sure you don't want to join us? We could use another man like you."

"Someone's got to stay and try to talk some sense into Fannin. But when you're done with your battle, come help with ours."

"Not sure about that. All I can say is maybe. I've got a girl back there and I've been away from her too long as it is."

"I understand. You two be careful. Kill 'em all."

"We'll try."

Miles and Matthews mounted up and rode off at a gallop. As they neared two miles, Miles slowed his horse then reined to a stop.

"What's wrong? I thought we were in a hurry."

"We are, but I've had a friend waiting for me out here. We'll meet up with him soon."

"Fine. Let's go."

"Hold on. I wanted to warn you that he's an Indian, so don't try to kill him when you see him."

Matthews stared for several moments. "An Indian?"

"He's friendly. Trust me."

"And trust me. I could have killed you many times over by now." Turtle appeared from behind a bush next to the road.

Matthews reached for his pistol, but Miles grabbed his arm. "He's my friend, Matthews. Don't try to hurt him. You'll only end up dead." Miles heeled his horse toward Turtle. "I gotta admit you're a scary sight, Turtle. If I didn't know you, I might try to shoot you myself."

"You would try." They shook hands then Turtle looked down the road. "You took a long time, my friend. Where is your army?"

Miles followed his gaze. "They aren't coming."

The expression on Turtle's face must have looked much like his when Fannin turned him down. "They will not help their fellow tribe?"

"No. They won't help." Miles blew out a breath. "Mount up, Turtle. I've been gone too long already. Let's get back." He turned to Matthews, still eyeing Turtle with suspicion. "You ready?"

"Ah, sure."

"Good." He looked again at Turtle. "I have food for you if you're hungry."

"Not hungry. Ate rabbit."

Miles laughed. "I should have known. All right then. Let's go."

They rode back to the Alamo much like they had when they were on their way to Fort Defiance in Goliad. Miles knew his horse was still tired from the ride there and pushed him only as much as he dared without taking a chance on losing him. During the middle of the day, they stopped at a stream to let the horses rest and get a drink. The men devoured the beef and biscuits in Miles's pouch before riding on to the Alamo.

The sun went down with so much color the ground appeared to be on fire. In minutes, they were surrounded by darkness. They slowed the horses for another rest.

"How much farther before we're there?"

Miles glanced toward Matthews, who sounded nervous, but only saw his outline. "We probably have a good seven hours yet. But before we get there, we have to get off the road. Santa Anna has men posted on this road. We'll have to sneak around them and then ride like a wildfire is after us to get through the last line."

"Doesn't sound like much fun."

"Running for your life never is, Matthews. But it's what we have to do to get back inside. Several of the men have done it, me included, so it can be done."

"Right." Matthews looked wary.

Miles smiled and heeled his horse back into a gallop.

* * * * *

Rosa quit rocking. She sat forward in the chair and listened again. Then she hurried to the window. "It's quiet out there."

Mama cocked her ear. "Yes, it is. I like it. All that constant booming is tedious."

"But why is it silent? The cannons have been going off since Santa Anna arrived." She looked at Carlos. "What does it mean?"

"I don't know, Rosa."

She didn't believe him. He seemed to know everything that was happening, thanks to his brother. He shook his head.

"I honestly don't know, Rosa. My brother never said anything when I saw him today. We only spoke for a few minutes. He said he was busy."

"Then why did it take you so long to come back and walk us to the house?"

He glanced at his wife. "I walked to the edge of town. I wanted to see what was happening at the Alamo."

"And what was happening?"

"The usual. Just the cannons firing at the fort."

Dread filled her heart. Though the quiet was nice, it seemed like a sign. She'd been through scary storms that started with calm weather. She shared a look with her mother.

"I'm sure it's fine, Rosa. Maybe Santa Anna wants to rest his men."

Rosa turned back to the window. There was only one reason his men would need a rest. She swallowed hard. Despite the silence, sleep would be scarce tonight.

Please Lord, protect Miles.

* * * * *

The trip seemed much longer this direction. Like Matthews, Miles felt like they'd never get there. About thirty miles from the Alamo, he reined to a stop.

"I'm not exactly sure where we are, but I think we're close enough that we need to get off the road. No need getting shot at in two different places. What do you think, Turtle?"

"I think you are right. I will lead. You have been away from our teaching for too long."

Miles chuckled. "You may be right. Go on ahead."

Turtle wound them through bushes and thickets far enough off the road that any of the Mexican troops wouldn't see or hear them. The going was slow at best because the ground was uneven, but Turtle's horse acted as though it could see through the dark and continued leading them northwest. They'd ridden for quite some time before Matthews rode up next to him.

"What time is it?" Matthews voice was barely over a whisper.

"I don't know for certain, but I'm guessing it's getting close to five o'clock and we're still several miles from the Alamo. We should be there right before sunrise."

"That's good. We can ride through the line in the dark."

"Exactly."

At least Miles hoped that was the case. The moonlight was bad enough. Full sunlight would make them too easy a target.

He reined to a stop. "There aren't any cannons blasting."

Matthews breathed harder, his fear palpable. "What?"

Miles strained to hear. "Santa Anna's had us under cannon fire almost around the clock since he arrived in Béxar. I don't hear anything."

"Is that bad?"

"I don't know. It's just unusual."

Turtle turned back. "You want to stop?"

Miles's heartbeat increased. "No, I want to go faster. Something doesn't seem right."

Turtle picked up the pace. In the distance, Miles caught glimpses of torches. He hurried to catch up to Turtle.

"You better stay here. I'll find you when this is over." He shook his friend's hand. "Thanks for all your help, Turtle."

"I will be waiting."

The sound of bugles drifted faintly over the hills. Miles looked at Matthews.

"We gotta go!"

They hadn't ridden more than a hundred yards when gunshots and cannon fire echoed toward them. They heeled their horses into a gallop.

Chapter Thirty-One

Miles reached the edge of the tree line on the hill east of the Alamo. He gaped across the plain as the thousands of Mexican forces attacked the Alamo on all sides, the weakened north wall taking the worst of the assault.

"Let's go!"

"What? We can't go down there now."

Miles glanced at Matthews then heeled his horse. He didn't get more than a few yards before another horse cut in front of him. His reins jerked to the right and Miles flew from the saddle to the left. He hit the ground hard, leaving him winded. He pushed to his feet. Turtle sat atop his mustang, the reins to Miles's horse dangling from his hands.

Unwilling to lose more time, Miles jerked his rifle from its sheath and started running toward the Alamo. Turtle rode in front again and launched from the mustang, knocking Miles to the ground a second time. Turtle stayed on top of him, keeping Miles from rising.

"Let me up, Turtle. I gotta get down there."

"You go, you die."

"I've got to help. I can come up from behind and surprise them."

"You get one, maybe two, then they kill you."

"I've still got to try."

"I will not let you die. It is useless to go there now."

Miles knew he was right, but he wanted to help his friends. He quit fighting, and Turtle let him up. He pushed to his feet, rubbing his hands on his thighs, wishing he could do something to help.

Through the torchlight and gun flashes, Miles watched the fight in the distance.

Cannons and rifle fire blasted from both sides. Miles was proud of the determined fight of his defender friends. The force of the Alamo artillery on the east and west side pushed the enemy back. The Mexican forces re-formed and attacked once more, only to be repulsed a second time. Miles's hope surged. But as the fighting wore on, the Mexican infantry on each side moved toward the north and merged with the men already fighting there.

The Mexican army now had such a vast number of men along the north wall that the defenders couldn't stop them. As the enemy attempted to climb the wall, men from both sides fell. The weakness of using the roofs and catwalks of the buildings became evident as the defenders had to lean over the wall to shoot, leaving their heads and upper bodies exposed to Mexican fire. Yet over and over, the defenders continued to reload and lean out to fire on the enemy.

Miles clenched his fists, silently cheering on the defenders. They were fighting for their very lives and it showed as they put up a tremendous resistance. He glanced to the south wall, especially along the palisade. From such a distance and with only a dim glow from the rising sun, he couldn't make out any individual, but he was thrilled to see his friends were keeping the enemy at bay. He said a quick prayer for Crockett, Hector, John, and Peacock.

He returned his gaze to the north wall in time to see the first handful of Mexican infantry break through the line of men atop the wall. Many of the defenders used their rifles as clubs, landing blow after blow on the enemy, cutting them down before they could enter the Alamo. The Mexican infantry fought back with the bayonets attached to the ends of their rifles, sending many defenders to their deaths.

The breach of the wall started as a slow leak but quickly became a flood as the Mexican forces poured over the wall. They rushed inside and swarmed over the defenders, firing shots and stabbing with their bayonets. The gunners along the south wall turned their cannons toward the north and fired on the advancing Mexican army. In minutes, the Mexican forces scaled the south wall and killed the gunners.

Many of the defenders retreated to the long barracks. Miles couldn't see the fighting, but the blasts, shouts, and noises sailing through the wind brought with it much despair. Flashes could be seen from gun barrels along the San Antonio River. Miles assumed some of the defenders went over the wall in an attempt to escape and were killed.

Some of the men posted along the cattle pen and horse corral crawled over the lower part of the wall and rushed toward the prairie. Miles reached for his rifle, prepared to help them make it to safety. Before he could take two steps, the Mexican cavalry advanced on the defenders. Miles lifted his rifle only to have Turtle shove the barrel to the ground.

"I've got to help them get away!"

"All you will do is give away our position. It is too late, my friend."

Moments later, the cavalry opened fire on the retreating defenders. The shooting continued until all the men were killed. The rising sun cast an eerie orange glow over the scene, as though accentuating the blood the defenders had shed.

Miles dropped to his knees, his chest and throat burning, his mouth dry as dust. He turned his sights to the palisade to check on the progress and safety of his friends. A group still fought along the low wall, only to fall back to the front of the chapel. Miles could no longer see any of them, but he was certain they had no time to reload and fire upon the enemy, which meant the rifle shots he heard had to be coming from the Mexican army. He could only pray they made it inside the fortified chapel.

Many of the enemy had turned the cannons toward the long barracks where the rooms were also fortified. One by one, they fired on the barracks. Some of the enemy attempted to take down the flag flying over the Alamo. Four of their soldiers were killed by the remaining defenders before one man succeeded in finally pulling down the flag.

A handful of the Mexican army worked to turn the eighteen-pounder cannon toward the front of the chapel. Minutes later, the cannon blasted, destroying the barriers, resulting in several more rounds of rifle fire.

Intermittent gunfire continued to go off. Miles could picture the Mexican army checking defenders' bodies inside the chapel, one by one, firing on those still alive. Inside the compound, they were doing just that, either firing on or bayonetting several of the Alamo defenders.

Dead inside, Miles wandered to the nearest tree and sat against it, unable to continue watching the defenders die. He ran his hands over his face. They came away damp from the tears he didn't realize had fallen during the massacre.

Matthews pushed to his feet. "I'm sorry, Fitch. That was brutal. But since there's nothing I can do here, I'm leaving."

"Going back to Goliad?" His voice sounded lifeless to his own ears.

"Probably."

Miles didn't even look at him. "Better take the route we used to get here."

"I will." Matthews took a step before stopping. "Come with me. There's nothing for you here now."

Words refused to pass his tight throat. He merely shook his head. A minute later and without another attempt to convince Miles to join him, Matthews galloped away.

Turtle sat cross-legged beside him but didn't speak, as though he understood Miles's need for silence. A bugle played in the distance, but the sporadic rifle fire continued. Miles flinched and his anger grew with each blast until he was ready to shake his fist at an uncaring God. If Turtle weren't there to stop him, Miles would be on his way to the Alamo to kill as many Mexicans as he could before they made him join his friends in death.

Chapter Thirty-Two

Rosa lifted her head from the pillow and listened. From the distance came the din of cannon and rifle fire, much different from all the days previous. Instead of one blast every few minutes, this was constant, steady. She knew she was hearing the sound of battle.

She threw off the covers and climbed into her clothes. Determined not to let Carlos or her mother stop her, she hurried to the door and ran out into the night. She couldn't just sit inside the house and listen to the fighting and not know what was happening. She refused to wait for Carlos to check the battle and return with bits and pieces of information. She'd watch and learn firsthand.

Certain she wouldn't get anywhere near the river by going straight east, she headed to the north end of town before veering east. She stopped behind a tree closest to the water's edge. After peeking around the side to make sure she wouldn't be seen by any of Santa Anna's men, she moved for a better view of the fort. She gulped back a sob as the Mexican army climbed the north wall of the Alamo. Like a slow flowing river, the enemy scaled the wall and disappeared inside. There were so many.

No, Lord! Please, no! Miles is in there!

She prayed for his protection, that Santa Anna would show compassion, rescind his orders that no quarter would be shown, and let the men inside live.

The faint glow of the rising sun could be seen, showing the stark outline of the fort, making it look much like it raged with fire. But the only fire was the one burning inside her with the desire to know whether or not Miles was still alive.

Cannons continued to blaze and rifles fired fast and steady. Then the screech and shouts of men in pain rolled across the river, raising gooseflesh all along her arms and legs. Like the gunshots and screams from the Alamo, her tears flowed in an unending stream.

A lifetime crept by before the cannons stopped exploding and the rifle fire slowed to an occasional blast. Even the shrieks came to an end. Rosa pushed to her feet, unaware of when her legs gave out and she'd ended up on the ground.

Her gaze adhered to the Alamo, and, unable to stop herself, she moved to the water's edge and forged the river. On the other side, she stumbled and righted herself in time to keep from falling on the bodies of several Mexican infantry. About to step over one, she paused when an idea came to her.

With a quick look around, she searched until she found the first man with a rifle ball to the head. He was slightly larger than her, but he'd have to do. She struggled to drag his body behind a bush then stripped off his uniform. Minutes later, she had her dress off and the Mexican uniform on. She returned to the fallen soldiers and found boots and a chacó. The boots were slightly large, but when she tucked all her hair inside the Mexican soldier's hat, it fit snugly.

She rubbed dirt all over her face, looked around, and then stared at the Alamo. Doubting her good sense, and in an act only a woman in love would attempt, Rosa made her way across the plain to the Alamo gates. She ignored the bodies of Santa Anna's men and forged ahead, determined not to leave until she saw Miles.

After passing over the small bridge crossing the ditch in front of the breastwork, Rosa walked through the gates crowded with Santa Anna's men and entered the fort. The bloody bodies of both the Mexican military and the Alamo defenders lay everywhere. She wandered around, looking for anyone wearing buckskin. She recognized several of the dead defenders as the men she'd helped with their laundry. But there was only one man she wanted to see, and she prayed he was alive.

Each time she spotted someone in buckskin, she lost her breath and didn't gain it back until she'd turned over the body and discovered it wasn't Miles. Fighting back the desire to sob over the waste and slaughter of so many good men, Rosa turned toward the chapel, continuing her search.

In the length of a few steps, she gasped and stopped, nearly falling to her knees. Only a few feet from her lay John Prine's body, riddled with rifle shot and knife wounds. Bile rose in her throat. She ran to the wall and emptied the contents of her stomach. The heaving continued until there was nothing left, and still her stomach rebelled.

She was crazy for being here. If the sight of John's body affected her so badly, there was no telling what would happen should she find Miles in the same condition, but still she had to know. She glanced around. Only Mexican military wandered the compound checking the bodies of both sides of the battle. There were no Alamo defenders on their feet.

Her vision blurred, her hands shook, and her head felt light. She had to find Miles soon or she'd make a mistake, like fainting, and she'd be discovered as a resident instead of a fighter. She took several deep breaths and prepared to move on. The area in front of the chapel was her goal, certain that's where she'd find Miles.

"*Deja de buscar heridos entre los defensores. Todos están muertos. Necesitamos buscar a los Mexicanos heridos y darles ayuda.*"

Rosa obeyed the Mexican officer's order to stop checking the Alamo defenders for survivors, but at his comment that they were all dead, she almost screamed. She badly wanted to take the sword from the belt of the uniform she wore and strike down the officer.

Sanity returned before she made such a mistake. To keep from being discovered, she started examining the Mexican troops for those that might still be alive.

"*Toma sus pies y ayudame a cargarlo a donde estan los otros.*"

Rosa cringed at the order to grab the wounded man's feet. She did not want to carry him to the others, nor did she care whether or not he lived. Not anymore.

Remembering to make her voice low to continue her ruse as a man, she prepared to lower her voice before answering. "*Espera, tengo que hacer mis necesidades.*"

The man grunted at her request for time to relieve herself and then turned away as he gave one last command. "*Busca a alguien que te ayude a cargar a los heridos.*"

With the officer's back turned, Rosa ran to the low wall and glanced along the palisade and the court in front of the chapel. To give herself more time, she knelt next to one of the dead Mexicans. Two officers led a group of women, children, and slaves past her and out of the gates. She recognized one as a cook for the Alamo garrison. Rosa blew out a breath of relief that they hadn't been killed along with all the Alamo defenders.

She took a chance and peered over the wall again. A man in an official and lavishly decorated uniform stood near the center of the court with several soldiers gathered around him. Instinct told her it was Santa Anna. Her fingers wrapped around the rifle on the ground next to her as she wished him dead. Sanity returned before she did something that would get her killed, though did it matter if Miles was gone?

That thought had her looking once again for Miles. There were two men wearing buckskins on the ground in front of the chapel, but before she dared an attempt to check them, the officer turned and scowled. She raced out the gates and headed for the front of the breastwork, her stomach once again demanding relief. When finished, she rose and wiped her mouth.

"*Que haces tu allá?*"

She spread her legs and grabbed at the front of her pants in answer to his question about what she was doing. "*Mis necesidades, pronto estare ahí.*"

After making certain her long hair remained hidden under the chacó, she headed to where several men were gathering the wounded and grasped the feet of one while another soldier hefted the torso. They moved him toward the river and laid him alongside many others.

She needed to get away before she was discovered. One of the men had already given her an odd look.

"*Voy a ir por mas vendajes.*"

Before anyone could stop her, she hurried to the bridge and crossed the river. She dashed along the water's edge to the north, refusing to stop for any reason. She made her way to Miles's house. His home was the only connection left to the man she loved. She shoved through the door, collapsed onto a chair, and laid her head on the table. Sobs racked her body as she emptied what was left of her heart.

* * * * *

Miles pushed to his feet. He'd lost track of time, but the sun was now much higher. He needed to get things done, though he knew of only one thing to do next. Beyond that, his choices were few. Trying to make plans for the future was impossible at this point. But as he took time to decide, he also needed to check on Rosa.

Turtle rose next to him. "What now?"

"I'm going to see if my girl is safe. You?"

"I will go see if I approve of your girl."

He tried to smile. The ache in his chest only allowed his lips to twitch. When he'd heard about the death of his parents, the pain to his heart was nearly unbearable. Watching the death of his friends was just as bad, except that this time he was a witness, making the pain run deeper. But if he stayed here much longer, he might do something he'd regret.

He moved forward to take one last glance at the Alamo. What he saw made him pause and stare. The Mexican army was stacking the bodies of the defenders into a pile and layering them with wood, which could only mean one thing. The desire to kill Santa Anna and his men grew until it filled every fiber of his existence.

Turtle moved next to him. "Wait for a better chance to get your revenge."

Miles had never known hate until now. The loathing increased to a taste of bitterness. "I'm going to kill him, Turtle. Santa Anna deserves to die. And I'm going to take out as many of his men as I can."

He stomped away to find his horse. They rode north until he thought it safe enough to head west. They forded the river and rode through the trees until they were close to his hut. They tied the horses at a distance and crept through the woods.

The door was slightly ajar. Miles gave it a push. A Mexican soldier rose from his table. Caught off guard, Miles raised and cocked his rifle. Without time to aim, he fired.

Chapter Thirty-Three

The musket ball hit the soldier in the side, spinning the man away from the table before he dropped to the ground. As soon as Miles had pulled the trigger, he started to reload while keeping an eye on the soldier. When the hat fell off and revealed a long cascade of dark hair, he froze. Then he took a step closer for a better look. It couldn't be. . . .

"Rosa?" Miles dropped to his knees and swallowed hard.

She opened her eyes and pushed away her hair. "Miles! You're alive!" She grasped at her side then glared at him. "You shot me. Why did you shoot me?"

He didn't respond as he examined the hole in the uniform. "Are you hurt?"

She tried to sit up then lay back down. She pulled her hand away to see if there was any blood, but the only blood on her hand was dry. Her eyes went to his. "No, I think I'm just bruised. The musket ball must have gone right through the cloth."

Miles stared at her clothing. Why was she wearing a Mexican uniform? His mind landed on only one answer. All the anger from earlier replaced his shock. He pushed to his feet.

She moved to follow. "Why—"

"Stop."

She obeyed, though her expression revealed her confusion and irritation, much like how he felt. What he saw before him was a traitor. The final, and fatal, knife was thrust into his heart. All the bitterness that had filled him spewed out.

JANELLE MOWERY

"I trusted you. All this time you've been lying."

"No!"

"Be quiet! How can you expect me to believe another word that comes out of your deceptive mouth? Just look at you." As he examined her from head to toe, his tongue soured. Her tears had no effect. "The blood of my friends stains your hands and yet you stand there trying to deny your deceit." He stood in a moment of indecision, but knew he had to leave lest he spew more venom. "I'm sickened at the sight of you."

Completely devastated, Miles left his own house, not knowing if he'd ever return.

"Miles, wait!"

Rosa's angry plea bounced off of him, leaving no impact. He kept walking without looking back. He never wanted to see her again.

* * * * *

Rosa demanded Miles stop. She needed to explain, and she needed him to explain. She started after him but stopped when a terrifying Indian stood in the doorway. A scream froze in her throat.

He jutted his chin. "You hurt my friend. You lost a good man."

Her mind scrambled. Miles knew this man! The fact that they were friends and he'd sided with Miles without hearing her side poured kerosene on her anger. She pointed her finger at him but didn't get any closer though she wanted to get in his face.

"Hold on one minute! I hurt him? He's the one who shot me! And then he didn't even stay around for an explanation after hurling those terrible accusations at me!"

The Indian only stared then shook his head before turning to leave. She started after him, frantic to tell her side of the story. When he stopped, so did she, afraid to get too close.

270

"But I didn't do it. I didn't kill any of his friends." She plucked at the uniform. "I only put this on so I could sneak into the fort to find Miles. . .*after* the battle was over. I give you my word! You've got to tell him!"

As fast as the Indian appeared, he disappeared. She hesitated several seconds then ran out the door. No one was in sight.

"Miles!"

Silence was her answer. Though Miles was alive, he could have just as well been dead, so great was his hate for her.

* * * * *

Hands on his saddle, Miles couldn't climb aboard. His chest was so tight he could hardly breathe. He'd never felt so deceived and betrayed. The depth of disappointment in himself, Rosa, and God, was bottomless.

His parents and most of his friends were dead. Rosa's treachery ended any kind of relationship possible. And with the defeat at the Alamo, he'd never see his land again. There was nothing left. Nothing but seeing to the death of Santa Anna for all the sorrow he'd caused.

Leaves rustled behind him, telling him Turtle had arrived. He didn't know what to say, and his friend remained silent. Birds chirped their merry tune as though nothing had changed, yet everything had. Life would never be the same.

Turtle moved to his horse. Miles could feel his friend's eyes peering into his very soul, waiting for the right moment to speak. Miles made it easier for him.

"Time to move on."

"Where? Goliad?"

"No. I won't fight under a man I don't trust or respect." That left only one other place. "Gonzales. Reinforcements arrived from there, which means they're fighters. I'll join whatever forces are there. But first I want to return to that hill to the east for one last look."

He would let the sight and memory burn an imprint that would last forever, though he knew he'd never forget, whether or not he returned.

Turtle rode up beside him. "Your girl wanted me to give you a message."

"She's not my girl."

"Do you want to hear the message?"

"Not particularly."

Turtle rode in silence a few moments. "Does that mean no?"

"That means no."

They crossed the river and Turtle joined him again. "I think you should hear the message."

"Not now, Turtle. I don't want to hear it right now." He doubted he'd ever want to hear from Rosa again.

By the time they rode the long way around to keep from being seen, the sun had dropped low. Miles dismounted next to the same tree as earlier and walked closer to better view the Alamo, the place he'd grown to love because of what it had represented. Freedom. Independence. Honor. All that was left was the honor he felt. . . at serving with fierce and upright men. . .and the place they now deserved to be honored.

Most of the activity centered around the pile of bodies. A thin stream of smoke quickly turned into a large blaze. His hands became fists at the way those incredible men were being disrespected. He turned away, no longer able to watch such mockery of brave men who'd given their lives for what they believed.

He climbed onto the saddle. "What're your plans, Turtle?"

"I will ride with you most of the way. When I am close to home, we will part ways."

"Good. I'll be glad of the company."

They rode slow and easy. They'd worked their horses much too hard for the last couple of days, and the poor beasts were due a much-needed rest. But the Mexican cavalry had other ideas. Miles heard the thunder of hooves before he spotted the enemy, close to fifty of them, coming toward them at a hard gallop.

Miles hesitated, his hand on his rifle, ready to turn and take out as many of Santa Anna's men as he could.

Turtle reached out and slapped the rump of his horse. "Move!"

They tore off as fast as the horses could run. Miles heard the buzz of a musket ball passing his ear, followed by the boom of the rifle, telling him they were close. More blasts went off. Miles heeled his horse faster, leaning low to help remove even the smallest amount of wind resistance and also to make a smaller target.

Another musket ball hummed past, only this one caught his buckskin cape and part of his sleeve. The force nearly knocked him from the horse. Turtle grabbed his arm and pulled, helping him catch his balance. Miles prayed his horse wouldn't stumble or tire too soon.

Minutes later, the sound of galloping hooves diminished. Miles peeked over his shoulder. The Mexican cavalry had quit the chase. With a cloud of dust surrounding them, the enemy watched as Miles and Turtle made good their escape. Miles reined his horse to a trot as he continually checked over his shoulder then slowed to a walk, glad of the chance both he and his horse could catch their breath.

He glanced at Turtle and smiled. "That was close."

"Too close." He shook his finger. "You must learn to use good sense of when to pick a fight and when to run."

"I know. I'm sorry, Turtle. My desire to kill them overshadowed my good judgment. It won't happen again."

After riding several miles to get far away from any more Mexican scouts, he and Turtle stopped near a stream to make camp. While he started a fire near a fallen tree, Turtle wandered off to round up something to eat. Miles expected him to return with his usual rabbit, but a turkey hung from his hand.

"You must be hungry."

"Like a bear."

Miles had no appetite, but he'd eat to make Turtle happy and to keep up his strength. While Turtle readied the bird, Miles found a stick, green and strong enough to hold the turkey over the fire. Then he went to have a good wash and bring back some water. If only they had coffee to brew in the morning. He had a feeling he'd need something hot and strong.

Hair still dripping, he moved upstream and filled his water skins then returned to the fire to get warm. The water felt cold enough to nurture ice. He sat on the fallen tree and set his rifle next to his feet.

"Smells good."

"Legs and wings will be ready soon."

"That won't be enough for you."

Turtle smiled. "No. But I am patient."

Miles crouched by the fire and held out his hands then rubbed them together before repeating the process. He'd be sleeping close to the heat tonight.

"Your girl said she put on that uniform to get inside the fort to find you."

Miles sighed. "I told you I didn't want to hear it."

"That was hours ago. I thought you might want to hear it now."

"You were wrong."

Turtle turned the bird. "I believe her."

"Then that's your first mistake. Same one I made. I won't make it again."

"Why would she put on that uniform?"

"To kill as many defenders as she could. She'd been digging for information to use against us. Her next step was to pick up a rifle and also use it against us."

Turtle tested a wing. He pulled it off and handed it to Miles. "I think you are wrong."

"Why? How would you know? You just met her. Trust me. She's not worth your confidence."

He jerked off the other wing. "I think you are letting your anger think for you."

Miles took a bite, finished with the conversation. Some people learned after getting bitten once. Miles was a slow learner where Rosa was concerned. He didn't plan to let her get another chance to bite him.

Turtle motioned to the bird. "Leg?"

"No thanks. I'm turning in."

Sleep had been hard to come by since Santa Anna laid siege to the Alamo. He doubted it would be any easier tonight despite the safety and silence.

"Since you will not be sleeping, you can take first watch."

He stared across the fire at Turtle and managed a smile. "You know me much too well, my friend."

Turtle pulled off a leg. "Chew on this to help you stay awake."

He took it then pointed it at Turtle. "One day you'll be wrong, Turtle, and I hope I'll be there to see it."

"Then you admit I am right about the girl."

Miles's mouth dropped open. He clamped it shut when he saw Turtle's smile. "Go to sleep."

"Keep the fire low and do not burn my bird, or you will not eat tomorrow."

Miles reached for his rifle and laid it across his lap. He decided against the blanket, hoping the cold would help him stay awake. With nothing but a crackling fire and cooking bird to keep him company, his mind wandered where he didn't want it to go.

Rosa's smiling face washed through his memory. He probably could have avoided thoughts of Rosa if Turtle would have stopped talking about her. But the shock of seeing her wearing a Mexican infantry uniform would stay with him forever. Not to mention the blood on her hands.

If what Turtle said about donning the uniform just to get inside the Alamo was true, the blood could easily have come from a man on either side of the battle. He would love to know what she saw while inside but would likely never find out. Nor would he ever know for which side she truly fought. The loss at the Alamo would keep him from ever seeing his land again. The best he could hope was that someone in Gonzales was forming an army to go against Santa Anna for his atrocities. If so, he'd join them for the chance to see that evil man dead.

Miles sensed rather than heard someone lurking nearby. He slowly cocked his rifle. The sound alerted Turtle, who tensed and gradually reached for his tomahawk but remained on the ground. As Miles tried to decide if he should dash for the darkness or turn and shoot, not far behind him a saddle creaked followed by the sound of steel against leather.

Chapter Thirty-Four

Rosa had run through the woods searching for any sign of Miles until she was out of breath and exhausted. How did he and that Indian disappear so quickly and quietly? She trudged back to Miles's house, tears wetting her cheeks. Discouragement warred with rage. Sure, she was wearing a uniform of the enemy, so she could almost understand why he pulled the trigger. But he had no right to leave when she actually could have been hurt and he owed her a chance to explain.

If only they could have talked. If only he'd stayed long enough to give them the chance. Her only hope was his Indian friend, but his alliance didn't seem likely. And since the defenders lost the battle, most settlers would never come back for fear of losing their lives, Miles included. She wanted to shake him for being so unfair. But at least he was alive. She could almost forgive him his injustice, because as long as he was alive, they still had a chance. Her immense relief made her feel weak as she fought tears.

She needed to change out of the smelly uniform, yet she'd left her clothing on the other side of the river, and all her other dresses were at Mama's house. With no other choice, she continued on, feeling safe in the borrowed uniform, certain no one would bother her.

She knocked on the door and waited. When the door opened, Mama gasped at the sight of her, even backed away before she recognized her. "What are you doing in that, Rosa? You could get into trouble." She grabbed Rosa's arm and pulled her inside then shut the door. "Why are you wearing that? And why did you run off this morning? I've been so worried." Mama examined her face. "You look terrible."

Rosa ignored the last comment. "When I heard all the shooting before sunrise, I had to know what was happening."

"Why the uniform?"

"It was the only way I could think of to get inside the Alamo to check on Miles."

Mama's mouth dropped open. "Inside. . .?" She stared, her eyes wide. "And? What did you find?"

"I'm not sure you truly care, but he's alive."

"Of course I care." Mama's shoulders slumped. "But how, Rosa? Carlos told me Santa Anna repeated his order of no quarter. No combatant was to live. From what Carlos was told, the men fulfilled that order."

"Well, Santa Anna didn't get his way, not completely." Rosa straightened her shoulders. "You should have seen it. It was awful." A lump swelled in her throat. "I recognized some of those men. Good men. And I didn't see any alive but women, children, slaves, and one of the cooks." She lifted a hand and let it fall. "In any case, I don't know how Miles survived."

Mama frowned. "Then how do you know he's alive?"

She swallowed hard. "I saw him at his house."

"You saw. . .and you didn't ask how he made it out of there?"

Rosa walked past her mother, unable to look at her while she tried to explain. She replayed the scene and crossed her arms in her attempt to ward off more frustration at the man she thought she loved.

"He saw me in this uniform and shot at me."

Mama gasped and rushed to her side. "He shot you?" Her eyes rushed over Rosa's body. "Where? Are you all right?"

"Yes." She showed her mother the hole in the clothing caused by the musket ball.

"But when he saw the blood on my hands, he became very angry. He thinks I was not only a traitor but that I'd been lying to him all along."

"Rosa, no. Surely not."

"Think about it, Mama. I'm sure he'd just seen all his fellow defenders killed, and then he sees this uniform. Why wouldn't he think the worst? And not only that but I gave him good reason to doubt what with all the spying I was forced to do when we met."

"But that was explained."

"I doubt that makes much of a difference after a battle like the one at the Alamo. I wish you and Carlos had seen it, Mama, so you could know how dreadful and appalling that battle truly was. It was the most terrible thing I've ever seen. I wish I could scrub it from my mind."

"You shouldn't have gone."

"I had to know. I love Miles—more than I love or trust anyone else."

Carlos pushed through the door. "Why isn't this door latched?" His entire expression changed when he spotted Rosa. "You're wearing a Mexican uniform. Why? Did you kill one?"

Mama scowled and swatted his arm. "Be quiet, Carlos. You know Rosa well enough not to ask that."

"Obviously he doesn't, Mama. We've been through so much over the past few weeks, and he still doesn't know or trust me at all." She glared at Carlos. "No, I didn't kill anyone, but after seeing what happened at the Alamo today, I wish I would have."

"Then why are you wearing that?"

"I took it off a dead Santa Anna man outside the Alamo so I could get inside and look for Miles."

Carlos's throat worked. "And did you find him?"

Her face heated. "Yes."

She didn't want to explain. He didn't deserve an explanation. All that had happened and then to be accused of killing someone made her feel mean. Let him think Miles was dead.

"He's alive, Carlos." Mama grabbed his arm. "We don't know how he survived, but he's alive."

Rosa was shocked to see Carlos smile. He actually appeared relieved. She would never understand him.

"I've got to get out of this uniform. It stinks. I don't know if I'll ever get this smell out of my skin."

She disappeared behind the curtain only to return a moment later. "Carlos, I saw Mexican officers leading some Alamo survivors outside the wall. Women, children, and slaves. Do you know what happened to them?"

"Sí. Santa Anna interviewed each of them and let them go. He sent some to Gonzales to spread the word of what happened here. He hopes it will put down any further uprisings. End the battles faster by forcing outsiders to leave."

The fact that Carlos still considered her father an outsider made her fume. But least Santa Anna let the civilians live. "Will it work?"

"I doubt it. Like losing the battle here in December made Santa Anna want revenge, I fear word of this bloodbath will only ignite the wrath of the settlers. I believe the fight will go on."

She clenched her teeth and returned to her room, glad the fighting here was over. She'd had enough. If it weren't for the tiny chance of seeing Miles again, she'd leave. But in a quick decision, she'd stay, at least for a time, to see if Miles ever returned. As mad as she was, her love outweighed the anger.

* * * * *

Miles stiffened, prepared to move and fire on their unwelcome visitor.

"I'll share my coffee if you'll share that bird."

Miles turned, squatted, and aimed. "Show yourself."

The man nudged his horse into the firelight. "I mean no harm. Just hungry and tired and in need of some company."

The visitor, old enough to be Miles's father, wore buckskins with leather shoulder straps to hold all his fighting gear. He reminded Miles of Davy Crockett.

"May I dismount?"

"Shed your weapons."

Turtle stood behind Miles, ready to back him up. The man lifted first one leather strap then the other over his head and lowered them to the ground.

"Better?"

Miles gave a nod. "What's your name?"

"Shad McCombs. I'm on my way to help the Alamo defenders." As he dismounted, he motioned to Turtle. "If it weren't for your friend here, I'd 'a thought you'd be doing the same."

Miles returned to his seat on the fallen log, his rifle still ready if needed. "You're too late."

"Too late for what?"

He was in no mood to discuss the battle with a stranger. "The Alamo has fallen. All defenders are dead."

The air left Shad in a gush. The man trudged to the other side of the fire and squatted, holding his hands out for warmth as he stared at the flames. Lines of too many life experiences traced a map on McCombs's face, some made more profound in the flickering firelight.

"When?"

The one-word question came from a voice so filled with pain and grief Miles wondered if Shad knew someone inside the fort.

"Early this morning."

Shad sat quiet, his expression blank, his gaze never leaving the fire. "You were there?"

And there it was. . .the question Miles never wanted to be asked. The question he continually asked of himself. The question that ate at the very core of his heart. Why wasn't he there? He should have been.

"No."

He couldn't get any more out. He'd never get over the shame of not standing at the side of his friends, fighting for their freedom, their independence, for their very lives. His friends deserved more than just a witness.

Turtle relaxed, broke off the last leg of the turkey, and handed it to McCombs before returning to his place on the ground. Shad took the meat with a nod but only stared at it for several long moments before the corner of his mouth twitched.

"And life goes on."

But his voice was dead. He took a bite but didn't appear to enjoy the simple meal even though he finished every morsel. He tossed the bone behind him then aimed his gaze at Miles.

"So what's next?"

A good question, though hard to answer, at least for his future. "Gonzales. I'll see if they're forming a group to go after Santa Anna. If not, I'll keep riding until I find one."

"You want him dead."

"Many times over."

Shad nodded. "Mind if I join you?"

"Not at all." He'd seen what a lack of manpower could do. "You said you had coffee?"

With a smile, Shad moved to his saddle then returned with a bedroll and a small canvas bag, which he tossed to him. Miles started some coffee brewing. As the aroma drifted into the air and started his mouth watering, he eyed Shad.

"You from around here?"

He shrugged. "All over, really."

A vague answer. His father told him more than once to be suspicious of such things. "And you're here because. . . ?"

"Read about the possible battle."

"And you thought you could help?"

McCombs rubbed his hands together. "Didn't figure I could hurt."

"You know someone in there?"

"Knew of. Thought it would be an honor to fight with Crockett."

Miles nodded. It was very much an honor. But he had no intention of telling McCombs that. If he did, he'd also have to confess he hadn't stayed. He poured coffee into two tin cups and handed one to Shad before sipping on his own. He nearly closed his eyes as he savored the brew. It'd been too long.

McCombs made short work of his coffee and tossed the remnants in the dirt. "Appreciate the grub and company, but if you don't mind, I need some sleep."

Miles nodded, and Shad hunkered down. In minutes, loud snores filled the air. Turtle sat up and tilted his head first at their visitor then at Miles.

"You had to let him stay?"

Miles smiled as he shrugged. "It'll help me stay awake."

"You don't want to sleep?"

He motioned to McCombs. "I don't know him yet. I try not to let a snake bite me more than once. Not ever if I can help it."

Turtle blinked. "Next time, find a quieter snake."

Miles eyed McCombs releasing vapors into the air with each exhale and hoped this man wasn't one of Hector's two-headed snakes. . .and a poisonous one at that.

Chapter Thirty-Five

Rosa opened the door only to have Carlos push it closed again. She craned her neck to examine his face. "Why did you do that?"

"You can't go out yet. It's not safe."

She frowned. "The battle is over."

"Yes, but the Mexican forces are still here and no doubt looking for. . .entertainment."

She groaned. "And so I'm still in prison. For how long this time?"

"Until they leave."

"And how long will that take?"

He lifted a shoulder. "My brother didn't sound in any great hurry."

Alarm rushed through her. "Days or weeks?"

"I honestly don't know, Rosa."

Mama finally joined them. "I wasn't happy either when I heard, Rosa. We'll just have to make the most of things until they decide it's time to leave."

Fuming, Rosa dropped onto a chair and crossed her arms. "Men! So quick to pull the trigger with no good reason or explanation afterward. They should let women make the decisions."

Carlos chuckled. "Not a good idea. You're too emotional. Just look at you. I think you'd shoot the next man who happened to cross your path."

Miles's face came to mind. "And he'd probably deserve it."

Carlos sat across from her, arms on the table and fingers clasped. He didn't say a word until she looked at his face.

"Don't be too hard on him, Rosa. I'm sure he had a good reason."

"For shooting me? Hardly."

"No, I think we both know the reason for that. I mean a good reason for leaving without listening to you."

"Not good enough. He has a lot of explaining to do." If he ever came back. And at the moment, she wasn't sure how much she wanted that to happen.

* * * * *

In no hurry to get to Gonzales in order to rest his horse, Miles rode between Turtle and Shad McCombs. They avoided all roads to keep from being spotted by the enemy. After four nights around a campfire, no one felt the need for much talk. When McCombs wasn't trying to get information out of Miles about the Alamo battle, he'd pull out a well-worn book and read. It took a few glances, but Miles finally discovered the book was a Bible. Shad offered it to him more than once, but Miles always declined.

"No thanks. I've read all of that I ever intend to."

His head knew he should dig back into the Word and look for answers to his anger and doubts, but his heart wasn't ready. God had him confused, and to read about His love was more than he could take at the moment.

Miles continued to ignore Shad's indiscreet questions about the battle. He wasn't inclined to tell him, or anyone, anything about the defenders' loss. Besides, he was too tired to think, let alone say anything that would make sense, especially with his emotions in such a jumble.

He couldn't get Rosa off his mind. His anger still simmered, but now his ire was seasoned with doubt. . .and a pinch of guilt. He could still see her wearing that Mexican uniform, making him grit his teeth. Yet, if she truly did only put it on to check on him, he could easily love her more for taking such a huge risk. But was that the case, or had she gotten so practiced in her lies they came quickly and easily?

Turtle reined in his horse. "Time to go our own ways, my friend."

Miles shook his hand. "Thank you for your company and help, Turtle. Say hello to your family for me."

Turtle dipped his head. "I will. You do the same to your girl for me."

With the slightest smile, he turned and rode away. Miles watched several seconds then shook his head and heeled his horse on.

McCombs did the same. "You have a girl? She in Gonzales?"

Miles never looked at him. "I'm not sure if I have a girl or not. Time will tell, I guess."

"You didn't say where."

No, he didn't. He hesitated, wary of more questions. "Béxar."

Shad's brows rose and he whistled. "And you're riding away from there." He cast a look at Miles. "You were at the Alamo."

"Not during the battle."

McCombs paused. "And you feel guilty."

Miles refused to talk about it. They rode in silence a few minutes, all the while McCombs rubbing his hand on his leg. Then his hand became a fist.

"I don't tell many people this, but I used to work on a place up near Chicago, a place next to Indian Creek. My boss, a settler in the area, dammed the creek, which upset some Indians living downstream. They complained the dam wasn't letting the fish get to their village. When my boss refused to dismantle the dam, one of the Indians tried to take care of it himself. He was beaten for his effort."

Miles quickly made the connection. Settlers moving in on territory where the Indians previously lived for years would certainly cause anger, resistance, and most likely uprisings, very much like what had happened in Mexican-owned Texas. He remained silent, allowing McCombs to finish his story at his own pace. He could see the man's jaw working. Several minutes passed before he continued.

"I was gone, went to town the day the Indians decided to get revenge for the assault on their tribe member. I came back to fifteen men, women, and children killed." His voice cracked. "They were mutilated and scalped. Two of the girls were kidnapped." He pounded his fist on his leg. "And I wasn't there to help." He blew out a loud breath. "That was about four years ago, and I still struggle with my feelings." He coughed. "I should have been there."

Shad's words echoed those of Miles's, whose heart stumbled before throbbing with a painful ache. The story was much too close to his own.

Knowing the outcome of the Alamo battle, Miles still wished he would have been at Crockett and Hector's side. "Even if it meant dying with them." It was a statement, not a question. If he had the chance to go back and do it all over again, he'd stay and fight. The guilt was too much to bear.

"I used to feel that way too."

"Sounded like you still do."

"Don't get me wrong. I still hurt every time I think about it. But then I wonder if maybe the reason I wasn't there is because there's still more for me to do. . .that I wasn't supposed to die."

If that's how McCombs made himself feel better, by lying to himself, who was Miles to say otherwise? He wasn't about to say anything to bring back the feeling of guilt to a man who'd been through something so terrible.

They rode into Gonzales and found a sea of disruption. Large groups of men, both militia and volunteers, roamed the streets in a jumble of confusion. Miles tried to spot someone who appeared to be in charge and failed. He shared a look with McCombs, who shook his head.

"Now what?"

Miles glanced around, trying to figure out where they'd get the best information. "Let's ride around a bit, see if anyone looks like they know what's happening."

As they rode down the street, the noise to their right made them turn onto another street then another until they came upon an open plaza filled with hundreds of men. There, they dismounted. Miles walked several feet until he found a group of smartly dressed military men.

"Do you happen to know if someone is putting together a group to fight Santa Anna?"

One of the four men turned and looked him up and down, nodding toward the holes at his shoulder. "You look as though you've already been in battle."

"Ready for one. Is this where I need to be?"

The man's brows folded. "Where'd you get that gunshot?"

"I was chased by some of Santa Anna's cavalry." He stuck his finger in the hole of his buckskins. "It was close, but I outran them. I'm ready for another chance."

With a nod, the man shook his hand. "Colonel Neill just returned from an attempt to reach the Alamo. He and his men were also chased away. He's in the process of organizing all the men willing to fight into a unified military force. Stay close and you can be a part of it."

Colonel Neill. That was good news to Miles. He liked the man and wouldn't mind fighting for him.

"Thank you." He turned to McCombs. "Let's see if we can find something to eat besides rabbit."

"You want good food?" The man they'd been talking to stopped them and pointed. "Turn left on that street right there, ride west a couple more streets, and then turn north. There's a hotel there that serves the best food I've had in a long time. Might have to wait for a table."

That sounded great to Miles. He nodded. "Thanks."

He led his horse down the street as McCombs followed. Once he made it to a clear area, he climbed onto his saddle and rode to the hotel. Just as the army man had warned, a group of men lingered outside the door. Miles considered riding on, but the incredible scent drifting from the building made him dismount. Sitting at a table instead of hunkered on the ground was too appealing to resist. He tied his horse and slid his rifle from its sheath.

After a short wait, he and McCombs were seated at the far side of the room with two other men. They didn't get to order. The waitress returned a few minutes after seating them with a plate of food. McCombs raised his brows.

The waitress mimicked his raised brows then added a snarl. "Look, mister, we're busy. No time for special orders. This is what you get. You want it or not?"

McCombs smiled and tapped the table. "Absolutely. Thank you."

Miles and McCombs exchanged a look as they grabbed their forks. "With service like that, the food must be excellent."

They tucked into the roast beef, potatoes, beans, and bread like they hadn't eaten in weeks. As told, the food was wonderful, and the line extending outside promised a booming business for a long time to come.

McCombs dropped his fork onto his empty plate and rubbed his belly. "Any cows in the area had better run at a stampede if they want to live. You ready to go? Those men out there look like they're ready to escort us out and won't be all that nice about it."

"Sure. We can camp near the river tonight. I doubt there's a room to be had anywhere in town."

After paying the waitress, they made their way outside to retrieve their horses. Before Miles mounted, commotion in front of the hotel made him glance back. Colonel Neill stood in the doorway surrounded by several of his men. For a second, their eyes met. As Neill craned his neck, Miles took a step toward him. The next second, Neill's men swept him inside the hotel.

Miles stood in indecision. He could try to make his way inside and ask to see Neill, knowing what he told the colonel wouldn't change a thing. Or he could stay in the background, bide his time, follow Neill to Santa Anna, and fulfill his goal.

"You going back in for another plate?"

Miles shook his head as he climbed onto the saddle and headed west toward the Guadalupe River. "No. I'm ready for a rest."

"You mean actually sleep?"

"I sleep."

McCombs squinted. "That's why your eyes are red with black smudges below, huh?"

"I get enough."

"You better figure out how to get more, Fitch. I've been where you are. It only gets worse if you don't deal with the guilt."

Miles nodded. Oh, he knew how to deal with the rage that kept him awake nights. He'd sleep fine after Santa Anna was dead.

Chapter Thirty-Six

The buzz of excited voices raced along the river. In minutes, men either ran toward town or were saddling their horses to ride. Miles stopped one man running past them.

"What's all the talk about?"

"General Sam Houston is in town. There's talk he plans to get everyone ready to fight Santa Anna."

Miles took his time getting his horse saddled. McCombs nearly tapped his foot waiting for him.

"What's taking you so long? I figured you'd be one of the first in line."

He'd been hiding it well, but Miles was anything but patient. All this waiting around for something to happen was eating at his gut. But every perfect plan took patience and time.

"If Houston just got into town, there's no way he has all his plans together yet. In fact, I'll be surprised if he's ready any time tomorrow. If he's wise, he'll gather all the information he can, then make his decisions. If he's ready tomorrow, I'd be hesitant to follow him."

McCombs eyed him. "You sound like a man who's been through this before."

"Maybe."

"You really don't want to talk about what happened back at the Alamo, do you?"

Miles mounted, his lips clamped tight. "We can spend the day in town, see what's happening. But I'm not expecting much."

The day dragged on with very little action or information until two Mexicans arrived at dark with the news that the Alamo had fallen. Houston demanded everyone remain calm, that he'd arrested the men until their declaration could be confirmed.

McCombs leaned against a building next to Miles. "You could have confirmed that story. Why didn't you?"

"Do you really think they'd believe me any more than those two men?"

"Maybe not, but you could have tried."

"I don't want to spend the night behind bars. The hard ground is better than bars."

They camped out at the river again. McCombs sat close to the fire, straining to read from his Bible. One of the men camping near them scooted closer.

"Read it out loud. I'd like to hear something nice for a change. Something from the Good Book."

The man got comfortable by leaning his head on a saddle and pulling a blanket over his chest.

McCombs flipped the page. "Blessed is the man that walketh not in the counsel of the ungodly, nor standeth in the way of sinners, nor sitteth in the seat of the scornful. But his delight is in the law of the Lord; and in his law doth he meditate day and night."

As Shad's voice droned on, Miles tossed the rest of his coffee onto the ground, placed the cup back in his pack, and dropped onto the ground. He hoped he could shut out the noise in order to get some rest. He wanted to move closer to the fire for the warmth, but doing so meant hearing every one of Shad's words.

"That was nice." Their neighbor rolled to his side to face McCombs. "Would you read Psalm twenty-three? It's one of my favorite passages."

McCombs smiled and nodded. "Sure thing."

Miles could hear Shad turning the pages and knew there was no way to drown out what he was about to read. Maybe for the first time since Santa Anna showed up in Béxar, he could fall asleep fast instead of thinking through the day. . .or the battle.

"The Lord is my shepherd; I shall not want. He maketh me to lie down in green pastures: he leadeth me beside the still waters. He restoreth my soul: he leadeth me in the paths of righteousness for his name's sake. Yea, though I walk through the valley of the shadow of death, I will fear no evil: for thou art with me; thy rod and thy staff they comfort me. Thou preparest a table before me in the presence of mine enemies; thou anointest my head with oil; my cup runneth over. Surely goodness and mercy shall follow me all the days of my life: and I will dwell in the house of the LORD for ever."

Snores from several men punctuated the air. McCombs had read them to sleep. With good reason. It promised provision and protection, something the men needed to hear, to believe in with all their hearts. Miles remembered his parents reading that same passage many times before turning in for the night. How could one not trust a God who promised to guard and shelter His people? Except that He didn't. At least not the men in the Alamo.

McCombs tucked his Bible back into his bag and climbed under his blanket. In minutes, his snores joined the others. Miles lay awake, replaying the words he knew well.

"*Though I walk through the valley of the shadow of death, I will fear no evil.*"

Miles had missed the shadow of death, though he'd seen more than enough of death and destruction to last him several lifetimes. But he was determined not to fear the evil of Santa Anna. He'd gladly face that evil and bring it to an end, if only God would give him the chance.

He didn't know when he'd actually fallen asleep, but he woke feeling just as exhausted as when he'd called it a night. He shared some coffee with McCombs and a few other men then headed back to town.

The day was a repeat of the first, slow and long. They were about to return to the river when a crowd rushed through town, all surrounding a woman carrying a child being protected by army scouts. They took her directly to where Sam Houston stayed.

Miles trailed behind, hoping to get a look at the woman. He got his wish when she stood in the light of an open door before being led inside. He would have loved a moment with her, if only to find out what she saw the morning of that awful battle.

"You know her?"

"No."

McCombs snorted. "You really need to work on your penchant to talk too much."

Miles took a deep breath. "I've seen her before, but I don't know her."

"That's better, and I bet it didn't hurt a bit."

Miles eyed the man then shook his head. "Time to get some rest. I have a feeling things will be picking up soon."

"You sure are a puzzle, Fitch. Promise me something. When you finally feel like talking, let me be there."

"Not much to tell."

"I doubt that, but then I'm a patient man. I can wait."

After a restless night, Miles and McCombs returned to town accompanied by wails and moans of women consoling each other along the streets. Miles understood. He'd felt much the same as he watched his fellow defenders fall. The women's cries and shrieks were like knives in his heart and gut.

"What happened?" McCombs craned his neck, taking in the scene of all the sobbing women.

"You remember me telling you we received reinforcements

from here? I would imagine word is out that all the Alamo defenders are dead."

McCombs blew out a loud breath. "Oh Lord, please pacify these poor hurting souls."

All the soldiers mustered in the open plaza. Miles dismounted, waiting to see if they were about to receive orders. Though he hadn't formally signed on yet, he fully intended to be with these men as they went up against Santa Anna. He'd even take the lead if possible, anything to be the one who put a musket ball in that evil man's black heart.

A handful of volunteers to his right murmured about fighting a battle that wasn't theirs.

"I ain't giving up my life like those at the Alamo. They were outnumbered just as we are, and look what happened to them."

Another in the group snorted. "If you're that scared, Bert, skedaddle. I sure don't want you running over top of me as you retreat in fear."

"I ain't afraid. I just don't want to die for a cause that ain't mine. Surely I ain't the only one who feels like this." He looked around and pinned Miles with his gaze. "How about you. You're young. I can't believe you'd risk your life for this piece of land when you got a whole lot more living to do."

Miles took the bait, ready to help this man and any others see what the battle was all about. "It's not for just a piece of land, though I'd like to get mine back. This fight is for freedom and independence and the right of choice. Those men at the Alamo knew that and gave their life for the promise of the liberty to live life as they chose. I'm honored to take up their cause and make it my own. I don't want to die, but I'll give up my life if it means protecting my country and countrymen."

While some of the men around him applauded or nodded, others still sided with the first man, looking at Miles as though he'd lost his mind.

McCombs moved closer and leaned on the post near them. "Heavens, Fitch. When you decide to speak, you roll out the words like precious gems. Very well said." McCombs set the stock of his rifle on the ground and gripped the barrel with both hands. "But there's something I don't understand. Maybe you can help me out." He turned slightly to better see Miles. "You're ready to take up the cause of the men at the Alamo and possibly even die during the fight, yet I've got to wonder if you're fighting for the right reason."

The right reason? What better reason than to avenge the deaths of his parents and his friends? "What do you mean? I just explained why I was fighting."

"I think you explained what you want to be the reason you'll go to battle, but is it the truth, or is there more behind it?"

"I don't know what you're asking, McCombs."

"I think you do. I think you went to the Alamo for the very reason you just gave, but now, after all your friends died, you have a very different reason. I can see it in you, Miles. You have an anger, a hate, boiling inside you and you want to put the fire out."

"Who wouldn't be angry? Those men didn't have to die."

"I see." McCombs looked off into the distance and paused for a long moment. "And if you go to battle for the wrong reason and win, in the end, are you really free? Will you truly have the freedom you fought for?"

Miles's back went ramrod straight. "Are you telling me not to fight?"

"Not at all. I just want you to be honest about why you're fighting." He clapped Miles on the shoulder. "I'm not admonishing you, Miles. I just want to caution you to think about the real reason you're continuing this battle. If it's for the wrong one, you haven't won a thing, and the peace that you're seeking will never be found."

McCombs left him then and checked his horse's gear. Miles knew it was to allow him time to think about what he'd said, but all it did was make him fume that McCombs doubted his sincerity.

As some men continued chatting about possible plans of action, others mounted their horses and rode away. Miles doubted he'd see some of them again. He understood the fear but not to the point of running.

"I've got to get my family away from here. I've no doubt Santa Anna's men will be on their way at some point."

The man left at a run. Once again, Miles had to berate himself for judging too quickly and harshly. Maybe McCombs was right. Maybe some self-examination was in order.

"Let me have your attention, please."

General Houston stood in the bed of a wagon. The men all made their way to him until it appeared he floated on a sea of humans. Houston raised his hand, and they all fell silent.

"Thank you. By now I'm certain everyone has heard what happened at the Alamo. I ask that you pray for the families of those brave men." He took a few moments of silence then looked around at the crowd. "I want everyone to get prepared to evacuate. By tonight, we'll be packed up and moving east. We want to help move all the women and children to a place of safety."

As Houston made his way back to where he stayed, the words *scared* and *retreat* followed him as several of the men disagreed with his decision. Thunder rumbled around them as if in agreement.

Miles didn't say a word. He didn't have anything to pack up, and he wasn't certain Houston's decision to leave was the best course of action. Granted, from what he'd seen, Gonzales was filled with women and children, and they wouldn't be safe if a battle took place in the town. After a few more minutes of thought, he decided Houston knew more about the situation than anyone and was making the wisest decision. He probably knew of a better place to fight.

As rain started to fall, Miles decided that, for now, he'd trust Houston's leadership. But at some point, he'd also better be ready to turn and fight.

Chapter Thirty-Seven

"I've been sitting here with so much time to think, Mama. Too much time. And still, I don't know what to think."

Rosa sat at the table wiping an area that was already spotless. With nothing to do when Carlos wasn't around to escort them through town, the house had almost been turned inside out from too much cleaning. They'd sewn every spare piece of cloth they could find into a quilt. All that was left was their own clothing, and they'd grown desperate enough to consider using their dresses.

"You're not saying anything, Mama. I've got to get out of here or go mad. When will Santa Anna and his men leave? They got what they wanted. They won. Why aren't they moving on to the next town?"

As soon as Rosa said the words, she wanted to take them back. In no way did she want anyone else to endure what their town had gone through. But she wanted the Mexican forces gone so she could get on with life, whatever that life might be now.

Her mother remained silent as she entered her bedroom and returned with a book in her hands. She laid the Bible in front of Rosa.

"Read, Rosa. It always helped your father."

Read. And just how did her mother think she'd be able to concentrate enough to read when all she could see was Miles's face, hear his voice, and think only of him, though she'd tried to scrub him from her mind?

"Start in the Psalms. Your father always found those passages soothing."

Rosa laid her hands on the cover as she recalled how her father would sit outside in the fading light of day and read to her. And if she begged for more, they'd move inside and he'd try to read by lantern light until he complained his eyes were too tired. Her father loved his Father and showed it in his everyday life, in everything he did and said. In all that had happened in the last few weeks, and especially the last week, Rosa had let her faith slide into the background. As she'd just confessed, Miles and the battle, the one at the Alamo and the one between her and her relationships, had been her focus.

Her father had always told her that if she put the Lord first, everything else fell into its proper place. It was past time to put that advice into practice. After a quick prayer asking for forgiveness and understanding of what she was about to read, Rosa opened God's Word and began to read.

* * * * *

In the dead of night, with a light but steady rain falling, Sam Houston led his troops, the volunteers, and Gonzales residents out of town. They headed eastward. Away from Santa Anna. Away from any confrontation with Mexican forces.

Miles sat atop his horse at the edge of town as streams of people moved past him. Some drove wagons or carts filled with belongings. Others were on horseback or on foot, all toting whatever they could carry. Children, some crying, clung to their mothers. Miles couldn't tell because of the rain, but he had no doubt some of the mothers were also crying as they left their homes, and probably many precious possessions, behind.

Beside him, McCombs tipped his hat in order to get the water to run off the back. "You gonna sit here all night?"

"No, but I am planning to ride in back in case any of these people need help. With this rain, any of the wagons could get stuck or lose a wheel. Or any of these on foot might not be able to go on."

"Noble. I thought we'd ride near the front in order to learn of any upcoming plans. I could learn a lot from you, Fitch. Guess I'll hang back and see if I can learn more."

"Right. I think you're the one wanting to do the teaching."

McCombs chuckled. "And astute. I'm glad I ran across you, Fitch. You make life interesting."

Miles shook his head and was about to heel his horse to follow the townspeople when flames caught his attention. One by one, from north to south, every house and business was set on fire.

A soldier riding by stopped and followed their gaze. "Houston's orders. He wanted the entire town torched so none of Santa Anna's men would have any shelter or place to lay their heads. I understand and agree, but that sure is a hard thing to see. The residents will have nothing to come back to."

As the soldier rode off at a gallop, Miles continued watching the flames increase. He hoped the families would get to come back, but with the way things were going, doubts haunted him. He'd seen this before. His own parents were killed for their land, and Miles had no idea if the small cabin he and his father built still stood. He'd even done just what the men in Gonzales were doing now. He'd burned the houses outside the Alamo just to keep Santa Anna's men from having places to hide, leaving many people homeless. As sadness filled him, the sight before him added fuel to his desire to see this battle all the way to the end.

Between the rain and lack of wagons or animals to pull them, progress was slow. More and more settlers joined them while others still deserted the group. Day after day, Miles and McCombs spent their time helping women, children, sometimes whole families, cross swollen streams or pull carts from mud holes. His heart hurt for them. Though the upcoming battle was just as much for them as it was for himself and all families who had yet to move west, these help-less refugees had no choice but to run.

Children clamored around him and McCombs, begging for rides, more for fun than necessity. Off and on, they'd scoop them up to ride for a short time then get back to work trying to keep the march moving.

At the Colorado River, they caught up with Houston's army, who helped all civilians cross. As Miles tried to leave, one little boy hol-lered his name and waved. Next to him was the little girl who'd stolen his heart. She ran up to him with her arms out. He leaned down and pulled her onto his lap. Her long dark curls and brown eyes reminded him of a miniature version of Rosa. The little girl wrapped her arms around his neck and placed a warm, wet kiss on his cheek, leaving both a hug and scar on his heart.

After saying goodbye to the children he'd grown to know and love over the last five days, Miles followed the army and McCombs to where they set up camp several miles downriver. For the first time since the fall of the Alamo, he had the feeling they were getting closer to the fight against Santa Anna.

He found McCombs near some trees and dismounted. The ground felt good after another long day in the saddle.

"I'd begun to wonder if you'd decided to stay back there with those children. I think they love you as much as you love them."

"It's my horse they love." He loosened the cinches then pulled off the saddle. "I think I love him more now too since I don't have to walk." He motioned with his head toward the soldiers without mounts. "One has to wonder how much longer their boots will last."

Miles removed a filthy piece of cloth from his pack and rubbed down his horse. He also checked each hoof to make sure he didn't end up on foot from not taking care of his mount. He led his horse to a patch of grass and ground tied him. When he returned to McCombs, his partner handed him a piece of dried beef.

"Where'd you get this?"

"Houston's officers sent a couple of men to a nearby town for food." He shrugged. "Not much to be found, from what I heard. I managed to wrangle us a few bites. I guess they consider us and all the other volunteers part of the troops."

Miles chuckled. "I'd imagine you'd be able to talk a bear out of his honey."

"Only if I had a hankering for sweets." He gnawed off another piece of beef. "What do you think of this Houston fella?"

Miles bit off a chunk of meat and chewed while he thought on his answer. He swallowed. "I'm not sure yet. I've been so busy helping those women and children, I haven't had much of a chance to watch him."

"Watching him helps you decide?"

"Couldn't hurt. You can tell a lot about a man by watching his actions and reactions."

"Yeah, I've noticed."

Miles eyed him, knowing exactly who he meant. "And what have you decided?"

"You've got a lot of love for people inside of you, but until you get rid of that huge lump of hate, you won't be free to truly love."

Miles shook his head. "You learned all that in just over a week?"

"That was the easy part. The hard part is trying to figure out exactly who you hate. Or more precisely, who you hate most."

Miles wanted to deny he hated anyone, but he didn't want to lie too. He thought if he didn't answer, maybe McCombs would drop the subject.

"I figure there's three choices."

Miles leaned his head against the tree and closed his eyes. His silence didn't work. Maybe pretending to sleep would.

"There's Santa Anna. He was the obvious one. Then there's God. I figured that one out when you refused to read His Word or listen to me reading it." McCombs paused. "You want to hear my third choice? It's you."

Miles opened his eyes and stared at McCombs. "Me? You think I hate myself?"

"Don't you?" McCombs chewed on his beef awhile. "So, of those three, put them in order for me. Which one are you most mad at?"

"That's easy. Santa Anna."

"Are you sure? What about you?"

"What about me?"

McCombs took a deep breath and let it out slowly, as if trying to decide what to say or whether to say it. "You've never come right out and said it, but you were in the Alamo, weren't you? Not during the battle, but before, when you got to know some of the men. Then somehow, for some reason, you left and missed the battle. And because you weren't there to fight with your friends, you can't forgive yourself. You feel like you should have died with them. And in a way, you have. At least a part of you has. I know, because I've been there."

Each of Shad's words was like a bayonet of accusation to his heart. He'd tried to convince himself it wasn't true, but deep down, every word he spoke was right on target.

His throat tightened. "You're right. I was there, and I should have been there that morning." He blew out a breath. "I was sent to Goliad for reinforcements. I didn't get any reinforcements, and I didn't make it back in time to get inside. Instead, I watched from a hill as all my friends were killed." He swallowed hard. "I should have been there." Just revisiting that morning made him relive it again along with all the pain. "I feel like the only way to redeem myself is to make sure Santa Anna dies."

"It'll help, but it won't get rid of all the guilt you're feeling. The only way to do that is to forgive yourself, even though you didn't do anything wrong."

"I shouldn't have left."

"You were following orders."

Shad's attempt at consolation didn't help because Miles was alive and his friends were dead.

"Have you asked yourself why you're alive?"

Miles snorted. "I'm alive because I wasn't there for them. I just told you that."

"Go deeper than that, Miles. Don't you think God wants you alive for a bigger reason?"

"Like for some sort of punishment? First I lost my parents, then my land, and now my friends." Not to mention Rosa. "How much more am I supposed to hurt? My father always said God gives and He takes away. Well, He's definitely proven that. His Word says He's a God of love who cares for His people, but from where I'm standing, that's becoming much harder to believe."

"You can say that after all He's done for us? Our Lord suffered more than we could ever understand. He left heaven to endure all the same things we have to, and to top it off, He was scorned, spat on, beaten to within breaths of losing His life, and then gave it up on the cross so we could have life, all out of love for us."

Miles was properly ashamed. He'd been taught all of that since he was old enough to understand. But the moment he was hurting, he forgot and blamed God for everything.

"You're right. I know that. But it's still hard to understand why God puts those He loves through so much pain."

"I know what you mean. But have you ever read about Job?"

"Yeah."

Job. He remembered his mother and father taking turns reading that book to him. Most times, it put him to sleep. But the last few chapters kept his attention. God called Job righteous then allowed Satan to test him. After losing everything, including his health, Job questioned why he was being punished. God finally answered by asking Job where he was when the world and everything in it was created.

"Job learned God was sovereign and was to be completely trusted. But that one request sure is difficult."

"Ain't it though?" McCombs tipped his head back, resting it against the tree trunk. "Seems to be one of the toughest things to learn. For me, anyway. After those Indians killed almost everyone on that settlement, hate for them grew until it filled every part of me. Killing those Indians was all I could think about."

Miles knew that feeling all too well. "What'd you do?"

"I fell in with a group of men who planned to go after some Indians. There were twenty or thirty of us. We cornered about a dozen of them at a bend in a river." McCombs paused as he voice thickened. He coughed and spat. "We didn't just kill them. We scalped them too."

"Sweet revenge."

"You'd think so, wouldn't you?" He stuffed the rest of his dried beef in a pocket then clasped his fingers together. "I couldn't get the picture out of my head. Still can't. What's worse, I don't even know if those Indians were a part of the bunch who killed my friends. I just wanted to kill some of them, give some retribution. But I learned vengeance isn't all I thought it would be. It ate at me worse than losing my friends." He rubbed his hands together as though trying to rid them of the blood he'd shed. "I guess there's a reason the Good Book says to never take our own revenge but to leave room for God's wrath. Took a long time to forgive myself for that."

"Sounds like it still eats at you."

"I'll never forget. Can't forget. The picture will remain with me forever. I think it's our discipline for our bad choices. But I can let the Lord work on my heart. Heal it of my wrongdoing. That's another choice."

Miles didn't respond, couldn't respond. The life of Shad McCombs so mirrored his own, what he was going through right now, the similarity was almost scary. And he was fairly certain the reason Shad told him that story was so he wouldn't go after Santa Anna for the wrong reason and then have to deal with the guilt afterward. Miles appreciated the thought and would have to do some thinking of his own. . .because he still wanted Santa Anna dead, and he'd love to be the one to do the killing.

Chapter Thirty-Eight

Rosa wandered the streets of Béxar in amazement. This was the same place it was mere weeks ago, yet it was completely different. Santa Anna and his men had set off for their next battle the day before. What they'd left behind was chaos and refuse.

Gone were over half the people who used to live here. After weeks of bombing and shooting and then another two weeks of thousands of military men wandering around, the silence now surrounding her was somewhat eerie. Would the town ever get back to normal, or was this all that was left now and in the future? Time would tell, but would she still be here to get her answer? This may be where she'd lived, but she wasn't sure she could call it home any longer. She'd managed to make some decisions, while others still waited for answers. In time, those would also come, some depending on whether or not Miles ever returned and his answers to her questions. Either way, there was a very good chance she and Mama would be saying their good-byes.

Carlos and Mama trailed her by several yards. They wanted to allow her some time alone but still weren't sure the town was completely safe. From what Rosa could see, there weren't enough people in town to cause any trouble. She missed the children running along the streets playing their games or chasing a puppy. No longer were there any vendors plying their wares to those passing by. Were there even enough residents to allow Carlos to make a living?

"Rosa!"

At her name being called, she stopped and turned. Ana waved as she rushed toward her. Rosa cringed. She hadn't seen Ana in weeks. At the sight of her, the vision of John lying dead at the Alamo returned, as did her annoyance toward Ana for using him. She tried to crush that feeling. Since she started reading the Bible, she'd been praying for tolerance and understanding toward those who'd deceived her. She had to forgive, and that came hard.

Ana stopped just short of giving her a hug. Her expression probably mirrored that of Rosa's.

"What's wrong?"

Rosa shook her head and motioned around her. "This place is empty, Ana. Look at it. It's sad."

"But it's finally over."

She looked around her again. "Yes, but at what expense? The whole battle seems like a waste. Did it really solve anything?"

"We got our land back."

"But no one's here to live in it." She shrugged. "I don't know, Ana. I feel as empty as this town." She hesitated but felt the need to say what was on her mind. "John is dead."

Ana had the grace to look down. She nodded. "I figured. My father told me Santa Anna stayed with his order of no quarter, which means you lost Miles too. I know how you felt about him. I'm sorry, Rosa."

Rosa didn't feel like correcting Ana's wrong assumption. She didn't want to have to explain any part of how he was alive, especially since she didn't have the answers. She remained silent.

Ana looked toward the Alamo. "I was upset to hear he ordered all the bodies burned."

Rosa hadn't heard about that order. Tears sprang to her eyes. The news added more weight to her heart. She needed to be alone.

She touched Ana's arm. "I'm sorry, Ana. I know we haven't seen each other in a while, but I need some time by myself. This just hurts too much."

With no idea where she was going or any regard for safety, Rosa walked away from Ana, Mama, and Carlos as fast as she could.

* * * * *

Now on foot, Miles trudged with the rest of the growing army. Because of lack of feed and poor grazing, Houston gave the order that the only horses allowed to continue with them were those used for packing supplies. Miles refused to give up his horse. He was the last thing Miles had left of his parents' possessions, so it now carried provisions for the men.

More and more troops were joining Houston's forces. The growing army raised everyone's spirits, right up until they received the news that Fannin and his men had been captured by a portion of the Mexican army.

Miles exchanged a look with McCombs. "That could have been me."

Shad nodded. "Looks to me like you have much to be thankful for. You escaped capture by leaving Fannin, and you escaped death by not being in the Alamo. That's a pretty small gap."

Only hours after Houston ordered one of the crossings to be burned, word quickly spread through the troops that some Mexican forces weren't too far away, just on the other side of the Colorado River. Miles's heart pounded. The time had come to fight, and he'd never been more ready. When Houston's order to continue retreating reached him, disappointment warred with anger. By the sound of all the murmuring, many of the men fought the same emotions.

Day after day, the retreat continued until some of the men started talking mutiny. Miles understood. He was ready to fight, be done with the battle. He was tired of walking and running away. Yet he'd been watching Houston. The man seemed completely aware of their surroundings, as though constantly measuring the benefit or detriment of the environment as a battleground. Miles began to look at Houston and the areas they passed in a new light and appreciated the general's wise strategy.

After leaving two groups of men behind to take up defensive positions, Houston led the army several miles up the Brazos River, crossed, and set up camp. Miles was glad of the rest, but the respite didn't last long. Houston ordered his army to drill in preparation for the upcoming battle. Any protest they might have made ended when word arrived that the men captured at Goliad had been slaughtered. The men trained all the harder.

During twelve days of drilling, several hundred more men arrived along with two cannons. For the first time, Miles felt confident they'd win the next battle. Not only did they have more men, but they were now more orderly, thanks to the calming hand of a good leader. Miles rubbed the stock of his rifle, eager for the fight to begin.

Then came the order to move on, but there was little complaining. Miles had the feeling all the men had begun to feel the same confidence in their leader. Two days later, the thought was confirmed when Houston led them down the road that would take them to the long-awaited confrontation with Santa Anna. The men's footsteps came a little faster, more sure and energetic.

After two more days of marching, they set up camp near Harrisburg. A buzz sped through the men about the capture of a Mexican courier who confirmed Santa Anna's presence and number of troops. Miles and McCombs exchanged a glance and smile. They were close, and Miles's excitement soared.

For the next two days, they marched with very little rest. At a wooded ridge overlooking a prairie near San Jacinto, Houston ordered them to set up camp. Mere hours later, Santa Anna and his army arrived. A line of the Mexican army formed and advanced on the Texian army with a cannon in tow. They fired several times on the camp. Houston ordered one of his officers to attempt to capture the cannon. The Mexican force retreated, taking the cannon with them, and the brief fight ended.

Miles enjoyed the encounter because Santa Anna had to retreat. To him, it was just a small taste of what he was sure would come.

He stood on the ridge and watched the Mexican army work to put up a breastwork of supplies and equipment in preparation of a battle. He examined the field before him and the position Santa Anna chose to camp. Beyond Santa Anna lay a marsh and a lake. A retreat would be difficult for the general and his men. They'd have to stand and fight or get bogged down in the water, in which case they'd be as easy to pick off as wounded turkeys.

He stared at the uniforms. He hadn't seen them since the Alamo fell. And he saw one up close when Rosa wore one in his home. That day came back to him with the force of a cannonball in his gut. He'd shot the woman he loved and walked away. He more than believed the message Turtle passed along from Rosa. All the days on the trail gave him plenty of time to think, to mull over their time together. Her very nature, the one she'd proven over and over, demanded he accept the truth. She had risked her life and donned the uniform for him. . .to see if he'd survived the battle. That fact made him love her all the more.

The ache in his stomach moved to his heart as he admitted he still loved her with every ounce of blood in him. Her face, her teasing smile, came easily to his mind, and the desire to hold her again made him long to be home. But the biggest question remained. . .would she have him? The venom he spewed at her had likely poisoned her against him. He had only himself to blame if he ended up living without the woman who would fill his life with love and happiness.

A twig snapped behind him. He didn't need to turn to know McCombs had joined him.

"So, what do ya think? Can we win this fight?"

Miles reached up and plucked a leaf from a branch of the oak tree hanging over him. "I think so. In fact, I'm sure of it. Of all the places we've camped on the way here, this is the most promising. Look at the landscape. There's very little room for him to retreat, and we have plenty of men to face him."

"I agree. And if Houston uses good timing, we could have the element of surprise."

"Yeah, like when Santa Anna chose early morning to attack the Alamo. A time when the men were probably least prepared."

"You sound ready."

"More than. I've been waiting for this for far too long."

McCombs clapped him on the shoulder and shook his hand. "I'm glad I met up with you, Fitch. I've enjoyed getting to know you. Maybe when this is all over, I can take a trip to the Alamo. You've given me the desire to show honor to the men who fought there."

"We'll ride there together. I'm ready to get back."

"To see your girl?"

Miles peeled his hat from his head and thumped it against his leg. "I pray she'll have me, Shad, but I don't deserve her."

"If she's half the woman I think she is, she'll see past your mistakes and focus on the man you are."

"I hope you're right."

The two made their way back to camp. Men everywhere cleaned and oiled their rifles, looking ragged and ferocious with shaggy beards and filthy clothing from over a month of marching eastward. Miles joined them to get ready. "So this is it, then. This is where we'll fight."

The man next to him spat on his barrel and wiped again. "Looks like. It's about time."

Everyone around them mumbled and nodded in agreement. Miles doubted anyone would sleep tonight. Between Santa Anna camping so close and the excitement of imminent battle, he expected the most they'd get was short slumbers.

As dawn arrived, the morning air was filled with the mouth-watering scent of bread and roasting beef. The men were allowed to eat their fill, as though Houston wanted their bodies reinforced to fight. Miles enjoyed every bite. Too many times he'd slept with an empty belly.

Once he'd finished his meal, he pulled out his rifle and checked to make sure it was in good working order.

"I thought you checked that yesterday."

McCombs sat next to him and examined his own gun.

"Just needed something to do. I wonder what Houston is waiting for."

"Like you said. . .the most appropriate moment. Take a deep breath, Fitch. We're almost there."

Midway through the afternoon, the order came to take up arms. Miles instantly broke out in a sweat. Under the command of Juan Seguin, he lined up with hundreds of other men to Houston's left and waited for the order to attack. And for the first time since the Alamo massacre, he sent a plea to his heavenly Father for forgiveness, strength, and protection.

Chapter Thirty-Nine

Heart pounding, Miles crept through the knee-high grass across the plain. What appeared to be such a short span from their camp now felt like miles as they moved in a crouch. Hundreds of men were doing the same thing, and it amazed him how so many could move so quietly at such a fast pace. From what he could see, none of Santa Anna's men had spotted them. Their campground was peaceful.

Around fifty yards from the Mexican breastwork, the order was given to attack. The two small cannons that had been pulled to the front blasted their rounds into the enemy's barricade. To the shouts of "Remember the Alamo!" and "Remember Goliad!" the entire army ran to within yards of the surprised enemy, and the first shots were fired. Santa Anna's camp sprang to life.

Miles stopped, took aim, and pulled the trigger. His man dropped. He reloaded and fired again. Santa Anna's men were falling all around the camp. Some picked up rifles while others fled toward the marsh. Miles quickly reloaded and raced over the breastwork.

Pain tore along his thigh, spinning him around. He paid it little heed and instead looked for the man who shot him. One stood reloading his weapon. Miles took aim and added another man to his tally. He loaded his rifle once again and ran after those trying to get away.

Houston's forces, who'd been waiting weeks for this moment, hollered as they raced after those retreating. Once they caught up to them, they beat the enemy with pistols or swung their rifles like clubs in a frenzy of rage that had built up for over a month.

Miles fired one last time then chased after more men with his knife, slicing and stabbing as he went along. One man slashed at him with his bayonet, leaving a gash in Miles's upper arm and shoulder. He spun around with his rifle and laid the stock upside the man's head and followed up with his knife blade into the man's belly. He grabbed the man's bayonet to make sure he wouldn't get up again. After pulling out the man's pistol and tucking it into his belt, Miles tore after more of the enemy, purging himself of the wrath he'd stored up since the Alamo massacre.

Hundreds of Santa Anna's men lay on the ground dead or dying. Miles ran past them, focused on looking for their leader as he continued chasing those in flight, knowing he'd never be completely emptied of his fury until their general was dead.

Some of the Mexican infantry ran into the marsh and became bogged down in the muddy water. Miles and his fellow fighters drew down on them and fired only to reload and repeat the process. Miles ran on along the edge of the water looking for any others trying to escape.

Time passed quickly yet stood still as Miles sought and killed Santa Anna's men. Finally, some of the Mexican men quit running and, instead, stopped and raised their hands.

"Me no Alamo! Me no Alamo!"

Miles lowered his rifle and stared. Try as he might, he couldn't pull the trigger. Not with them standing with their hands up in surrender. Before he could wave them out of the water, other fighters ran up beside him and fired on the men.

More and more of Santa Anna's men gave up only to be shot by the furious Texians. The marshy water turned red with their blood. His own rage spent, Miles dropped to his knees and witnessed the slaughter of terror-stricken Mexicans. From what he could see, the battle was over, yet for almost another hour, Houston's militia sought and shot any fugitives they found trying to run or hide.

Miles shoved his knife into its sheath and reached for his rifle. For the first time, he noticed the blood covering his hands, sleeves, and shirtfront. He pushed to his feet and limped to the edge of the water. Again, he dropped to his knees and washed the blood from his hands then splashed water on his buckskins in an attempt to get rid of the blood. Try as he might, his clothing remained stained and discolored.

Too tired to care, he headed toward camp. His shoulder and thigh burned from the wounds. His throat also burned. They'd won. They'd defeated Santa Anna's army and found justice for the men who died at the Alamo and Goliad. There was one more thing Miles wanted before going in search of Rosa.

As Miles sought his horse to retrieve some bandages from his pack, he spotted General Houston leaning against the tree where he'd slept the night before. A handful of men surrounded him and appeared to be working on his leg. Miles moved closer and noticed bloodstains around his ankle. They shared a nod before he moved on.

After yanking some strips of cloth from his pack, he finally took the time to check the gunshot wound on his leg. McCombs arrived and took a look.

"That's not too bad. In and out right along the edge. Bet it's gonna burn like fire in the morning."

"It already does. It's gonna be stiff tomorrow. They ever find Santa Anna's body?"

"No. But one of his generals surrendered along with all his men. Several hundred of them. The battle's over."

"I know. But I want to see Santa Anna."

"Winning isn't enough?"

He couldn't answer. He didn't know what to say to that question. He was thrilled they'd won, but it didn't seem complete without the death of the man who led the enemy.

"Let me see that arm."

While McCombs checked his shoulder wound, Miles wrapped the strips of cloth around his leg and tied it tight to keep it from bleeding.

"You got another one of those? Your upper arm could use some bandaging."

Miles pulled out another strip and handed it to him. He winced when McCombs jerked it tight.

"That's about all I can do for ya, Fitch. You all right?"

"Yeah. Let's get back. I want to hear what all's happening."

"You mean whether or not they found Santa Anna?"

He shrugged and winced at the pain. "That too."

They joined the growing crowd around Houston, still sitting at the base of the tree. He commanded one company to watch the prisoners. Word quickly spread that Santa Anna had escaped.

McCombs stood at his shoulder. "Look at 'em, Fitch. Some of them don't look old enough to hold a weapon, let alone shoot a man."

Miles examined them for the first time. From what he could tell, the ages ranged from about fourteen all the way up to fifty. They looked just as worn down as Houston's group of fighters. And what held just the smallest bit of surprise for him was. . .they were just men. No different from the ones Miles fought with in each skirmish and battle.

"Gotta feel for them just a bit, don't ya think?"

Miles craned his neck to look at McCombs for an explanation.

"Think about it, Fitch. They were fighting for what they believed just as you were. They wanted to keep what they thought was their land and you fought for what you knew to be yours. They fought for their fallen comrades, and so did you. What makes them so different?"

"We never gave the order of no quarter. They're still alive while my friends at the Alamo and the men at Goliad are all dead."

"You're right about that. There's probably mistakes made that both sides can claim."

As much as it irritated him, Miles had to admit McCombs was right...on all counts. Now that he'd examined the faces of the enemy, he could hardly look away because they didn't look like an enemy any longer. Not to him anyway.

Houston had his men return to the Mexican camp to capture all their weapons and supplies. McCombs told Miles to hunker down and rest his wounds, that he would take care of the search. With his thigh throbbing, he did just that and ended up sleeping until early the next morning, at which time Houston ordered the men to do a thorough search of the area for the missing Santa Anna.

Well-rested and determined to help find the man, Miles labored to saddle his horse.

McCombs helped him onto the saddle. "You know you don't have to do this, right?"

"I want to. I got plenty of sleep. I can't walk far, but my horse is rested. There's no reason why I can't help."

"All right. Hold up, and I'll get mine saddled. We can look together."

In the midst of many other men, they rode toward the marsh and meandered along the edge, sometimes riding into the water and through any tall weeds in case someone was trying to hide. They made their way west behind Santa Anna's encampment. While Miles checked the trees, McCombs continued in and along the marsh. At the end of the encampment, Miles reined in his horse.

"I've got to get off this saddle. My leg is on fire."

"All right. Let's go back and get it rested. We can start looking again later."

Back at camp, Miles checked his wounds and applied new bandages before dropping next to a tree for a rest. He hated feeling weak and unable to help but allowed his wounds a chance to rest and heal. McCombs left him alone and returned to the search for Santa Anna.

About midafternoon, a shout went up. The men had found another fugitive. They brought him through the prisoners toward Sam Houston. Miles struggled toward Houston's tree for a look. Disappointment filled him when he saw the common soldier's uniform instead of Santa Anna's colorful and lavish costume. He was about to return to his horse when the buzz of excited murmurs reached him.

"The prisoners called him *El Presidente*! That's Santa Anna!"

As a whole, the group tightened as it moved closer to the new captive. After his wounds had been bumped too many times, Miles moved around for a better vantage point. Houston still sat on the ground looking up at the prisoner, who started talking with an arrogant voice in his own language. All Miles could understand was the name spoken. Antonio Lopez de Santa Anna. They had him. The president of Mexico and leader of the Mexican forces was now their prisoner.

Miles squinted to better see the man's face. He'd dreamed of this moment, though in his dream, the two were alone and Miles was standing over the man's body.

Houston called for interpreters, while all his men crushed closer for their own look at the Mexican president. Houston finally ordered them to get back.

In search of an opening, Miles circled the group. Many of the men wandered off in pursuit of food and rest, their curiosity sated. Their departure left many gaps in the circle of men. Miles's eyes never left his prey as he moved around. And then he found what he sought. . .the perfect space for the ideal shot.

Miles pulled the pistol from his belt, checked the powder, and then took careful aim. A few of the men around him watched without saying a word, even moving aside to give him more room, as though encouraging him to pull the trigger.

Miles cocked the hammer and looked down the short barrel. In seconds, the man he'd detested for weeks would be dead. But the man in his sight suddenly became just that. . .a man. No longer in a battle situation, instead of an evil tyrant, Santa Anna had been reduced to a meek prisoner. If Miles pulled the trigger now, he'd be no better than Santa Anna declaring no quarter. He'd be a murderer.

He lowered the gun. The faces of Crockett, Hector, John, and Peacock raced through his memory, and the gun barrel rose again. But he no longer felt the rage he once hung on to with desperation. Somewhere along the miles and miles of roads they'd traveled, listening to McCombs talk about his own torturous experiences and the reminders in God's Word, Miles had changed.

Releasing the hammer, Miles tossed the pistol aside. With the plan to ride out and return to Béxar and Rosa, Miles turned. McCombs stood behind him, a smile on his face and tears in his eyes. He nodded and shook Miles's hand before the two of them walked away from hate, anger, bad choices, and Santa Anna.

Chapter Forty

Rosa strolled toward the well in the center of town, swinging the bucket in her hand. Béxar was still quiet and empty after the Alamo battle and Santa Anna's army had left, but she'd grown used to the calm, even enjoyed the peaceful tranquility. She had no doubt her newfound serenity stemmed from time, weeks, spent with her Lord.

Still undecided about where her future lay, she continued toying with the idea of heading east in search of her father's family that she'd never met. Mama spent every possible opportunity trying to talk her into staying. But Rosa couldn't see herself in Béxar without Miles. The memories, though they'd fade, would be too painful.

Her anger toward him had dissolved, replaced instead with a large dose of doubts that they'd ever really loved each other. She understood his actions a little better, though she still thought he'd acted too impulsively out of hate, which also made her doubt whether or not he had really been the man God intended for her. And she'd probably never truly know the answer since she believed she'd never see him again.

Once she reached the well, Rosa stood along the side and peered into its black depths. She used to avoid standing too close to the edge for fear of falling in and drowning. And at times in the past weeks, she thought landing at the bottom would be the perfect ending to her miserable life. Now, she couldn't get enough of trying to spot the bottom that was too far away to see. The seemingly bottomless pit reminded her of her Father's love. Nothing, no height nor depth, not even all the mistakes she'd made, could separate her from His love. As deep as it was, the well had a bottom. Her Lord's love for her didn't.

She bent down and picked up a stone then let it fall into the well. She leaned far over the side to be able to hear when it splashed.

"You're not thinking of throwing yourself in there, are you?"

Alarmed, Rosa gasped and jumped, nearly losing her footing and tumbling into the black pit. As she caught herself and pushed away, another pair of hands grasped her and pulled her back. She tugged away from those hands and turned toward the voice she knew so well.

Miles's throat worked as he took several steps back. "I'm so sorry. I didn't mean to frighten you like that."

She stared, taking in every inch of this worn, filthy, and yet magnificent man. His buckskins were torn and stained with mud, sweat, and blood. His face, though apparently scrubbed clean, still bore the signs of pain and fatigue, barely visible through the months-long growth of beard. And when their eyes finally met, she knew beyond any shadow of doubt that she still loved this man.

She didn't move or say a word, content to take in the very sight of him. He peeled his hat from his head and twisted it in his hands. He licked his lips and looked away before gazing at her once again.

"I owe you so many apologies, Rosa. It's hard to know where to begin, but I'll start with apologizing for shooting you and then leaving without allowing you a chance to explain or giving you any reasons for my actions. I wouldn't blame you if you never want to see or hear from me again. Just say the word, and I'll be out of your life."

She continued to stare, heart in her throat that this man she loved so deeply had returned to apologize, and loved her enough to walk away if she only said the words.

"I guess I've hurt you so badly that you won't speak to me." He gazed at her a moment longer as though waiting for an answer, and then he looked down at his hands and paused before nodding. He turned away.

Her heart skipped a beat then throbbed into double action. She ached at the thought of losing him yet again, but he also owed her an explanation.

"I'm sure I know why you pulled the trigger when you saw me, but I'd like to hear why you left so quickly."

Miles turned back to her, hope radiating from his eyes. She saw him swallow hard as he mangled his poor hat. She truly felt for him, but she wasn't about to make it any easier either. She'd prayed about this moment many times, even though she'd been certain it would never come. Now that it was here, their admissions had to be made.

"I'd been sent as a courier to Goliad for reinforcements. The battle started right before I made it back." He looked away and shook his head. "I watched from a hill as all my friends and fellow fighters were killed. Slaughtered." His throat worked again. "I should have been in there with them. My insides were torn with guilt that I wasn't."

Anguish poured from his voice. She wanted to go to him. Hold him. Try to remove his pain. But she also knew how healing it was to purge oneself of guilt and anger.

His eyes returned to hers. "When I saw that uniform standing inside my home, every ounce of my fury was poured into the moment I pulled the trigger. Then when I saw it was you wearing the uniform, you became the target of every emotion raging through me, and I couldn't get away from you fast enough." He took a step toward her then stopped. "I accused you of some horrendous things and treated you—" His voice broke. He looked down at his hands. "I became the kind of man I despised and have earned every bit of your disgust. I don't deserve anything from you, Rosa, but I hope one day you can forgive me."

She tried to smile, but instead her lips trembled. "I already have. Weeks ago."

His head jerked up and his eyes peered into hers. "Thank you."

She waited, but he didn't say anything else. "Is an apology the only reason you returned?"

He plucked at the rips in his buckskins. "I thought maybe you could mend these for me."

She stood dumbfounded. Of all the nerve! She crossed her arms. "Or maybe we could just throw them away and start fresh and new."

He scanned his clothing before looking at her again, this time with tears in his eyes. "We could do that. Or we could mend these, hang on to them as a reminder of the mistakes we've made so we won't make them again. Maybe they'll remind me to be more appreciative of what I have." He took another step toward her. "I left the battlefield and gave my hard and beaten and broken heart to the Lord. He removed the stone and returned it to me fully renewed. And now I'm offering it to you, whole, healed, and complete. If you'll still have me. I love you, Rosa. With everything in me, more than my own life, I love you."

Tears sprang to her eyes, and he blurred in front of her, but she still took the final steps in order to touch him, be held by him, for the first time in too many weeks.

"I'll still have you and your heart. Forever and always."

Author's Note

While the cover depiction of the Alamo represents a modern-day rendition, the building at the time of the battle did not yet have its sculptured roofline. The building in San Antonio was originally constructed as a mission for Indians. The complex once covered close to four acres of ground containing the chapel, workrooms, storerooms, and housing, all surrounded by an outer wall, which became used as a fort during the Texas Revolution.

About the Author

Award-winning novelist Janelle Mowery is the author of ten novels and novellas. Her first novel, a mystery co-authored with Elizabeth Ludwig and titled *Where the Truth Lies*, was published in 2008. The second and third mysteries in the series, *Died in the Wool*, a finalist for the ACFW Carol Award, and *Inn Plain Sight*, released in 2011.

In 2010, Summerside Press published Janelle's *Love Finds You in Silver City, Idaho*, which received a four-star rating from RT Book Reviews. Three novels in her Colorado Runaways series followed in 2011 with high ratings. Janelle has also contributed novellas to two Christmas anthologies; *Christmas at Barncastle Inn* made the ECPA bestseller list.

Janelle has been married for twenty-four years and is the mother of two sons. She is a member of Sandy Point Bible Church and participates in the church's bell choir. To learn more about Janelle and her work, visit her on the web at JanelleMowery.com.

*A*merican *T*apestries™

Each novel in this line sets a heart-stirring love story against the backdrop of an epic moment in American history. Whether they settled her first colonies, fought in her battles, built her cities, or forged paths to new territories, a diverse tapestry of men and women shaped this great nation into a Land of Opportunity. Then, as now, the search for romance was a major part of the American dream. Summerside Press invites lovers of historical romance stories to fall in love with this line, and with America, all over again.

Now Available

Coming Soon